FIVE-STAR REVIEWS
FOR *MENDEL AND MORRIS*

Lively Dialogue

The author of *Mendel and Morris* lovingly portrays the friendship of two elderly (although the characters would HATE that characterization!) men. . . . The friendship of these unique characters—unflinchingly portrayed with warts and all—comes alive through their lively and authentic dialogue with one another as well as with the women who befriend them.

Growing Younger with Age

Fred Sokol's sparkling new novel had me hooked on the first page, where he launches us straightway into the hilarious and no-holds-barred dialogue between two men friends who are well beyond middle age (but don't dare call them elderly!). . . . With humor worthy of Woody Allen and a poignant tale of friendship that could have come from Mitch Albom, Sokol takes his narrative beyond the level of a "buddy road trip" and eventually introduces Zena and Gilda into the mix . . . the romantic twists and turns will upend any expectations you might have, as the human issues that older people face in real life intrude into the hopes and dreams of each character. . . . It is like a fresh breeze to see an author's imaginative powers focused . . . on the metaphorical goblins and trolls that face us everyday humans as we grow into old age.

A Great Read

Not only are the characters a hoot; so are many of the predicaments they get themselves into. But this book also takes a serious look at the opportunities and limitations of old age, which may slow us down even as it opens new doors and renews our appetite for living. Sokol has a real talent for writing realistic yet distinctive dialogue. By the end I had grown to love the characters and wanted the story to continue. . .

Destiny

A Novel

Fred Sokol

Bellastoria Press

ISBN: 978-1942209775

Cover photograph by Fred Sokol

Bellastoria Press
P.O. Box 60341
Longmeadow, Massachusetts 01116

Destiny sweetly recalls a generation of individuals
who were 75 years of age and older
during the early portion of the 21st century.

As I wrote the novel, I thought of my grandchildren:
Allison Harper Sokol, Summer Aurelia Sokol and Arlo Morrison
Sokol.
With good fortune, all will live well into the 22nd century.

Destiny, both the book and her character, celebrate life's joy.
Thus, much appreciation to the parents of the grandchildren
for bringing the little ones into the world.

AUTHOR'S NOTE

During Labor Day weekend of 2018, this writer received a serious medical diagnosis. The generous response of a multitude of friends, truly heartwarming, carried Fred Sokol through an evolving recovery period. He attributes a vigorous return to health, in part, to those (it would not be fair-minded to single out or prioritize names) who were there for him during those pivotal days. For speaking with him by phone, for sitting with him, for writing him, he says, to each individual, thanks, thanks, thanks. . . .

A GLOSSARY OF
MORRIS AND MENDEL EXPRESSIONS

alter kocker	old geezer
amain	amen
bopka	sweet braided bread
bubee	darling, dear, honey
Capisce	understand
chazzerai	trinket, knick-knack
chuppah	wedding canopy
farhblunget	lost, befuddled, or confused
farshtinkener	stinky
go know	go figure; believe it or not
gonif	thief
goyisha	gentile; non-Jew
kibosh	put an end to
L'chayim	to life
mensch	honorable, decent person
meshugge	crazy
mishegoss	craziness, madness
mitzvah	good deed
nakhes	pleasure, especially in a parent from a child
nu	well? /so? /what's going on?
nudnik	a boring person, an annoying person, a pest, a nag
oy	oh! / ouch!
Oy! Vey ist mir!	woe is me

GLOSSARY (CONT'D)

schlemiel	bungler, ineffectual person, inept person; a person who is easily victimized
schlep	pull, drag, tug, yank
schmatte	rag; anything worthless
schmendricks	fool; inept person, nincompoop
schmucks	jerk, fool, contemptible person
schnoz	nose
shiksa	non-Jewish girl
tsimmes	dish of mixed fruit and/or vegetables; stew; (colloq.) fuss, something that has gotten blown out of proportion and turned into a very big deal
tsuris	trouble, distress
tuchus	rear end, butt

Definitions of Yiddish words from
http://www.yiddishdictionaryonline.com/

Chapter 1

"Morris will get stuck in purgatory," whispered Mendel, just loud enough for Morris to hear. "You got yours now, but within ten years the light will shine on my bald head, not your thick curls. I will have angels in short robes dancing around me while you're hurling red and black devils' pitchforks or whatever those gizmos are."

"You shut up, you tired little monkey, and let me shoot," yelled Morris as a bevy of older, ample, dimpled women surrounded him. Morris lifted his cue above his head and walked toward Mendel, scowling. Mendel looked over Morris's shoulder and smiled.

Morris assumed his stance anew. Since wrenching his left knee, he found it impossible to effectively push off. To adapt, he first tried positioning his right leg behind him. He hoped for thrust without pain. "No go," he said to himself. Morris wanted to use his left leg for propulsion, as he had since he began playing "this goddamned game" twenty-five years earlier.

Finally, Morris was ready to shoot. He exhaled with an audible whoosh, as his shapely physical therapist had once advised. The disc, however, toppled and then skidded to a halt onto its side and perched itself alongside the border of the court.

"That's it, I'm through," Morris proclaimed. "I'm not playing until they fix this knee or get me a new one. No more embarrassing moments for me." He looked over his shoulder, sensing Mendel's presence. "Maybe Mendel will fill in for me?" asked Morris.

With that, Morris folded his cue, cradled it beneath his armpit, and walked to the entryway of Phases, the senior center he and Mendel had developed. He turned briefly, looked at Mendel, thumbed his nose, and went inside.

The Lewis sisters were sitting opposite each other, a chessboard dividing them. "Zena, I say Zena, remember when we used to play while listening to the radio?"

"Morris, hello, what's wrong?" asked Zena. Without moving her head, she looked across to her sister. "Mother always had the radio on, always. News. John Gambling, even during that President FDR. No wonder I was never much of a reader. But it did not seem to affect you, Gilda."

"My left ear was always the better one. I would turn it to the radio and concentrate on whatever I was doing with my brain. Maybe that makes no sense to a scientist. I felt that I could divide myself."

"Nobody pays attention to me, a man who has twisted both his neck and back. Not to mention that fake heart problem of mine," said Morris. "I feel like a warped pretzel."

"That is you, Morris," said Gilda. "If you felt fine, you would have nothing to talk about. It used to be just Mendel who was such a needy showman. Now, it's both of you. So, what is it this time?"

Morris thumbed his nose at both of them, spun on his heel with surprising fluidity, and walked out the door. He attached green clip-on lenses to his eyeglasses to block the sun, placed the retro Cleveland Indians cap firmly upon his head, and headed for the park. He hummed as he walked across Sumner Avenue in Springfield, Massachusetts, staring at birds he called red-tailed hawks. "A summer beauty of a day if ever I saw one," continued Morris.

"Hey, you know what happens to people who talk to themselves?" said an approaching man Morris knew but whose name might as well have been Methuselah for all Morris could recall.

"Don't worry, my brain locks just the same way. I'm Kiley—shuffleboard Kiley. Well, it's more like cockeyed Kiley since I can't remember the last time I won a game. Talk about senior moments."

"Hello, Kiley. My mind plays tricks. Sometimes I look in the mirror and a fat, overstuffed owl stares back. I wonder who he is."

"Let's go to the courts and have a friendly game."

"No game could be worse than the one I just left. Mendel appreciates nobody but himself, and I will never speak with such a liar again."

"This is your best friend?" asked Kiley.

"That has nothing to do with it."

They walked along side by side, although Morris's waddle frequently pushed Kiley off the concrete and onto the dirt beside. As the Forest Park shuffleboard courts came into view, Kiley suddenly jumped in front of Morris and raised his hand as if in class.

Morris played along. "Yes?"

"I would like to become a Jew," said Kiley.

Morris smiled, then laughed, rumbled, and coughed till he gagged. "Whatever for?" he asked.

"Warmth, rituals, life, and maybe, to tell the truth, death. I don't want my body out there for everyone to look at after I'm gone."

"This is why you want to be Jewish? To get a closed casket?" Morris began to shake. "If I were you and I wanted closed, I would write it on my order. Just like dry cleaning. If you don't want starch, you tell them soft, no starch on the collar."

"The only thing is," said Kiley, "if someone gets it wrong, I won't be there to tell them. I mean, I will but I won't, if you catch my drift."

"Why don't the two of us play a game? Then we'll schmooze." Morris, known as a charmer, an easy talker, shut down a conversation when the topic didn't suit him. Now, he was hoping to avoid or delay while he contemplated his thoughts.

They went to the shed where Kiley, slim and WASPish, stored one of his prized sticks. Morris had stationed his at the Phases courts. Now, he wished he had a spare with him. He hated generic models as much for the grips as the action. When he had played tennis as a younger man, Morris had fiddled with his racket grips constantly, before the practice became fashionable. Before playing a friend, even, he would tape over an existing surface. He might rip off the tape mid-match, even if he realized it probably had little if anything to do with his performance.

Now, Morris fished in his wallet for one of the large Band-Aids he always carried. He placed it over a worn section on a cue. "Ready for action," he pronounced.

Kiley, by far the more skillful of the two players, easily trounced Morris. Morris tried to overpower him and sent discs flying off the court. Kiley noticed that Morris was holding his cue with both hands but chose not to ask why. Kiley, meticulous of style, dress, and demeanor, held to that sartorial standard whenever he played shuffleboard. Placement was everything to him. He would stick a disc in a 10, then block it from harm if he could. In a seeming flash, Kiley accumulated the necessary 75 points for the win. The big man accepted defeat easily. If ever a match counted, as in tournament play, he could out-psych Kiley without too much trouble and take him. Let him gloat, thought Morris. But, Kiley wasn't paying attention. He was filling time, staying patient so that he could research his explorations of Judaism more extensively.

"Okay, nice game," said Kiley. "Now we talk."

"It's such a sweet day," said Morris. "Let's walk to the X and sit in that new Starbucks. They have latte, *schmatte,* soy, no soy, skim or not. If we get those two easy chairs, I got to shield my forehead. I'll get such a burn by the window or, worse, the Big C. It's worth it to relax, though."

The men walked side by side, slipping into single file only when bicyclists approached them. Otherwise, the resurfaced pathway provided ample room for them to stroll and talk. Midway through, Kiley plucked a folded Yankees cap from a rear pocket and placed it backwards on his head.

Morris squinted and looked directly at him.

"In honor of Junior Griffey, whom I once predicted the Bombers would land before mid-summer," Kiley explained. "He wore his hat like this during his salad days with Seattle. I liked him because I liked his father, who, if you remember, played out the string with the Yanks."

"I seem to recall, but I have to tell you: I've hated the Yankees ever since the late 40s when Raschi, Reynolds and whatshisface beat my Tribe."

"It might be Eddie Lopat. Steady Eddie. That's the lefty who balanced out the staff. At least, that is what I've been telling myself."

Starbucks, thankfully, came into view.

"It's still a goddamned shame they had to remove drugstores—people owned these pharmacies before CVS and Walgreens—to make way for Starbucks," said Kiley. "Dunkin' Donuts, over there, was good enough. Correction: It's been top of the line."

Morris did not respond, since he had become nearly addicted to Starbucks coffee. He drank it black and always without flavoring or sweetener. Kiley took note when Morris held his cup with both hands.

"This is not Parkinson's," said Morris, anticipating a comment. "Years ago, when I was playing basketball, I came down hard on my right hand and crushed some bones. Since then, the goddamned tremors come and go. They began a few years back, after the Trade Center bombings. This is how I respond. Go figure."

Kiley said nothing and nodded his head. "It's just that every time I've been to a Jewish funeral, not one person stands over a coffin bawlin' out their eyes the way they do at Catholic funerals," he said. "What I want, after I go, is some respect. That day and for a couple days later. After that, don't matter."

"Ah, now I get it. You want to be Jewish so that no one will see what happened to you—no dimples, no blue eyes, just cracks and crevices in your skin," said Morris. He liked the way the Starbucks looked. It was stylish but not huge, comfortable yet not too fancy—like Cleveland but unlike New York City, which had too much of everything to suit Morris. "Although I would never pretend not to be Jewish, I would also never convert. These women who join up because of a man? That makes no sense to me. Follow your own map, I say."

"I am not a woman, and enrolling now is not the issue. What is important is eternal rest."

"Spoken like a true Christian," said Morris. "Stay where you are is my advice to you. Don't mess. On a nice day like this, let's go outside."

Morris held the door for Kiley and, without saying so, led the way to Phases.

The Irishman hadn't been to the community center since the opening gala. Kiley couldn't explain why, but he had chosen to stay away. Ten minutes later when he stepped in the door, he knew he'd missed out.

The chess set, which looked to be hand-carved, dominated the room. Those playing had left the game for other pursuits. The pieces rested, as if contemplating next moves. Kiley, a chess champion when he was a young teenager, had not played for many years. Nobody he knew was interested. He eagerly sat in one of the hard-backed chairs to get a sense of the contest.

As a former high school history teacher, Kiley was forever reading. He had a tendency to dream, book in hand, about something he had read long ago or about his life in the past, present, and future. The decision to tackle the Talmud was instrumental in his decision to investigate Judaism. Kiley wondered if Jews were good at chess. To him, this only made sense. After all, it was about intellect.

A photograph of Albert Einstein hung from the peach-colored wall behind the chess set. Morris was watching Kiley and anticipated his question. "I know," said Morris. "Whatever happened to white walls or does anyone still use wallpaper?"

"Listen to the Talmud," said Kiley.

"Whatever. Why do you say that?"

"Because it tells us that Jews should give every man a break. Even the one who used that orange and pink color for the wall," said Kiley. "Really, you should read it."

"I can tell you for sure without even asking that Mendel made this decision."

"And where is your best friend?"

"I imagine he is in here somewhere. I left him when I walked away earlier today from the shuffleboard court."

****

Mendel, however, had ambled off, taking a couple of cues with him as walking sticks. For some time now, he had been thinking predominantly of his demise. It wasn't his hip or shoulder or twitching thumbs; nor his perpetually bobbing chin; nor even his aching back, which flared up early and pained him in any sub-tropical temperatures. Hobbling and kvetching—these had become signature style identifiers. People knew, down the block, when he was coming.

At this very moment, he was squeezing himself between ragged chicken wire fencing which separated the manicured terrain of Forest Park from the overgrown, weed-ridden hillside. As he drew clear enough to feel assured that no one was within earshot, he let out a loud yet scratchy, "So where are you, dear deer of yesteryear?" It sounded rehearsed but was, to Mendel, an easy end rhyme. The first of his family born in America, he took pride in elocution and enjoyed playing with the language.

Mendel was now aware of mind slippage. He could cope and even conceal memory lapse, but he would never allow himself to witness self-erosion of the brain, especially not *his* brain.

Craning his neck to be certain no one could hear him, Mendel began to mutter as he stumbled down a gentle hillside. "So, *nu*, I would like to be buried somewhere in this park. Maybe here where real animals used to roam, before they were locked up in cages. Or walk around without leashes, at least. First choice would be the shuffleboard courts, but these are filled with poison ivy or sumac and I don't especially like the idea of carrying a rash with me into the next life." Nearly toppling, he grabbed a wilted, dead tree to steady himself. "This might be me in a couple of days: on the way out, but not past the expiration date. But, this is a long-term plan. In the meantime, I am writing"—here, he raised his voice—"a list of instructions." Then, realizing he was alone and could not be heard, he lowered his voice again. "Or a couple of months or maybe even years. However long it takes to write these commandments. Number one: Honor all women—young, old, timid, bold; it doesn't really matter. But let me say that we are the weaker sex. Men—we think we are *gonifs*, but we are really *schmendricks*. Women are not so strong, at least not most. Women must always be on the lookout and in the ready position for an attack. Who is going to rob me, to even guess that I have money socked away under the mattress, in bonds, in the bank, in the market? I look like I am ready for assisted living, but I will never be there."

Mendel, wandering downward, never thought to check the hovering sky. He was startled to see that black and blue canvasses seemed to have taken over when he heard shrieking birds above him.

"Looks like Europe during The Blitz," he said. "Either that or something already blew up and this is the end of life for humans and animals, too. I am half-deaf and still, this hurts my ears, so shut up," he said, thinking something from above had cursed him. This was not the case, but Mendel was uncertain. "Not so fast. I got some living to do," he replied, contradicting his self-examination and virtually everything he had been thinking. "No cockeyed wonder of an explosion from the heavens will put an end to my reality. No! I will take myself out when the time comes, which is not now!

"All my life people been calling me a pipsqueak. Well, I got news for them. This scrawny bag of bones has a head. Yes, call me scarecrow or whatever, since I know that I look like a Yiddishe bat. Mark my words that in the end, my brains will win out."

Mendel lurched forward with a creak. Having been so consumed with his footwork in order to avoid toppling over, he was oblivious to claps of thunder until this very moment. Suddenly, the skies opened above with a monsoon and drenched him. He looked up and saw a graceful, watchful bird sitting on a branch near the top of a tree.

"Herring, blue herring?" he queried. The bird flew lower, temporarily swooping close to him. "You don't speak and, I have to tell you, having seen you skimming along more than one of the park ponds, I think you are mute. What do you say to that?"

The wild blue heron spread its wings as it dropped even closer to Mendel. With a whoosh, it took off with great thrust.

"Don't say good-bye, but, I will say, certain people say too much. Probably better off being silent. Anyway, I will miss you.

"Goddammit to hell," he muttered and then, more loudly, "Just my luck to have a shining head when I need one of my thirty-five caps. Caps for sale, even, I would take that," he continued, recalling the children's book he was hoping to read to a grandchild—if only one little one would come along. "Cannot believe these old, tired eyes. Will you look at that?" he asked, gazing toward the sky.

A full rainbow, boasting red and orange highlights, had spread across the seemingly rear portion of a long sky. "Never did I see something like that," said Mendel. "Well, maybe once when we were at a circus when I was ten or twelve. Such a terrible storm came along that it shook the tent and scared the living piss out of me. My mother took me outside and there it was, just like this, a golden rainbow. I will miss this when I am gone. But, then again, I will not know what I am missing. Will I?" he looked to the sky. "This is where I want to be. I can say 'pissing' without every Tom, Dick, and Harry passing judgment. Before humans took over this park, animals ruled. I know this as sure as I am Mendel— Mendela, as my mother used to say. I hear that the lion was king. Hard to think about now, probably lock him up. Our world is a scary place. Maybe the next one will be better. Only one way to find out."

With that, Mendel took a step downward, and then another. He saw a ravine below and knew that he needed to explore. "I will probably come up with some case of itches, but who cares," he said to himself, realizing he did not have what he treasured—a live audience. "If only we still had the goddamned menagerie every old-timer tells me existed here a century ago. Then you got something. This? I like trees and bushes as much as the next guy, but it ain't like having friends who show off all those feathers and spots and teeth which make such noises you never heard," he said, out of earshot of every living soul.

It began to rain on a slant and Mendel could only kneel beneath a tree. So Mendel spoke to the tree: "You, my friend, are nearly as stooped as I am; not stupid, but bent over. You will remember me when I am gone, kaput. The only problem is this: I will miss everyone else, even that plump, bagel-eating good-for-nothing. He grows on you, if you know what I mean. So, I ask myself how long I should continue with the *schleps* to the doctor, the seven-pills-a-day regimen, the pretend workouts with the one-pound weights. The answer is, I don't know what the answer is. But, I can still sing." With that, Mendel began singing, "Sit down, sit down, sit down, sit down, sit down, you're rocking the goddamned boat!"

****

Kiley smiled and said, "Morris, you see that white-haired, white-bearded gentleman sitting over there on the bench—right by the old courts, the weedy ones?"

"I do and, so help me, he must sleep there. Every day I walk past him and he smiles, never says hello. I don't get it," said Morris.

"Sphinxie is what they call him," said Kiley. "He is always sitting there, observing. I believe he likes animals, especially large dogs."

"Ones, I assume, who look like him? Like those snowy huskies and Saint Bernards? I bet his name is Bernard," said Morris. "And, by the way, someone told me that a place called Jinxie's, which rhymes with this Sphinxie, was a jazz/booze hangout in Springfield before I even heard of the place."

With that, he took Kiley by the arm and steered him toward the bench where Sphinxie was primary resident, twirling in his hand what appeared to be an old baton. As they approached, the previously stone-faced one said, "Company always is a special treat. Welcome. Plenty of room to spread out." He pointed to the seats beside him. "Make yourselves comfortable and watch, with delight, with me. It's a smorgasbord of people: races, ages, genders, sizes. Little ones are the best, definitely the most adorable. As we grow older, this is what matters, don't you think?"

Neither Kiley nor Morris said a word. Sphinxie interpreted this as a signal to continue and, as oppositional in personality as his nickname would suggest, picked up on his monologue. "I sit here and they come and go, wondering who I am and why I remain in this very spot, nearly motionless, for hours. I assure you, the pose is well-thought-out."

"Are you thinking about what is going to happen to you?" asked Morris.

"I sit here to avoid that."

"I see," said Kiley. "This is Zen."

Sphinxie gazed beyond Kiley's line of sight and held his stare, blinking only once.

Finally, Morris broke the silence, "Well, what is this? A séance?"

Sphinxie erupted with laughter. "A calm before a volcanic outburst," he said.

Just at that moment, a masked couple, seemingly out of nowhere, appeared. He wore a white, form-fitting suit which flattered a muscular physique while she, too, was trousered. Her top, loose and revealing, was embroidered with leather trim. Her jet-black hair was pulled back and strapped close by a headband. They held hands as they approached Sphinxie, who immediately greeted them with, "Got it! Lone Ranger and Tonto. Kimosabe, how are you?" The woman answered in a much deeper voice than Kiley could have imagined. Morris elbowed him, cupped his mouth around Kiley's ear, and whispered, "I am not so sure that is a woman. Could be my problem." Kiley shushed him but did not disagree.

More people followed behind the twosome, predominantly couples, all in costume.

"Parade of the crazy animals is what this is called. But they are tame and they are not real. Even more important, this does not matter. Only the imagination matters. Who cares what is real and who knows what is real? Not me and not anyone." Sphinxie was just beginning to roll. "I sit here every day except for blizzards and, soon enough, performances blend like a speeding train that whizzes by before you know it."

"So, Sphinxie, have you seen anything of that spider, Mendel?"

"Mendel? Just yesterday, he said his customary hello and cut across the ball field. Last I saw of him, he disappeared behind that hill over there." Sphinxie waved vaguely forward. "Mendel, he takes great joy in fooling people into thinking he is a curmudgeon. Never did I meet a more generous fellow," said Sphinxie, who moved his limbs as this assessment amused the others. "Time to make a move," said Sphinxie, while Morris and Kiley stared into each other's eyes. "Well," he said, "don't just stand there. We should make an inquiry, look after your friend." With that, Sphinxie began walking across the baseball diamond and toward the region of the park where Mendel was last seen. "If I am up and ambulatory, the least I expect is my able-bodied colleagues to follow. Come join me, boys."

****

At that very moment, Mendel surprised himself by resisting the impulse to slide swiftly away, since that was an option, and instead decided to slowly climb a hill.

"For now," he announced to no one, "I choose life above the alternative. For now."

Accordingly, he placed one foot after the other, breathing haltingly with each laborious step upward. Instead of moving vertically, he made his way on an incline. "Stairway to heaven?" asked Mendel. He took note that he had never paid special attention to the many birds he now suddenly saw. "What's your name?" he asked a streaking silver blur of a thing that swooped low enough for him to feel a whoosh of air. Mendel stopped and took in a panorama as he pivoted slowly, gauging his and others' past. Mendel wandered and wondered which animals had preceded him. He allowed himself to speculate about lions and tigers; why not a ferocious community? "And what if there were a herd of zebras stomping on this ground beneath my feet? I know nothing. Did they have families then or what? Where have they gone?" He stopped talking and picked up a thick branch to use as a walking assistant. "Stick, listen to me since no one else will," he said. "I am an old man who is useless. I am using you, stick, not merely to navigate but to help me figure out a situation, a bind, a conundrum, as they say. There is no good reason for me to push on, but, equally, not the strength to seriously consider otherwise. Even if I might want out every so often, I am, dammit, too healthy and having too much fun to go. *Oy*."

Just then, a wrought iron, black jagged object quickly rose to Mendel's left and sped seemingly for his head. "Out, forget it, did I not just say that I intend to remain on the planet for a while? Shoo, shoo," he called. Sure enough, the flyer zoomed onward, disturbing nothing, exasperating one cranky old man as it marked a most unusual presence and then disappeared.

"Eh, shoo yourself," came the reply from afar. At least, he thought this was what he heard. Could it be that he had lost his mind?

Mendel startled and reversed his course. "Whadya want, cowards? Put up or shut up," called Mendel. "You *schmucks*."

Mendel continued his trek upward, his actions speaking more acutely than his philosophy. Thinking he saw an owl, Mendel chortled "hoo" and laughed at himself, since this might have been anything, even an illusion. He knew enough to doubt himself. "Maybe hoot is more like it, you goof. Speaking of which, I wonder . . ." he said and thought of his best friend (never would he acknowledge this) and *nudnik* enemy, Morris.

"Such a clown that no one would know he was the class brain. His hand must have shot up even when teachers did not exactly want or beg for students' answers."

He continued, slowly, to make his way toward the crest of the hill. He squinted, not trusting come-and-go eyesight. Then he said, loudly for him, "Christ, this looks like my two best friends, but who can that third human be? I pass by that stationary object every day in this park, but I swear he has never moved an inch. Now, he is some kind of general, leading forward such a pack?"

Sphinxie smiled from afar, deliberately raised his right arm, and slowly waved it at Mendel.

Mendel grinned widely as he lifted his walking stick, pointing at his oncoming friends. "This one"—he nodded at Morris—"makes even you, the Sphinx, seem like a speed demon," he said. "Then we change your nickname to Flash."

The two old men embraced before Morris shoved Mendel away and said, "I don't want anyone to get the wrong idea. Next thing you know it's in the Springfield Onion or back page of whatever the hell that arts paper is—and we might as well stand on our heads. Everyone gets the wrong idea!"

"If we could," said Mendel. No one responded. "I mean, if we stood on our heads, like Laurel and Hardy, people would think we were on new meds or something."

"Excuse me, but what were you doing by yourself in a ditch? If I didn't know any better, I would be suspicious," said Morris.

Ignoring that comment, Sphinxie said, "Since I see you are okay—well, normal for you—I got to sit." With that, he slowly ambled back toward the ball field bench.

Mendel waved behind him toward the downward slope. "You would not believe—technicolor, as we said sixty years ago: birds I did see and a strange mechanical gizmo heading toward me; and then I imagined zebras, giraffes, elephants, even lions. Morris, come with me, this is like that Fantasy Land we saw at Disney. Remember that tournament in Florida when we took a side trip? You can close your eyes and see all of it right here in this park. Nobody ever goes there, and they should. We should."

Mendel made sense. Morris was forced to acknowledge his friend's perception and consider the value of Mendel's accrued knowledge. He was jarred back into the here and now as Mendel poked him hard in the ribs with a tree branch.

"Still not ticklish there, you rascal," said Mendel. "One of these days I will reach, God help me, a couple of bones and then we will see just how stoic you are." Mendel had left his contemplative time in the woods behind him and now simply wished to play shuffleboard.

"Two on one, I will trounce both of you," he said to Kiley and Morris.

"Which reminds me, Morris," said Kiley. "I never knew you to cut short two games in one day. I say that your hand is bothering you and nobody will ever know for certain."

"Some private eye you would make," Morris replied. "I, on the other hand, walk around like a sun cloud is blinding me. I mean, on the way over here I noticed that the video store does not exist and here I was hoping to rent out a movie like *On the Waterfront*."

"You like Marlon Brando?"

"He has always been my favorite, even when he got old and fat. Look at me," said Morris. "But, as I was saying, I saw that the shoe store is replaced but not the jeweler. I ought to pay more attention."

"Probably so," said Kiley. "Prepare yourself for the worst, though. This is not the world we lived in when we were growing up."

Mendel hobbled toward them, leaning on the cue he had exchanged for the tree branch and was using as a makeshift crutch. "This is what is left of me," he complained.

"Don't give us that," said Morris. "After that romance of yours in the woods, no less. You will outlive all of us bastards and you know it. Just tell me that when you bury me, you'll make sure they don't put me in low ground. I don't want to be underwater in the next life."

"Just maybe this makes sense. We have to get somewhere after we live seventy, eighty, ninety, even more years on earth," said Kiley. "Judaism explains that this is not the end. That, for me, is too much to swallow."

"Swallowing is something I don't talk about with Morris in the room," said Mendel.

"You are one weasel, and there is no way you can deny that. You cheat on a woman, even. For your age, you got the market on lying. Then you stop by the door so nice and sweet," said Morris. "Kiley, would you excuse us? We got something to settle."

"Where should I go?" asked Kiley.

Mendel took him by the arm and escorted him to the café section of Phases. "This, my friend, is our jewel. You can get hot coffee, tea, and most days we used to bring in Danishes from Gus & Paul's. That place will never be replaced. Drop whatever you think this is worth in that cigar box. We do okay. Most people give what they can and it balances out. Meanwhile, you see we carry books and headsets so that you can listen. Take a snooze."

Mendel began to walk toward Morris, who intercepted his friend and blocked the exit with his body. Without exchanging a word, they went out the front door.

"I got a problem," said Morris to a man he forever taunted yet fully trusted.

"Speak now," said Mendel, "or forever hold or hold forever—whatever."

"Sex is an issue for Zena."

"You ain't a kid, Morris," said Mendel.

"This is not so simple. I got plenty of colored pills and they do the trick. That is not what I mean."

"What about Kiley?" asked Mendel. "You planning on leaving him there forever?"

"Don't worry about him. He's the kind you leave in a Borders and he gets lost. We got plenty of stuff to keep him going for hours." Morris raised his already thick shoulders and shrugged.

"Borders is no more. It's your heart I worry about, Morris. Sex is not so easy on people like us. I know," said Mendel.

"What is this? I knew about that Southern trash you had a date with. Don't tell me you had sex with her?"

"No, not that I couldn't have. I got plenty left in the tank," said Mendel.

Kiley came trotting out to see them. "I wish to check out some books and CDs from your store," he said.

"We have no policy. Leave us a note or something," said Mendel.

With that, he put down his cue, took Morris by the arm, and steered him down the street away from Phases and back toward their Forest Park house. Kiley was left to stare at the pair, then picked up his album and CDs and moved along.

"Morris, let's go somewhere, the country or something."

"Ah, a road trip is what the kids call it. I'm all for it. Such a gorgeous summer day, we should enjoy ourselves."

At the house, they got into Mendel's brand new Prius. Soon, they were off, agreeing to explore the shore north of Boston, each claiming to be the expert!

"Listen, Mo," said Mendel, "you are seated in a new Prius. Only fifteen or twenty thousand of these babies in this country right now and I got one of my city cronies to save one for me. It might not look like much and back seat's kind of squished in but a thousand miles to a gallon, this number's got anything beat. If either of us do manage to live another ten or fifteen years, mark my words, Prius, originally from Japan, will rule the road."

"Yes, and you got a bridge in Brooklyn to sell me, too, Mendel," said Morris.

"You will see," said Mendel. "Maybe if 9/11 never happened, we would have more of these cars. Who knows?"

****

After thirty minutes, and at Morris's insistence, they pulled over on the right side of the Mass Pike. Morris made off. This was known territory, a path he had explored before. He needed, once again, to locate a small, sweet body of water. There it was, and he was at its edge.

Morris felt compelled to call Zena. No whiz with his flip cell phone, he was relieved to hear her voice. "Yes, my dear, this is Morris. Who did you expect, King Farouk? No, I do not know where Mendel is, and I care even less. Zena, listen. I wish you were here. Plenty of fish in this little pond. Like on some postcard or TV commercial. Zena, do not defend Mendel. He is nothing more than a shyster." Morris's bad left knee gave out from under him, and that side of his body slid into the water. "Dammit, I am now some kind of wet mammoth," he said.

"You are one hoot and a half, Morris," said Zena. "I would give a thousand bucks to see you."

"A genie I am not. Otherwise, no way I'd turn down any reasonable offer."

Mendel, who was left in the car to ponder, felt the tic around his right upper lip activate. When this occurred in public, he could simply lift a hand to shield the involuntary tremor. In private, however, he cursed the stupid twitch, stamped his foot, and scratched at his face. The more agitated he grew, the worse the spasm. Once he began, however, Mendel could not desist.

"Morris, get outta there before I croak," cackled Mendel, lifting his head above the top of the vehicle. "Look, Morris, you had your way. I know what this is like. A few times in my life—not often, mind you—I have done just the same. For spite, I admit. Every time, though, I retraced my steps. We are on the way to the beach, goddammit. Come out!"

Morris pretended to hear nothing—not one word of it. He was overjoyed to return to this pond, where he scooped up some water and sprinkled it over his head. "Jewish made up ceremony and, to tell the truth, I feel no different," he said aloud. As he turned his face to the sun, he saw a structure standing up tall, like a statue, out of the corner of his eye. He quickly tried to rise but, like a bowling pin just struck by a speeding black ball, toppled headfirst onto the ground. Gathering himself, he slowly lifted his body and arranged its parts. He walked to the structure and saw that something had been written upon it. Morris removed a handkerchief from his back pocket, dipped it into the water, and wiped at the lettering. He could decipher just this: "And Eternity in an hour." Then the initials WB. Beneath, scripted SAK and AW. Perhaps those letters were encircled or placed within the outline of a heart, a broken heart. This meant nothing to Morris, who nevertheless told himself to figure out the phrase when he returned to civilization.

Just then, wondering if he was daydreaming, heard what he thought was a thud beyond a pocket of birch trees. Wringing out the soggy handkerchief, he turned and walked toward the thicket.

Mendel pressed his palm flat upon the car horn and blasted away. He did not move from behind the steering wheel until he saw Morris emerge. Mendel rolled down the driver side window.

"Get in. I saw Dunkin' this side of the Pike. We'll go get coffee and donuts."

Morris pulled his friend's head halfway through the open window and cradled it. When Morris let go, Mendel, who had opened his door, slid off the seat onto the ground. Morris engulfed Mendel with a hug, lifted him, placed him behind the wheel again, and asked, "One question: Does this joint have any chocolate coconut? I will take three."

Neither man spoke as Mendel maneuvered the Prius back onto the highway. He drove directly to the take-out window for donuts.

"I need to go in and wash my hands," said Morris. "They smell like pond."

"What were you doing in the water?"

"I was not exactly in. The big news is that I discovered an ancient ruin."

"Tell me."

"Well, maybe it isn't quite that old, but it's a statue with writing on it."

"A gravestone?"

"Not so much. More like a marker, a special marker. It said eternity for sixty minutes. I think that was it."

"Sounds like some commercial for getting your snapshots developed. Nothing new about that," said Mendel.

Stuck behind five cars in the drive-up lane, the men were surprisingly patient. Mismatched bookends, they needed each other to be complete.

Before long, Morris had his three donuts and Mendel one. Each ordered a large coffee, Mendel drinking his black and Morris pouring cream and sugar into his. Morris went to wash his hands in the restroom and then Mendel edged the car, once again, back onto the Massachusetts Turnpike.

"Morris, I think maybe you were dreaming this whole thing. Not walking into the woods, but everything else. You were napping and you kind of thought up the rest."

"Shut up, weasel," Morris replied.

"Dreaming," repeated Mendel. "I been reading. Dreams tell stories."

"As sure as my name is Morris Kahn, I saw a stone statue with something about eternity written across its front."

As if Morris hadn't said a word, Mendel continued with his thought, "Morris, do you suppose people dream after they die? In the next world, in purgatory, under the ground? In heaven? In the ocean, if someone scatters your ashes? Cremation—I don't want to think about."

"Maybe," answered Morris. "And I don't want to hear of cremation, which seems to be the latest fad, either."

"That is no answer. You say maybe to everything. Where do they dream? You realize your answer could influence my choice. So far, I got a plot in Brooklyn. And listen to this: I am considering doubling, to make room for Gilda. And for your information, not that you asked, we sleep in the same bed. It's warmer that way. Why not continue?"

"I agree, since you push it, to make a trip to whatever— some kind of bird beach. I can't even remember the name now, and I was the one between us who knew that much. What do I get as a reward? I must provide information on the next life. As if I haven't got enough troubles here."

With that, Morris picked up the car phone Mendel had installed in the Prius. Morris plucked a wrinkled slab of paper from his wallet, held it toward the windshield, and dialed a number.

"Kiley? Yes, it's Morris. I was just wondering what you were doing." He paused. "Looking at women, no matter what age, is a good thing. But, I just wanted to tell you that most of them who buy the *chazzerai* that we sell at Phases, these are Jewish girls." He paused again. "I forgot, that's what you're looking for. Anyway, we won't be back anytime soon." Morris hesitated. "I understand: music, books, Danishes, and now live ladies. You're not bored." He hung up, having satisfied himself that Kiley was fine without them.

"Okay, Morris, do you think we will dream about girls after we're dead?"

Morris smacked the padded dashboard in front of him with such force that Mendel swerved. "How should I know? What do you think? I got a hotline to God? I will say yes to all of your questions. There is an afterlife, many more women than men, all of us are back in action, so to speak. It's one big party. Is that what you're looking for?"

Mendel smiled and pursed his lips as if to kiss Morris. The big man waved forward hoping to catapult the car onward. "Just drive! Speed! What the hell? So you get points on your license. What are they going to do to you?"

Mendel, while still competent behind the wheel, often strayed toward the white line that divided the highway lanes. This was an irritant to other drivers, but Mendel could just not understand why people honked at him. This always surprised him. He shot dirty looks at each driver who passed him. If he drove sixty-five, everyone sped by. If he drove seventy-five, still he found himself lagging behind many. Morris was pushing him now, and Mendel secretly wondered if the Prius would blow apart into a thousand fragments if he broke eighty. Still, he pressed his foot down on the accelerator.

A couple of hours later, Morris, map in hand, navigated their way to Ipswich and the sign to Crane Beach. After three wrong turns and three queries to locals, the pair reached their destination.

Mendel stopped the car and strapped on his wrap-around, extra-large black sunglasses.

"Tell me what you're doing. You got those wings cutting into the side of your head, but you need a string to hold them in place, too?"

"This is insurance," said Mendel, fingering the elastic band.

"But, there's no sun," said Morris.

"There will be. Look up there and you can see the dark spots breaking up and moving away."

"It's already, what, past three o'clock? No way we could get sunburned out here. Why, again, did we make this trip?"

"Sightseeing. Those birds, high school girls in bikinis, also," said Mendel.

"Mendel, we're grown men. No, we are old, grown men who, speaking for myself, at least, have trouble down there." Morris pointed to his belt.

"For once, I am not in disagreement," said Mendel. "That is why I took you here—to gaze at some bathing beauties. For your information, they got pills these days, blue ones, to help us out. You said so yourself."

"The place is deserted," said Morris, hoping to change topics.

"Give them time to get out of school. They will come," said Mendel. "Meantime, let's walk."

"I got no shorts, no trunks," said Morris.

"This did not stop you when you took your little stroll to the pond and dipped in or whatever you did."

"Shush," said Morris.

Mendel made his way to some bushes in search of anything made out of wood. He wanted walking sticks. "We will need strong poles to hold us up. Otherwise, we get sand in our teeth when we fall. Neither of us is that solid," he said.

"Mendel, here's another trip you've gotten me into. The water is blue, the land is tan, I'm getting cold, and we are too old, to be tempting our fates all the way across the state. For what reason?"

"Such a poet. I never knew. This is what they taught you in Cleveland? To end sentences with rhyming words? Still, I am impressed. As Terry whatever-his-last-name-is, that Brando character, says, 'You coulda been a contenda, you coulda been somebody.'"

Morris grew more perturbed with each passing moment.

Unsuccessful at finding them walking sticks, Mendel opened the trunk of his car. He removed two long stakes, gave one to Morris, and kept the other. "These helped some luscious tomatoes reach for the sky. Maybe they will keep us vertical," he said.

Morris took the dark green pole and raised it to the water. "Just trying something, Mendel. You remember Moses and the parting of the Red Sea? I thought maybe it could work for me."

Mendel looked away to cover his grinning face, unwilling to grant Morris the moment. Sure enough, cloud cover had yielded to bright, blue sky as far as Mendel could see. Gazing forward, he saw that the ocean and sky had merged and he wondered if this was truly so or if his failing vision was playing tricks on him. No matter, he thought. This is my reality and that is what counts. He was certain his long-range view was diminished. So, too, Mendel understood that he could never express himself clearly enough, through words, to convince anyone else. If he could perceive clearly, though, why could he not think with such specificity?

He asked Morris again, "Moishkie, what happens next?"

This time Morris, hoping to shut Mendel up for a time, responded directly. "Each one of us dies, God willing, before the generation behind us. You want my opinion? If we do good here, we got a much better chance the next time around. That's all."

Mendel simply nodded. Morris continued. "I got Kiley on my brain. He wants to be a Jew. I am sure that, once upon a time in another incarnation, he was a priest or something. Now, I am worried about him back at Phases."

"Let's go for a swim. Then we can lie down, dry off, and wait for girls," said Mendel.

CHAPTER 2

Zena and Gilda, sisters into their seventies, still considered themselves girls. Girls in waiting—for Mendel and Morris. During the dreary days of January, when it seemed that spending winters in Springfield was a death wish for the middle-elderly, the sisters had convinced their men that dinners together were necessary. For the next few months, no fewer than five evenings a week, they would eat at home, rotating the organizational responsibility. Mendel was allowed to fetch Chinese food, but only if it was his treat. Morris could cater from Gus & Paul's, but the full tab was his. Zena and Gilda chose to prepare. Getting groceries and working through late afternoon helped ease the blues. After all, the sun set before five. The downstairs of the house never really heated up, even if Gilda set the thermostat at 72 or more. The women, who had flown from their Florida nests, grew weary of the weather and wary of prospects.

Spring, however, was rebirth and the months following even better. Once the weather improved, Zena and Gilda struggled to keep the dinner collective alive. On this clear summer Wednesday afternoon, the men could not be found.

"Could be they both turned off their cell phones," said Zena. "What do you think of that?"

"When they roll in at eight, they can fend for themselves. That's what I think," said Gilda.

"Would you say they take us for granted, big sis?"

"They know a good deal when they have it," said Gilda. "Not that we have it bad, either. I suppose it works out for the best."

"Agreed. Men, though, they tend to care about themselves first. Granted, some exceptions. Whose night is it to prepare?"

"That would be Morris, who, no doubt, does remember. What he has in that swollen head of his I never can guess," said Zena.

Morris, at that moment, having switched on his phone to make one essential call, was dialing the number for Frodo's, the new Mexican and Italian place located at the X, the major commercial intersection of the Forest Park neighborhood.

"Mendel, what are they going to want?" he asked when a voice demanded an order.

"Just order an extra-large pizza."

"Why extra?"

"Whenever we do get home, we want leftovers," said Mendel.

"We would like one extra-large pizza. Could you put some pepperoni and hamburger in a plastic bag and include it? That would be terrific. Deliver to Lewis, 36 Forest Drive, near the park, Springfield. That's it."

Neither Mendel nor Morris thought about payment. Forty minutes later, dinner arrived at the front door for Gilda and Zena Lewis.

"That will be $17.80," said the delivery man.

"But this is not our order," said Zena.

"It was phoned in by somebody. I heard the call come in. They sent me over as soon as the pizza was ready."

"All right," said Gilda. "I got some idea of who set this up and conveniently forgot about the check. Typical of that money bags. He's loaded until it's his turn to pick up a tab. I will get it." With that, she gave the man a twenty-dollar bill, took the food, and brought it to the kitchen.

"He remembered," said Zena.

"An elephant, even an ancient one who no longer hears, does not forget," added Gilda.

****

"Mendel, it's getting late. The sun is down. You must be a bit chilled, colder than I am, and not one woman is here. I know you got a thing for girls younger than you, like that Lucy, but there's nothing doing here. Gilda and Zena should be fine for dinner. As for me, I could eat. You ready to go?"

Mendel nodded. The boys gathered a couple of towels they had spread on the ground and slowly ambled toward the car. They opened doors almost in unison, then sat down in silence. Each slumped into his seat.

Mendel said, "I'm tired, Morris. Bushed. You want to drive this new-fangled machine?"

"You do remember that I have a lead foot? If it's okay with you, the Prius will get tested. Sure, I'll drive," said Morris. "Where to?"

"Food. I assume you're hungry? Me, too," said Mendel.

"Of course I'm hungry. But where should we go?"

"Woodchuck's or Woodruff's, whatever it's called."

"Okay, boss," said Morris. He wheeled the car around and gunned the engine.

"You know the way?"

"No, but we'll get there fast if I keep this up," said Morris. Fifteen minutes later, hopelessly lost, Morris pulled into a Dunkin' Donuts. "What goes around comes around. Here we are for a snack," said Morris. "Maybe someone inside can get us on track."

Several minutes and a few donuts later, they were back on the road. "The key is 133," said Mendel, waving a limp wrist forward.

"Allow me," echoed Morris in a deep baritone.

"Set me free," yelped Mendel.

"For posterity!"

They were off, ever the best of friends, chortling, singing, exchanging end rhymes and gibberish as if they were cornball freshman roommates in college during the 1930s or 40s.

"Okay, he said to stay on 133 East and keep staying on 133 East. Nu? We've been on that for days, it seems to me," said Morris, who continued to spin blindly around curves.

"I would like to live to eat one fried clam," said Mendel.

"All I can say is that if that do-gooder Paul Newman can make money even after he's gone, so can I. Mind you, I got nothing against him, but he used to tell everyone all the time about all of the wonderful things he did," said Morris.

"There's got to be a catch. Salad dressing now, too. Pretzels, cookies, popcorn, you name it. The man was a mensch."

"I like his wife. What's her name? Again with Wood. I dunno. Maybe she's Woodrift. It is Joannie something."

"Joanne Newman is her name," said Morris. "For your information, she's in our age group, at least almost. Couple of years back, go know, I would dream about her. Now, she is a senior citizen just like us, just like Zena and Gilda."

"Maybe she is related to this Wood. Wood on wood, if you know what I mean," said Mendel.

Morris accelerated and, veering into the oncoming lane, sped past a tiny foreign car. "Cooperman mini," he said.

"It's just Cooper, like the scooper."

"More rhymes?" said Morris. "You know what precedes scooper, and I'm not going to say it."

"Could we possibly get out of third grade here?" asked Mendel.

"What do you think, Mendel?"

"I think I see a sign for Woodman's, and that is our place. What are we talking with Woodcut's or Woodchuck's?"

Morris wedged the small car in between a tank-like SUV and a golden VW bug. The drive seemed to have exhausted him.

"We made it easily," said Mendel.

"What, as if we're racing the clock? Where would you be, if not here?" asked Morris.

"If I had my way, I would still be on a beach blanket, dreaming of things to come—of the possible," said Mendel. Morris ignored him.

It took a while for the men to realize that they would have to sidle up to the counter so that their order could be taken. Mendel asked for a fried clam dinner plate while Morris went for a large clam chowder and steamers. They went halves on a pitcher of Coke and argued about who had the healthier meal. Morris predicted imminent heart trouble for Mendel since the smaller man chose to eat fried. Mendel noted the size of Morris's portions.

"Morris Kahn, you will split your pants and bust a gut."

"At least I will be living long enough to do so," said Morris.

For two minutes, they ate in silence.

"Mendel, maybe we could do a mitzvah if we had better food at Phases."

"Like fried clams, you mean?"

"That was not exactly what I had in mind. Something other than an artery clogger. But, could we get any of the feel of this joint at our place? The answer is probably no. It seems so comfortable here."

"I like it here too, Morris, but this is nearly on the water. For all I know, it *is* on the water. Springfield is not, unless you count the Connecticut River with all of its dirt and garbage."

"Since you mention water, what about one more peek at the ocean before we go home. We're not gonna see this baby again for a while, and I want to drink it in."

"If you can drive some, the answer is yes. You realize that we are at an hour when the young kids go to the beach to drink and so forth?"

"All of a sudden, Mendel, you're an authority on teenagers. What is it with you? You go to look at young girls, and I will gaze out at eternity. You know, like the saying I saw on the stone statue earlier today."

"We're both poets. I dream about what might have been for me and, I suppose, you dream about what might become for you. This is not so bad: we got the past and the future covered."

Morris added, "Through the present—which is now."

Mendel nodded and extended his hand, palm down, to Morris. The big man removed his right hand, slapped Mendel's hand hard, and gunned the motor.

"You broke my wrist, you ape!" yelled Mendel. His grin, however, betrayed him.

Morris had a good memory for driving directions, and he drove swiftly back to Crane's Beach. He called it that even though it was actually Crane Beach. A small sign advised that the grounds were closed after sunset. The boys had an hour of daylight left.

Each man slid out of the car with surprising ease. Morris saw before him two glorious Labrador retrievers, one black and one yellow. Their owner must have been off walking the beach. "Here boys, here boys," called Morris.

"You are positive these are boys?" asked Mendel, arching an eyebrow.

"Obviously, and this I already knew: You are not a dog person. Who from Brooklyn might be? Where and how I grew up, you called a dog a boy until proven otherwise."

The dogs dashed hard and fast toward Morris. He gathered them both with his large hands and pulled them to his body, much to the animals' delight. Morris began to scratch the dogs behind the ears while Mendel drew back.

"This is Uncle Mendel," said Morris. "Mendel, come over here for God's sake." When the slighter man inched closer, the sandy-haired dog jumped up on him with both paws and immediately began licking Mendel's cheeks. "Down, Rover," said Mendel. Morris doubled over and tumbled onto the sand, drawing the black Lab with him. Morris and the dogs playfully wrestled while Mendel looked at his watch and said, "We got fifty minutes, Morris. Let's go."

Morris dusted himself off and edged toward Mendel. The dogs, spotting their master, who was retracing her steps, hesitated. The woman swiftly ran toward the men and her pets.

"Thank you so much for playing with them. It's actually illegal to have them on the beach now," she said, pulling her dark hair, streaked with red, out of her face. "But, I cannot stand to have them wait in the car. They wouldn't hurt a fly."

Mendel swiped at his face. "What are these things—yellow jackets?"

"No," said the dog lady. "These are green flies, which are not supposed to get here for another few months. I thought they bite hardest in the morning. Guess I was wrong all the way around. Anyway, you two are sweeties for playing with Polly and Jess—that's short for Jessie. They want me all of the time, and I desperately needed just a few minutes to myself, so I ordered them to stay back here."

"We were just coming back from Woodcliff," said Mendel, suddenly poised and conversant.

Morris rolled his eyes backward, realizing that the younger woman, clad in a well-worn BU T-shirt and cutoff shorts, was inspiring Mendel. Morris thought she might be 45 but maybe a very youthful looking 50.

"Where are you from?" she asked. Before anyone could answer, she continued, "I'm Annabelle Winthrop, but everyone calls me Annie or Belle. It doesn't matter. Just that my real name makes me seem like I'm from someplace in the South. And I'm not. I'm originally from Lincoln, which is upper-crust but liberal. More than liberal, if you know what I mean."

Morris and Mendel looked at each other. Mendel lifted an eyebrow, this time in delightful surprise. Morris knew.

"Could we get you—you and your dogs—something to eat?" asked Mendel. "We're starved. And you?"

"Sure. I know a place close by, but suggest we go by car, since the footpath is challenging. And let me drive," she said. "I have a van, you know, for the dogs. They can go in the way back."

Mendel threw back his shoulders, Morris sucked in his paunch as well as he could, and the two of them followed Annabelle, Polly, and Jess. She walked with conviction while the dogs, covering twice as much territory, circled around and back, urging Mendel and Morris to keep up.

"Maybe we could just sit down and order in Chinese or something?" said Morris, grabbing onto Mendel's shoulder with such force that the slighter man nearly toppled over.

"Jump in!" called Annie, unaware that Mendel and Morris had dropped fifty yards off her pace. When they did not respond, she quickly turned and began to laugh. The M&M Boys lurched forward and stumbled into a half-jog as they approached the vehicle.

"What is this?" asked Morris, gasping for air.

"It's an old VW bus that my parents handed down. They were hippies, sort of, in California. They kept this and"—she wiped the bottom of the driver door—"no rust because no street salt, you see?"

"Do you live in this thing?" asked Mendel, noting the built-in bed as he craned his neck to access the interior.

"I've been known to spend an evening inside here, with the dogs of course, when I need to get away," she replied.

On cue, the Labradors, bumping into each other, clamored into the van. Polly bounded toward a water trough while Jess leapt toward the back of the vehicle.

"Better than children, no?" asked Mendel.

"I wouldn't be able to answer that one," said Annie, as if she had more to say. "Anyway, if you"—she motioned to Morris—"would flip down that middle seat, one of you could sit there and the other up here with me."

Mendel eased himself opposite the driver as Morris snapped the bench seat behind him into place.

Morris saw that Annie had a tattoo on her neck and it seemed to continue downward to her lower back. The big man felt certain that she was not watching him watching her as he lowered his eyes to get a full view. Morris had always covered that expansive area on his body by either tucking his shirt into or flopping it over his pants. These days, kids, especially women, were careful to expose. Morris told himself that they wanted to be seen. This, he rationalized, allowed him to lean forward for the view without being labeled a voyeur. Morris, aware that this was marginal behavior, nevertheless persisted. He was positioned on an angle to eye the driver's seat. Morris decided that Annie had a tree engraved all across her back, from the base of her spine to her shoulder line. The bottommost portion featured a mixture of greenery and floral highlights. These, he imagined, were roses, tulips, daisies. The arrangement surrounded the brown base of the tree. Morris wondered what precious treasure the rest of her back held since all he could discern, at the apex, was a culmination and conjunction of forest green leaves. He admitted to himself that he wished to rip off her shirt and get the full effect. Suddenly ashamed, he averted his eyes, glanced out the window, and saw that a bright orange sun was in descent. The perfect ending to such a dream. Why not think these thoughts? After all, Morris thought to himself, if Mendel were in this spot, his friend, too, would yearn to crawl forward. Morris desperately fought to obliterate his impulse to tug down Annie's top.

The truth was that Mendel had fallen soundly asleep. Polly and Jess, if they hadn't, were glad to catch the rhythm of a familiar drive.

Morris was heartened to have some time almost alone with Annie. He would get to know her even if he had but ten minutes.

"Do you come here by yourself often?" he asked.

"Almost always with my dogs. It's anything but isolating. They're my family."

"Someone like you must have many friends."

"I'm just this girl from a rich suburb, like I told you. I've always loved dogs and now that I live somewhere else, I knew that I would need someone or something for companionship. Polly and Jess are my best friends."

"We had a collie in Cleveland," said Morris. "Not Mendel. He's from the city. Brooklyn."

"My parents met in California," said Annie, "but they're both from, well, they went to college around here, in Boston."

"This country, out here, this is where God must have a summer place," said Morris, trying to be funny.

"I live here now," said Annie.

Mendel stirred. "Morris, where are we? What about the girls?"

Annie glanced back at Morris. "I wasn't aware that you two are married."

"We both were, but neither now. We live in a house with sisters we're dating," said Morris.

"And you thought I was kinky because of my tattoo," she said.

Morris blushed as Mendel shot him a look.

"I missed something?" said Mendel.

"Not as much as you would like to think," said Morris. Mendel wet and smoothed a dozen or so hairs, trying with futility to slick them down.

"Here we are," Annie said, driving up to a shack.

"It doesn't have a name," said Morris.

"That's because only a few people actually know that Destiny serves food and drink. You have to come to her door and ask," said Annie. The dogs jumped up with absolute glee. They ran out of the van and sped to the tiny house. Polly yelped, and Jess scratched on the screen door.

A small, soft woman, whose smile ran from ear to ear, peered out. She swung open the top half of a wooden door, keeping the lower portion in place. Destiny's long, nearly platinum hair, attention getting, dominated her upper body. Her bottom portion shook and seemed to dance when she came out to greet the dogs and Annie. Barely over five feet tall, she nevertheless enveloped the three of them with one hug.

Mendel and Morris slowly approached. Mendel's arthritic knee throbbed and caused him to limp. Morris, eager to eat, dragged his friend along.

"Where'd you find those two? Washed up on the beach, sweetie?" she said to Annie.

"Not far from the truth. They left their honey buns for the day to go for a swim and eat some fried clams. Something like that, Des. Anyway, we're all hungry. What you got?"

"The usual, but I've been experimenting with chocolate chip pancakes; also seafood quiche. Boys, join us in the dining room," she said, waving them in. Mendel saw a golden plate adorned with red roses beneath an outside light. "Welcome to Destiny's Place. Relax," the plate read.

The interior appeared to be one large room. An oak table was surrounded by six large wooden armchairs. A huge basket of fruit (apples, bananas, pears, grapes) and a free-standing pineapple beckoned. Annie quickly pulled out a chair and sat as the dogs lay down with the seeming intent to block the front door. Mendel and Morris stood next to each other, as if awaiting orders.

A series of clock chimes, bells, and cuckoo calls simultaneously went off. It was six o'clock. Mendel murmured, "I guess, Morris, all is well. Maybe we should start back?"

"You forget that we left our car at Crane's," said Morris. "Anyhow, let's get something more to eat."

"Why not? You really need it," said Mendel.

Destiny, who had vanished to the rear, returned with a set of hand-painted glasses and a large decanter of red wine.

"I am Destiny, and this is my home," she said, this time smiling simply and serenely.

"Morris Kahn, and this is Mendel Greenbaum."

"You are my guests," said Destiny. "Annabelle brings me only those she trusts. Usually just the two dogs. Sit down. Let's eat and tell stories," she said, laughing once more.

With that, Mendel and Morris sat opposite Annie, with one chair between them. Destiny took that seat.

"Like Annie said, we are just two old men who went away to explore," said Mendel. "Morris and I, we've been friends for years and now we met two women. Life has changed, but sometimes we need to just be the M&M Boys, as we were."

"You two sound like little pieces of candy. Hardly the way you look," said Annie.

"Closer to Mickey Mantle and Roger Maris, if anything, than to those little tidbits," said Morris.

"I don't get it," said Annie.

"But I do," said Destiny. "Anyone who has followed the Red Sox since the late 1950s knows Mantle and Maris, those Yankee sluggers. Did you know that Mickey Mantle was drunk all the time? Now, everyone says he died more of a hero than when he was the big and golden god of a baseball player."

"Keep going," said Annie.

"His last advice was his best to young kids. He told them not to be like him," she said.

"Excuse me, but why are you such a baseball nut?" asked Mendel.

"My own father," said Destiny. "He played in the minor leagues—on the Boston Braves farm team."

"I never knew," said Annie.

"Why would it have come up?"

"What's on the menu?" asked Morris, hoping to change the subject and get some food.

"I am not ignoring your wish for food. But first, what is your sign?" asked Destiny.

"Come again?"

"When were you born?"

"December."

"And you?" she glanced at Mendel

"June," said Mendel who wondered about this magnetic woman's age. To him, she looked 50, but she must be a decade older — what with her baseball recall. Okay, maybe 63 tops but so stunning?

"Good, we can have pancakes. A better bet than the quiche. You two have compatible signs. As far as Annabelle and me, we should be fine."

"I might be allergic to chocolate," said Mendel.

Morris, having shared ice cream desserts with his friend for decades, shrugged his shoulders and laughed.

"Does it offend you that I don't want to break out in a rash?" asked Mendel.

"Rash, schmash, you'll eat what she serves."

"I will make them with fruit instead," said Destiny. "Actually, this is even better. We haven't any fresh berries yet, but melons are ripe early this year."

"So, you like cooking, baseball, and Annie and her dogs," said Morris. "How did you ever get a name like Destiny?"

"My first name hadn't been the right fit for quite a while. A long time ago, I shifted to Destiny. It feels like me, and it suits what I do. When I get to know you better, I will tell more of that story."

"So, Destiny," said Morris, "you are giving us one hint about your work?"

"Foot massage, one of my strengths-of-giving, is both functional and spiritual. Through it, people come to talk about themselves," she explained. "That's how I came to know Annabelle. She heard about me and thought all I did was serve breakfast and lunch. That, technically, is true. But, people come in from all over when they hear I can calm down their feet. The message travels upward through the spine, through tissues, organs, and then to the head. When they realize I can help them, they trust me. Then, they talk. Respect and trust, respect and trust," she said, repeating the mantra. Annie stirred, slid down to the floor and over to her dogs, and immediately began to play with the affectionate Labs. The more she scratched them, the more they licked her cheeks and lips.

"Destiny and I met at a psychology class we were both taking at Salem State. Actually, there is another story behind this. One night after class, she invited me here." Annie spread her arms wide, as if to take in every cranny within the shack.

"I thought I wanted to be a shrink. She was one and maybe she still is, but she talked me out of years of graduate school," said Annie. "Didn't you, Des?"

Before Destiny could answer, Annie plucked a couple of purple tennis balls from one pocket of her shorts and tossed one to each of the dogs. The catches made, the animals jumped for joy. Annie knew just when her Labs could use stimulus. After a bit of play, they were ready to settle down for an hour or so.

Morris's cell phone rang. He fumbled while flipping it open.

"Yes, Zena. I'm glad you got the take-out we phoned in. No, we're not stuck but, as usual, I'm too hungry to drive back right now. We're getting dinner. I think the answer is pancakes. I know that's breakfast food. Didn't you ever get some after an evening shuffleboard match in Florida? This is the specialty of the house. Destiny. No, she's not a hooker. I love you. Mendel says he loves Gilda. We won't be home until very late, so do not—I repeat, do not—wait up. Yes, we will drive carefully. No, we don't know yet which one of us starts out behind the wheel. Goodnight."

Destiny brought in what looked like a vat of batter. She began to shake it above her head, then at shoulder level. Finally, she placed the bowl on the table and let the mixture settle. She lifted her face above the bowl and moved her lips. It seemed, thought Mendel, that Destiny was talking to the pancake batter. He looked at Morris, who raised his eyebrows but said nothing. Annie observed Destiny, her friend, and, in another context, a mentor.

Finally, Annie said, "For Des, the act of preparing a meal is a mystical experience. She sees it as a communion of food, soul, spirit, and people."

Destiny, as if in a trance, nodded. Soon thereafter, she opened her eyes fully, placed her palms downward to hold everyone in place, and began to sing in a rich alto voice. The lyrics were from a tune Mendel and Morris vaguely recognized. Annie harmonized above the melody. Mendel and Morris chimed in on the words that were familiar: "you've got a friend." The rest of the time, the two old men moved their lips in mime and occasionally hummed. Destiny, watchful, raised her arms to the low ceiling, looked upward, and smiled.

She then turned and appeared to vanish at the back of the room. Several minutes later, carrying a platter full of pancakes, she returned. Annabelle stood, went to a cupboard, and came back with plates and silverware, which she swiftly distributed. She began to sing "Amazing Grace." This time, Destiny harmonized. Mendel and Morris silently observed.

Destiny distributed two oversized pancakes to each of her guests, saved a couple for herself, and doled out one each to Polly and Jess, who wagged their tails gleefully and ate ravenously.

By the time everyone finished eating and drinking a concoction of iced tea, lemonade, and seltzer Destiny had produced, the sun had set. Mendel and Morris needed to make the journey back to Springfield, but the Prius remained at the beach. This time, Destiny, Mendel and Morris, and the dogs all wedged into Annie's bus for the ride to the shore.

"This smells like the sea," said Mendel, scrunching up his nose.

"Saltwater does this at night," said Morris.

"Since when do you, landlocked for your entire childhood, become an authority on the ocean and its appeal to the senses?"

"We made plenty of trips," said Morris.

This ride to the beach seemed half as short as the trip to Destiny's had been—especially for Mendel and Morris, who slept throughout. Neither man was aware of the surroundings as Annie announced, "Last stop! Everybody off!" The dogs barreled out, Destiny launched into "Well he never returned, no, he never returned, and his fate is still unlearned, poor old Charlie." The boys looked at each other, simultaneously pleased with and puzzled by the scene.

Mendel and Morris, each creaking, stepped out of the vehicle. To their astonishment, the Prius was not where it had been.

"This is not so bad," Mendel explained. "We can collect insurance, and I will go back and buy a Lexus or something even better."

Annie added, "If you have that money, get an SUV but only if you're sure you can get more than a few miles on a gallon of gas, and they do look smart."

"I was just wondering," said Mendel, turning to look at Destiny, "whether you would care to share that recipe for pancakes. We have a place where people can come and get coffee or tea, maybe a Danish. It would add something if we could serve one dish, such as your pancakes."

"I could eat a dozen more. That's my two cents," said Morris.

"Maybe I could visit you," said Destiny. "Annabelle, how about that? See these fine men and maybe the Berkshires sometime this summer?"

"James Taylor lives out there. Why not?"

"I know—'the Turnpike from Stockbridge to Boston.' And, for sure, the reverse is true," Destiny added.

Annie asked, "The dogs okay with you? I mean, if we visit?"

"We got plenty of dogs in Springfield. All sizes, many personalities. These are two of the finest young ladies I have ever met," said Morris. "But now, we definitely need to move on. There are two women and there's one man named Kiley, who for all I know is still reading a book in our little community house."

"Listen to him, will you?" said Mendel. "A community house? This is a little room in Phases, which—who knows?—might actually work out. And Kiley is mixed up. An Irishman who wants to become a Jew. What next?"

"What is next? Look out there on the marsh. I see our car," said Morris.

A few moments later, the boys discovered the vehicle, which someone had rolled forward along a dirt path—and left.

"Such is life," said Mendel. "I suppose this vintage car is much sweeter than one of those fancy-dan model jobs. Good enough and it looks fine."

Mendel slid behind the wheel and Morris into the passenger seat. All aboard, they began the drive across the state.

CHAPTER 3

Morris insisted when they stopped for coffee and, in his case, a Cinnabon, that he drive the final hour home. By the time they reached the duplex in Springfield, Mendel was curled into an asymmetrical ball, wedged against the passenger side door.

Correctly prognosticating that all would not be well, Morris killed the engine, hoping he could silently glide into the driveway. Gilda, however, led the charge out the front door, with Zena at her heels.

"You couldn't get home before midnight? You two are teenagers who need curfews? You don't remember we got a big event tomorrow?" Gilda accosted the men with her barrage of questions. "You had to eat for three hours? You don't know it's not good for people your age to drive at high speed at night? You don't think about us?"

This spurred Zena. "You really are the most inconsiderate men I have ever met in my life, and I have met plenty," she said.

By now, Mendel was awake. "We could say we got a flat tire and you would never know," he said. "Instead, we're telling you the truth." Then he lied: "The service in one of those, whatever, Legal Fish places is awful. It takes forty minutes to get seated, then another twenty before someone takes your order. Then, I don't know, maybe they have to catch a lobster so that they can serve it." He eyed Morris, who pretended to yawn.

"And the portions you don't want to know about. Not big enough for a ten-year-old on his first lobster. Tough it was, too. Not sweet."

At that very moment, the front door opened and out strolled Kiley.

"What in the blaze of fire is he doing here?" asked Morris.

"Waiting for you. What do you think?" replied Zena. "You just left him in Phases. We didn't know what to do, and he was happy to come with us. Here he is. And, by the way, where did you get that blaze of fire business?"

Kiley had a book in his hand, a tattered hardbound copy of *Exodus*, the novel.

"You know, I never knew the story," he said. "Of course, I saw the movie, with that beautiful music, maybe forty years ago or something. The pages, though, allow you to dream, to imagine. I've had a fair amount of time to pass."

"Anyway," said Mendel, looking back at Gilda. "Why make such a *tsimmes* about tomorrow?"

"This is opening shuffleboard tournament day. We got three matches, maybe more, ahead of us."

"Which is why I say that all of us better go to bed."

A year earlier, after deciding to share the house, both couples had lived upstairs in bedrooms at opposite ends of the hallway. It was Mendel who, one day, put the kibosh on the scheme.

"Up and down, up and down the stairs, not to mention the hallway in the middle of the night when I need to pee. This is no good. My hip tells me, 'Mendel, at your age, you should know better. Find yourself a place where you don't have up and down, up and down.' Gilda, we can't stay up here," he said, awakening early one Sunday morning. It was his ritual to arise before all, in the hopes that the Sunday *New York Times* would arrive on schedule, before seven o'clock. If it had, he would sweep it up, get to the business section, and look at the magazine well ahead of his housemates. "Gilda, if we were down there, I wouldn't have to fall down a flight of steps just trying to find out what to do with RCA stock."

"Mendel, calm yourself. There are people sleeping."

The problem for Mendel was that a first-floor bedroom did not exist.

"We will have to renovate, adapt, expand, make a place for ourselves," he said.

That night, at Wednesday group dinner, he explained further. "I am a wreck—my joints, my behind, my knees. I cannot live on the second floor forever."

"So?" asked Morris.

"So, Gilda and I will move down here."

"And just where do you plan to sleep?" asked Zena.

"We will take this little room with music and computers and adapt it, as they say, into a bedroom. There's a bathroom nearby."

"And just how much will this cost?" asked Morris.

"I don't think much more than a grand," said Mendel.

For the next few months, carpenters, an electrician, and a plumber shared the Forest Park house with its occupants. Mendel, especially, and Morris, as a follower for once, grew testy. Zena and Gilda seemed more than pleased.

On a certain weekday morning, the boys left for the bank and a surefire argument about rent on a property Mendel held. The girls soon greeted all of the workmen with donuts and a drink of choice. Then, the sisters retreated upstairs.

"You know, I sort of like the one with the long ponytail and the frizz just above his upper lip," said Zena.

"The one with the big arms does it for me. So what if he'll go to seed in the next ten years?" said Gilda. "We won't see him when he fattens up—packs on the tires—just like Tony Soprano did."

"Gilda, is it cheating to watch these guys with the hair and the muscles when we're with Mendel and Morris?"

"You know, given our age, it is not against the law to look. In fact, this is probably natural, even healthy. It shows we still want something from men."

"Something we are not all that likely to get from ours," said Zena.

"I wish I could say 'Speak for yourself.' Then, however, I would be a liar."

Within three months, the expansion had been completed. Mendel and Gilda moved downstairs.

Now, each person got ready for bed. Kiley slept on the living room couch.

****

They had not played shuffleboard all that often at Forest Park since the Phases courts had been completed. Lately, Park and Rec had organized a seniors' tournament and promoted it throughout western Massachusetts and northern Connecticut. Zena and Gilda had registered all of them for both same gender and mixed doubles. Women's matches were scheduled for the following day. Today were the men's matches.

Kiley, up before everyone, arrived early. Mendel had heard the courts were rough and he wanted extra practice, while Morris claimed he needed to work out a kink in his shoulder. Zena and Gilda, carrying iced tea in a thermos, sat on their folding chairs across the ball field as the men limbered up. Kiley took out his dog-eared copy of *Exodus* and found a partially sunny spot beneath an old maple tree where he could read.

"Dammit, they don't keep up these courts," said Morris, whomping a disc that flew true until hitting a crack and subsequently skidding far right.

Mendel limbered up by extending his cue, kneeling a bit at the waist, and pointing the stick forward and outward from his midsection.

"What is this?" asked Morris.

"Before everyone else gets up some mornings, I see this man, maybe from China or somewhere, doing what I think they call High Chee. Anyway, he has a staff from time to time and holds it like this," said Mendel, giving a demonstration.

"What does this have to do with shuffleboard?"

"You got to have your mind and body in perfect karma," said Mendel. "This is what Chee said."

The comment drew Kiley's attention. "Yes, this Eastern religion is somewhat like the Middle Eastern, which is what I've been studying."

Morris eyed the two of them as if he might smack one, the other, or both if this kept up.

Kiley continued. "I've been reading about this Kabbalah, you know, like Madonna, the sexy singer. She used to wish she was a virgin, but now she connects to Jewish mysticism. You left me alone in your little community room the other day, and I spent a lot of time thinking about a better way to find God, relate to God. Maybe this, Mendel, is like your High Chief man."

Morris could not stifle a roar as he listened to Kiley's confused interpretation.

"Kiley, Mendel, this is Tai Chi," said Morris. "I know only because I have a niece in New York, Mendel, of all places, who teaches it. Not High and not Chief, but Tai Chi!"

Just then, a loud bell rang three times. Years earlier, the Forest Park Shuffleboard Club had decided this sound would indicate the beginning of a match. Mendel and Morris, ready as they would ever be, sat on a bench awaiting their opponents. At the final gong, two men emerged from the small brick building near the courts. They wore identical shirts and khakis. Their shirts were monogrammed, each with HFD JCC in bold lettering across the front with their names in accompanying script.

"Abraham Hammer," said the man with "Abe" on his chest pocket. "And this is Greenie." Greenie's shirt, however, said "Mordecai."

"I'm Mort Greenberg, but only my wife called me Mort. Actually, she said Morty, which is confusing, since my parents named me Mordecai. On the other hand, in our age bracket everybody thinks all the time of mortality, so maybe it's appropriate. But, I've been Greenie to all since I was a kid." Greenie extended one hand to Mendel and the other to Morris.

Morris, amused, shook Greenie's left hand. Mendel looked away.

Once the game began, the Hartford pair was no match for Mendel and Morris.

The M&M Boys got off winging as Mendel landed an immediate 10. On the rare occasions that Abe Hammer scored, Morris, shooting with gusto, knocked his disc off the court. Neither of the Hartford men seemed to care. Greenie was more interested in socializing, while Abe, sensing early on that his team hadn't a prayer of winning, smiled and played through as if blissfully content.

Mendel and Morris won by more than 30 points. As they shook hands, Abe said to Morris, "I believe you were using an illegal substance on your cues. While we were waiting, I noticed your friend apply lubricant to the bottom of your implements."

"What, this is nothing," said Mendel. "I have always wiped down my cues with a bit of lemon concentrate. Nobody ever said one word until now."

"Nevertheless, New England Shuffleboard Bylaws prohibit foreign substances of any sort."

"Mister," said Morris, "you better be careful. Lemon juice is like water. But, it stings when it hits your eyes, sir."

Greenie tried to maintain calm. "To me, who cares? We met, we can go to a diner or something like that, and get a couple griddle cakes. Nu?"

Kiley, who had been alternately watching the match and reading *Exodus*, interjected. "This is a perfect time to remember that religion, even if it disrupted the world during the Crusades and again and again during our lifetimes, also helps with community. Even celebration. For all we know, shaking hands after a sport is completed could be a mystical experience. Friends, let's explore this park. It could be a mystical stroll."

Greenberg once again extended a hand toward Mendel, who took it and examined the man's palm but said nothing.

Hammer added, "A walk is good. A walk is better if, at the end of it, you find some girls. This I learned as a young boy growing up in Chicago."

"You are from Chicago? I am from Cleveland. We are practically neighbors," said Morris. "We need to get my good friend Abraham a stiff drink—and soon. Let's go find Zena and Gilda. Then, come to our house and get to know these women. Maybe we can find more, even, for you. Our girls know plenty. Just tell me one thing, Kiley. How is it that Jews spend so long getting a place to live and as soon as they get one, they move on?"

"This is what *Exodus* is all about," said Kiley, waving the book above his head.

****

Zena and Gilda rose from their folding chairs, placed the collapsible furniture in sacks, and slowly began to saunter across the lawn. Zena's trick knee had prevented her from playing shuffleboard when the season began. She knew that a knee replacement might be in order. Gilda held to her belief that Zena's extra weight caused the strain on her knee. Zena, however, thought otherwise. "A bum knee is better than a bum ticker," she said.

At this moment, though, she was having difficulty making the walk across the field. Zena wanted nothing more than to be driven home. This, she fully understood, was not a possibility. Morris, waving them in as if he were guiding an aircraft to the departure gate, shouted, "Girls, we got new friends to take out for something to eat. Maybe we can find them some companions, if you know what I mean." At last, the women arrived at the grandstand near the shuffleboard courts.

"Morris, be careful," said Gilda.

"Mort Greenberg, Abe Hammer, meet the Lewis sisters, Zena and her big sis, Gilda."

"Speaking for Zena, it is a pleasure to meet you," said Gilda.

"You are the little sister," said Greenie, extending a hand to Zena. "But, you're not as big as Morrie said. My ex-wife, she was what you called big. As in zaftig. When I think about it, that is not exactly bad."

"Morris is what you would call fat," said Mendel.

The big man was not self-conscious about his size, unless someone called him fat. This set him off. "At least I don't look like a skeleton," said Morris. "Hello, Bones."

Mendel knew enough to be quiet.

Zena said simply, "His name is Morris, and a few friends call him Moe. Not Morrie. He is not a Morrie."

"I am sorry for this," said Greenie. "Anyone who calls me Mort, watch out."

Kiley signaled the contingent forward. "This is the way to Pulpit Rock," he said. "I know. I used to worship it when I was a Christian. Now that I am studying the Hebrew tradition, it takes on a new meaning."

Mendel and Morris, the Lewis sisters, and Abe and Greenie walked slowly to the crest of a hill where Kiley, walking stick in hand, motioned them to follow. As they approached, Kiley began to descend.

"Wait a minute, Kiley," called Mendel. "We got to see what this looks like, what we're getting into, before you drag us somewhere."

"Fair enough," said Kiley, whose head reappeared above ground level.

When everyone had gathered, he spoke. "It isn't very hard to get to Pulpit Rock. You walk down here, maybe twenty or thirty feet down. You stop, go to the left, and follow a little winding stream. Then, you see what looks like a stone platform. That's it. I been there maybe eight times. Never has anything happened. Way back when I was in the church, though, people in the parish told me to come here and wait. They claim to have seen wild animals. Someone even said he thought he saw a mirage or had a hallucination. I never really believed in that until Kaballah. Now, who knows?"

Morris drew Mendel to the side. "I cannot believe that it was just yesterday what with the pond and the inscription, Woodchuck's, the beach, the girl with her dogs, Destiny and her food, the drive home. We did all of that and now we're with our girlfriends and this *meshugge* Kiley, who is a born-again but I don't know what or when for that matter. Mendel, we're acting like a couple of teenagers. I watch you sneaking glances at anything female that moves. The reason I know this is I'm right behind you. Even if you cannot perform, you never lose the urge to lust, correct?"

"Unfortunately, I am an expert when it comes to this topic. For a big fat guy from the Midwest, you're no dummy," replied Mendel. "I think, though, we better pay some attention. Otherwise, these girls are going to think something funny is up." Mendel and Morris joined the group just as Kiley, demonstrating, shifted his weight upward to avoid a spill as everyone maneuvered down the hillside.

A large rock with a blue arrow greeted them as each member survived the short trip to the valley. "This must be your rock," said Greenberg.

"No, this is a rock giving us directions to The Rock."

"I don't know what we're doing here, Greenie," said Abe.

"Would you rather return to the dependence of independent living or have some fun?" asked Greenberg.

"Follow me," said Kiley.

A small, nearly camouflaged snake appeared next to Gilda's shoe. Unfazed, she picked up a branch and brushed it away.

"Me, I would have keeled over if that rattlesnake jumped me," said Mendel.

"I love you, Mendel, but you are a coward, except maybe when it comes to the stock market," said Gilda.

"There it is!" shouted Kiley.

The rock looked like anything but a pulpit. A slab of stone, it extended halfway across a running stream. Pulpit Rock could have been a bench. At the very least, it afforded walkers and explorers the opportunity to sit and rest, watch the water, and bathe in sunshine peeking through treetops. On the negative side, they also had to swat an army of flying insects for whom this was home base.

Zena, who had bravely trundled down the slope and continued along the path, lurched toward the rock, eager to take the weight off her dysfunctional knee. Gilda wedged beside her. Abe Hammer sat next to Gilda, a portion of his bottom hanging off the sitting area.

"What's that, over there, in those woods?" asked Greenberg.

"Allow me," said the invigorated Kiley. Mendel and Morris, curious, followed while Greenberg stood next to Abe and watched.

The investigating trio stepped across the water hazard en route to the distant object. Morris attempted to leap over it but gauged poorly. His heel landed smack in the muck of the swamp.

"Nobody can maintain nothing!" he shouted. "They pay those guys an arm and a leg and all they do is go to Dunkin', which, as a matter of fact, is where I would rather be."

Mendel pulled his friend along in pursuit of Kiley, who, like a retriever, made a beeline for his prey.

Ahead of the pack, Kiley announced, "This is a baby carriage—maybe thirty, forty years old. I think there's some writing inside it. Wait a minute." Kiley went to work, narrating his discoveries. "There's a little mattress here, and underneath I think this is a newspaper. It's crumbling and yellow. Someone circled things on a classified page."

"Who really cares, Kiley? Let's get on with the walk so we can go home and eat," bellowed Morris.

"You be quiet, you buffoon," said Mendel. "Don't be a *schlemiel*, Kiley. Take your time and tell us what it says."

"This is a Jewish newspaper and whatever is marked here, I have no clue," said Kiley. "But, I take this as a sign of destiny."

"Destiny, again!" said Morris.

"You know, I think Morris is right. We ought to get home, and I don't know if you two"—Gilda motioned to Abe and Greenie—"will be able to make it, but I got plenty of brisket, enough to feed an army. You want to join us for dinner later, that would be my pleasure."

Kiley wasn't paying attention. "What do you mean about destiny again?" he asked.

"You will find out at our house, and so will we since this is yet another Mendel and Morris mystery tale," said Zena. "I think if we can possibly walk over that way, we just might be able to climb up a hill and land at the clay tennis courts. It's not more than five minutes from that point on to the duplex."

"Abe, we on any schedule?" asked Greenie.

"It's your car," said Abe. Then, looking at everyone else, he added, "Greenie has one of those new Camry hybrid jobs. Not at all bad, if you ask me." The Connecticut visitors chose to walk to the collective household and pick up the vehicle later to drive back to West Hartford.

Thirty minutes later, everyone but Zena and Gilda had arrived. Zena, her foot blistering, complained to her big sister, who had little sympathy and nothing but hardened advice.

"This is what you get when you allow him to buy you cheap shoes. Mendel would do just the same, maybe worse."

****

Kiley opened a bottle of white wine, and Gilda supplied seven glasses of different sizes and shapes. Kiley carefully placed one ice cube in each and paid no attention to those who claimed lack of interest. He meticulously filled one after another to an identical spot just above the halfway point.

Zena, however, interrupted his trance when she turned on Morris. "Okay, that's enough, Mr. Big Shot! Who is this Destiny woman? Since you been home, it's either you or your friend, Mendel, who speaks of this person as if she's some angel from heaven. What gives?"

Mendel answered, "She is what you call a spirit or something. Not that I am religious, but when you are with her, there comes a point when you think to yourself that maybe life has meaning. I never met a person like this before."

"Would everyone please sip just once?" asked Kiley. "This is religion."

Abe and Greenie lifted their glasses immediately while the rest hesitated.

"Please," said Kiley. "I have been studying many Christian religions for years and just recently Judaism. Ceremony, no matter what faith you've chosen, helps people to calm down and center—as Eastern religious men say, to find focus."

"Gibberish, but I will do as he wishes," said Mendel.

Morris lifted his cup and said, "*L'chayim.*"

Everyone toasted, but not one of these exhausted seniors had the energy to say anything more.

Kiley broke the silence: "Now then, Morris and Mendel will tell us of this Destiny."

Mendel, seizing the opportunity to save face, immediately began to revise the quite recent past. "You see, both Morris and I heard of a little tournament for people in our age group, men in this case, in Arlington. For those who don't know, this is west of Boston. We took off yesterday with every intention to play. Along the way, though, Morris noticed a sign pointing to the North Shore. Cape Anne, I think it is. We decided to go exploring. This is some country, let me tell you. You drive along for a ways and pretty soon you feel like maybe a horse is going to bound right over one of the white rails along the side of the road. I suppose this is comfortable for some people. For me, a little Jewish guy from Brooklyn, I would have been scared, if that scenery did not knock your eyes out of your head."

Here, Morris jumped in. "I just want you to know that this was not my big idea to play a tournament. But, when Mendel heard of it, I went along. Why not? It's always that

Springfield is second fiddle. Nobody out here can be any good. I figured this would give us a chance to do the city proud, not to mention anyone, let's say, over seventy-three. He's right, the sky seems a brighter blue out there. If you ask me—and this is a person who grew up going to Lake Erie for fun—the ocean plays this trick on you. You see the ocean blue and, all of a sudden, the sun juts right out at you. Anyway, I had to wear those big wraparound sunglasses and I was driving by now."

"I thought you just said you were going to play shuffleboard," said Zena.

"We decided to follow the signs to Cape Anne," said Mendel. "It was a joint decision, one which was not a question. I don't know exactly why. But, with a cell phone and help from information, I could call that group who sponsored. I didn't actually get a live voice. I left some story for them about why we couldn't come. I will tell you the truth. I said we both got food poisoning from some fish we ordered."

"Meanwhile, you two liars were off on some joyride to the beach. Probably you hoped to see some sweet young things in sexy bikinis. I wouldn't put it past either of you," said Zena.

"Listen to me, Zena," said Morris. "I have eyes but, in this case, they were meant for checking out scenery, not body parts."

"Sure, you convinced me," said Zena, sounding unconvinced.

Kiley tried to maintain the peace. "This is a great story. Let's sit longer and drink more wine."

"As long as one of us is sober and able to drive, we are not in a hurry," said Greenie.

"Anyway, let me continue," said Mendel. "We were driving along these twisting roads in search of the beach when, again, we saw a sign for Woodman's, and we knew about this place."

"But, we chose to go to the beach first to get the good light," said Morris. "Besides, it was getting kind of late in the afternoon and I felt we might lose the best view."

"When we reached Crane's Beach and parked, the first thing we saw was a fisherman who maybe had a big one hooked," said Mendel as Morris shot him a look. "I don't know fishing, but they tell me this is some thrill. You, the fish—it's a struggle, and this is the first time I have ever seen such a thing," continued Mendel.

"Will you please get to the point?" asked Gilda. "There is only one whopper here, and it is your story. I would like you, Mendel, to be truthful. Did you hear of some girl or something?"

"Nothing you heard so far is a lie," Morris lied. "Let me speak for just a second. So, we went to eat. Such fried clams you've never tasted! I wish he would open even a shack like this out here. I would be there every day for lunch or early bird if they had it. Anyway, we ate, we went to the beach. Yes, we met a girl, a young — she was a middle-aged woman really, who, with her two gorgeous Labradors, brought us to a little house later. This is called Destiny's, so now you know."

"Now, we got some puzzle here and to fill in the pieces will take all night. What about these guys from Hartford? You men, why are you staying here?"

"Girls," said Greenie.

"He means we are lonely," added Abe. "The only reason we ever came up to Springfield was we thought we might meet someone. You wouldn't know since you are all attached. But, it can be a desert out there. I been divorced for nearly twenty years, and I'm ready. Greenie lost his wife not long ago, and he has been by himself or with me ever since.

"Like I said, maybe it's time for me to get, as they say, back into circulation. I got some problems with that anyway. But, I don't think this is the time for that. Actually, we ought to get back on the road before long. So, could one of you please tell us about this Destiny and the other mysterious woman?"

"This is precisely where I was headed," said Mendel, "before every single one of you had to add your two cents."

Morris nodded in support and added, "Anyway, this woman—and this is where you come in, Kiley—she has what I think they call an aura. Such a nice person and not too skinny. Nu?"

"I just read where it says if you got a bit of fat, you live longer," Zena interjected.

"You will live for a while then, dear," said Morris.

"And you, with your paunch, will live forever," she returned.

"I wanted to say that Destiny is some lovely woman," said Mendel. "To me, it seems she has some kind of prophecy but is based on a feel for people and what is going on."

"Sounds like hocus-pocus to me," said Abe.

"And, at first, to me," said Mendel. "But, the longer I stayed, the more I liked it. Now, a day later, I miss it and her. I wouldn't mind going back there. She has a style that grows on you."

"Most people who are not men grow on you, Mendel. This is nothing new," said Gilda.

"I second that motion or emotion, whatever," added Morris.

"Nevertheless, a trip to Ipswich would do everyone in this room good," said Mendel.

"Again, I second," said Morris.

"I'm in," said Kiley.

"But not us," said Abe. "Miles to go before we get to the Insurance City. Imagine, it takes thirty minutes to get from the City of Homes to the Insurance City. Greenie and me have to get going. But, we need two rain checks, actually three. We would like to stay over with you sometime. Play a full round of shuffleboard. Meet this Destiny, too."

"Don't leave out the Labradors. They are always a canine-lover's delight," said Greenie, a bit of a dandy who twirled the ends of his silver handlebar mustache. "A couple of man's most trusted friends can add years. We need every extra day we can get."

****

Finding an appropriate time and corresponding excuse for Mendel and Morris to leave Springfield and journey back across the state was perplexing and difficult. Phases, their contribution to society as a club for elders, needed them. Mendel led investment group meetings Monday and Friday mornings. The girls taught shuffleboard Monday through Thursday. Morris led his beloved "Sounds of the Past" workshop just after lunch each weekday. He took great pride in never having cancelled. Held in the warm, fully carpeted Gillespie Grove (so named, by Morris, for Dizzy), every session began with the trumpeter's classic "Salt Peanuts." Morris passed out nuts and asked if anyone wanted coffee, tea, or non-alcoholic beer. That was the scene the next day as Morris, the teacher, spun some old long-playing records featuring an early, live Modern Jazz Quartet. Morris might have been lecturing to an audience of hundreds in a university auditorium. That he had two students, one perpetually dozing, meant nothing to him. He could listen to jazz records all day and talk all night about what he had heard. He considered this a treasured moment.

Mendel decided to take the new Prius to be cleaned and waxed at the only touch-free car wash he knew of—one across the river in West Springfield. He stopped off for a Memo's muffin, which he combined with a large Dunkin' Donuts black coffee. This, to him, was altogether heaven.

****

Zena and Gilda sat opposite each other in their kitchen. The elder sister began working on the Thursday *New York Times* crossword puzzle. When stumped, she silently passed it to Zena, who took a welcome break from her romance novel. Since they had been girls, Zena had felt compelled to follow her big sister's lead.

The puzzle out of her head and hands, Gilda felt the need to speak. "Maybe we should go visit this wonderful Destiny sometime this weekend."

"Gilda, do you notice that these men of ours always seem to be fascinated with one woman or another, most of them much younger?"

"I gather that Destiny is no spring chicken."

"She's the exception, but she has other things going for her. According to Morris, she's half-prophet, half-goddess."

"You're right, Zena," said Gilda. "When I walk with Mendel, his eyes go right to every belly he sees. You know, these girls hang out no matter what—I mean their middles. They don't care what slips over, they show it. And Mendel, for some reason, he seems to think this is the cat's meow. He is obsessed. I could understand better if he stared at their chests even. What is it with this man?"

"Morris always tells me he doesn't mind my weight, but I'm not so sure. There's a limit. Anyway, same story here. His eyes bug out when he sees one of those teenagers in a tank top skating around in the park. If you ask me, though, he likes skinny just as well, maybe more."

"You don't think they'll get tired of us, do you? Sex is not exactly what we got to offer. I should speak for myself."

"You assume correctly—for me, too. Maybe they see us as mother figures. As I say that, I really don't know what I'm talking about, Gilda."

"They never mention anything about their wives," said Gilda. "It's a mystery."

"Sometimes, it seems to me they have a pact. Certain topics are taboo; others are okay to discuss. Like they've worked this out for years. And, never should they even mention who they were with. Like we do not think about it? They must know we do."

"I say we should ask them. See how they handle it. You think?"

"Tonight, at dinner. I'm preparing, Gilda. You get some extra-special wine. It probably wouldn't hurt if each of us indulges just a bit before you bring this up."

"I will go right to the store. Tell Mendel, if he asks, I'm just out for my afternoon walk."

"Another chapter, sis?"

"About to be written," said Gilda, gently closing the back screen door behind her.

Mendel chose to postpone his return home. Instead, he drove to Phases, where he was certain to find Kiley, who was spending nights either at the Forest Park duplex or in the Phases common room. At the latter, he monopolized a well-worn sofa that worked better as a sleeping rather than reading couch.

Kiley was sitting on the floor with his legs partially crossed. Even from a distance, Mendel recognized the tattered copy of *Exodus* next to him. Kiley had something on his lap. From across the room, Mendel thought it might be a large, spiral-bound crossword puzzle book. As he approached, Mendel saw the top of a blue Scrabble box leaning against a corner of the sofa.

"You cannot take me, Kiley. I will even give you odds. It's not for no reason that, at age twenty-one, I vowed that I would study the dictionary and commit each definition to memory."

"And how far did you get?"

"The point is that I tried, Kiley. Who else even made the attempt?"

"Mendel, this is Hebrew Scrabble."

Edging around the sofa, Mendel saw that this was true. Each tile had a Hebrew letter etched upon it. "Now I know for certain that you are crazy. The headshrinkers should come and put you in some van and take you away."

"To learn a language, you need to immerse yourself. That is how I mastered Latin."

"You mean they got Latin Scrabble, too? Shoot me now and save me months of agony," said Mendel.

"Latin, after a short while, I began to read, Mendel. Hebrew, with its own alphabet, isn't so easy. So, I figured if I could learn the letters, then maybe . . ."

"Yeah, and assuming you do? Then what?"

"I begin to read Hebrew and next year go to Israel."

"What do you want—to get killed? You are a Christian, Kiley. Even if you convert, look in the mirror. You got that sweet Irish mug. Go to Israel. By then, the suicide bombings will be back in full force. This is just a lull. But, let's talk about why you would ever want to become a Jew. Morris told me that you think we Jews live another lifetime. Maybe so but, believe me, there is no guarantee. Why would you want to take on even more guilt? You quit one religion, then you take up another. What if this one is no better than the first?"

"I explained this to Morris, and now I am telling you, Mendel. Judaism is just a better match for me. I think of poets—even that Allen Ginsberg is more interesting to me than any of those Catholic stiffs. I mean, Ginsberg wrote that 'Kaddish.' You should read it."

"Him, with his hair, with his boyfriend, the one with that accordion. Ginsberg and his Peter friend never did appeal to me," said Mendel.

"Mendel, I am just trying to find a way to live on and even on again. Nothing in Christianity gave me any hope. This"—he pointed to the Scrabble board—"does."

"Listen, Kiley, I could be wrong, but from what I know of life, the idea is to live each day for what it's worth and not worry about what comes next. This goes for both your brain and body. This business of where your soul goes, that's another ball game. Who cares what religion you got?"

"Precisely, Mendel. I want some part of me to go forward. If that is my soul, so be it. I will take it. I just cannot think that one day I will go poof like a dead lightbulb and that will be that."

"Save this for another day, Kiley. The girls are cooking dinner, and we are expected. If the two of us are late, I will pay for that."

"Am I crowding all of you?" asked Kiley. "I don't want to cause any trouble."

"Kiley, you're like a cousin. We've known you forever. Now we just know you better."

Mendel and Kiley had forgotten about Morris's class, but they were reminded as the sounds of a trumpeter wafted from one room to the next.

Within minutes, Morris and his student, Hy, appeared. Morris snapped his fingers while Hy seemed mesmerized.

"Greetings. This has been some session. It put Benny to sleep. But Hy, here, is getting with things. As soon as I turned off that MJQ record and slipped in a Miles Davis CD, he came to life."

"You can't go wrong with Miles," said Kiley.

"Since when are you an aficionado?" asked Morris.

"I used to play," replied Kiley.

"When you were an apologetic goy, you mean?" cracked Mendel.

"Don't tell me he brought up this conversion again," said Morris.

"I caught him playing Hebrew Scrabble," said Mendel.

"Maybe we can paint some Hebrew letters on one of our shuffleboard courts. What do you say, Kiley? You want to crown some Jews on such a court?" asked Morris.

"Listen, I happen to think your faith has much to offer. So sue me, if you will," added Kiley. "As the song goes."

"Enough. I think we have to get going, all of us," said Mendel. "So, if you will be good enough to make certain that Hy and whoever else it is you are teaching are taken care of, the three of us need to see the ladies."

Morris insisted that they drive both Benny and Hy to their homes. That accomplished, Mendel, Morris, and Kiley doubled back from Longmeadow to Forest Park, where the women were waiting.

The men were surprised but delighted to find five filled wine glasses set on the dinner table. Mendel and Morris had already fabricated a story since they were certain it would be impossible to slip in nearly an hour late without receiving barbed commentary. They worried for naught. Zena, wearing a full apron, and a seemingly relaxed Gilda were more than pleased to greet them. Kiley, too, received a full hug from each woman. Mendel brought a finger to his lips to shush Morris.

Kiley, however, did not receive the message. "Gilda and Zena, we would have been here earlier if Hyram hadn't fainted during Morris's jazz class."

"What happened, dear?" asked Zena.

"He takes an inhaler twice a day, and he forgot. It was kind of musty in that room and, wham, he just passed out," said Morris, staring at Kiley.

"That's so sad," said Zena.

"So, did you take him to emergency?" asked Gilda.

"He recovered, according to Morris, in a minute," said Mendel. "He even walked down to visit us, didn't he, Kiley?"

"Oh, yes, he is in good health."

"Since when are you a doctor?" asked Zena.

"His color came back in seconds. It was as if nothing had happened," said Kiley.

Zena walked off and returned carrying a large platter of brisket.

"Before we eat, let me toast all of you and this Destiny, too," said Gilda.

Mendel shot a look toward Morris, who rolled his eyes. A different sort of session was about to begin.

"My big sister and I, we would like to celebrate. Five of us in this room are in decent enough shape, with most of our faculties intact. This is nothing to sneeze at," said Zena, lifting her glass.

The men began to drink immediately while the women continued.

It was Gilda's turn to speak. "It is many months since we began this experiment, the four of us. So, I call it the half-year anniversary."

"Maybe I should excuse myself," said Kiley. "This is a special dinner, an occasion. I'm afraid I don't belong here."

"You haven't any choice, my friend," said Morris.

Mendel seconded. "You want to be a Jew? If you're at a party or something, you don't leave early. This is rude."

"No, I wasn't attempting to be impolite," said Kiley.

"Stop that foolish talk, Kiley. We want you here, isn't that so, girls?"

Gilda smiled as Zena inched her cup upward in salute.

"If that is true, I don't mind staying. It's very generous of all of you," said Kiley.

Zena went back to the kitchen and returned with large bowls of fresh beans and mashed potatoes. Gilda passed around the hot rolls and salad. The men helped themselves to significant helpings of brisket. Zena explained that she "had prepared for eight—no need to skimp on portions."

As they ate, though, the conversation was limited to jazz masters, the unseasonably cool weather, the condition of the park, and speculation about the prospects for the city of Springfield.

Each drank fully of the wine. Gilda took a breath just before finishing her second glass of cabernet. "We are supposed to plan a trip to see this Destiny. So?"

"Gilda, you've never met anyone like her."

"Alright, what is it with you men? You meet a woman, always it's a woman, and there's no one like her. Cleopatra is back, yet. Am I wrong ?"

"I have to agree on this. She has such a great body in the front, is that it?"

"If you like teddy bears," said Morris.

"So, why *this* Destiny? Isn't there some kind of rap singer or something named Destiny? Destiny and Her Children?" asked Zena.

Nobody responded.

Mendel tried to be serious. "It doesn't matter that she is a woman. This is not a usual person. It's almost as if she is from somewhere else, like a spirit," he said.

"Now, I'm interested," said Kiley.

"And I cannot believe my ears," said Gilda. "Mendel, this one who will milk a buck from his best friend if he needs to, has found a spiritual leader—a large woman, no less?"

"You will just have to meet her," said Mendel.

They ate and drank, and talked of movies and children. All avoided further mention of Destiny.

Zena offered options for dessert: apple pie with vanilla ice cream for those who wished to indulge; raspberry sorbet for those paying attention to health and fitness.

Morris wolfed down two portions of pie. Finishing the last, he said, "I would let out a belt notch if I were wearing one. I got these warm-up pants on, which expand."

"In your case, this is a blessing. I mean that you got more room to grow. Look at you," said Zena.

"If I were in your condition, I might not speak so fast," replied Morris.

"I still love you," said Zena.

Having heard enough, Mendel moved back from his chair and rose, seemingly one joint at a time, until he was mostly vertical. He then began to gather plates. Each of his friends followed his lead.

"You will all excuse Zena and me," said Morris. "We got to talk in private."

With that, he took her hand and escorted her upstairs. He opened the door to their bedroom and shut it behind them. Morris then sat on their four-poster bed, which Zena had picked out. Morris began to take off her shirt.

"Just what are you doing?"

"I thought maybe we could spend some time in bed. Early. Before one or both of us falls asleep, which happens every night."

"I'm stuffed. Open your eyes. I look like a fat hen," she said.

"I love you, Zena," said Morris.

When she heard that, Zena took off her clothes, letting them fall to the floor, and slid beneath the covers.

"I took one of my blue pills before dinner," said Morris, as Zena pressed her palm softly on his big belly.

"For someone pushing eighty, you still got that extra oomph, which stirs me up," said Zena.

Morris smiled widely, turned to Zena, and kissed her hard on the lips.

An hour later, they went back downstairs and found Mendel sitting by himself in the living room.

"Where's Gilda?" asked Zena.

"She and Kiley went for a walk," said Mendel.

"But, your hip hurts, with arthritis, yes?" said Morris. He looked skyward, hoping, perhaps, to clarify his comment.

"That's the least of my troubles," replied Mendel.

He refused to elaborate, preferring instead to begin discussions about the return visit to Ipswich—and Destiny.

That Saturday morning, at Mendel's insistence, all five of them jammed into the groaning Prius, which was about to either split or quit. Ignoring Zena and Gilda's suggestion that they rent a minivan, Mendel coaxed Morris and Kiley to take his side in the matter. Finally, he said he would not go unless the Prius was the vehicle of choice. Mendel refused to acknowledge he had insisted that everyone meet Destiny but was flexible as to where or when. During the past few days, speaking with Annabelle, who was serving as Destiny's voice, Mendel had realized that a weekend rendezvous was the only option. Annie worked evenings at a Cambridge bookstore/café, and Destiny went to bed early during the week. During the weekend, however, Destiny seldom slept.

Mendel and Morris continued with the bluffing charade. The men hardly knew Destiny or Annabelle. Yet, they proceeded as if Destiny were a genius—part goddess, part prophet.

As Mendel sped past the portion of the highway where Morris had discovered the message upon the stone pillar, the big man rolled down his window, put out his hand, and waved. The women watched and laughed but said nothing. Mendel, relieved, sighed to himself. He suddenly pulled the car over to the side of the road.

"Just back there, when Morris poked his hand out, there's a beautiful pond. Someday, we should stop to see it," said Mendel.

Morris glared at him but said nothing.

The skies soon darkened and, without warning, let loose with shots of thunder and multiple lightning flashes, followed by a brief, violent storm. Mendel put his hands over his ears. Everyone else waited silently for the downpour to cease.

Nearly thirty minutes later, the rain on the wane, Morris spoke. "If you look to the right rear, you will see three-quarters of a rainbow. That is a sign."

"Of what?" asked Zena.

"Destiny, my dear," replied Morris. "Look at those rose, orange, and pink hues."

"This is some mystery," said Kiley. "At what point in this game will one of you clue us in?"

"In time," said Mendel, stepping on the accelerator and swinging the hybrid vehicle back onto the Massachusetts Turnpike.

CHAPTER 4

As a teenager, Deena Tina Yates was known as DT. Destiny came later. DT grew up in wealthy, liberal Lincoln, several miles west of Boston. The daughter of a charismatic junior high school English teacher and a man known for his integrity through his work, she was allowed to think that any achievement was hers for the taking. She had smarts, charm, and golden good looks. Plus, her parents provided her with a financial base that enabled her to find and then be herself, regardless of societal norms and conventions. She dreamt daily and recorded many of her dreams in a notebook binder. On the outside of the book, she wrote "Destiny." She cut out pictures of multicolored flowers, taken from the pages of glossy magazines, and mounted them meticulously along the edges of the notebook. While living with her parents, she hid the journal under her bed at night, made an entry when she woke, and then moved the book to a special spot beneath a rug in her bedroom closet. Before reading in bed each night, she carefully placed the book, razor-point pen attached to the inside cover, in its place.

When she was seven years old, Deena's parents, Marsha and Henry, bought a home in Chatham, on Cape Cod. Every year, she, her parents, and her little brother, Todd, four years younger, summered in Chatham. There, she claimed to have first communed with the ocean. She did not, however, take to boats. Todd learned to sail early on, but Deena never showed any interest. She liked to sit in a life raft on a salt pond and dream. If she was lucky, she would get there before the boaters had charged up their crafts. Deena always brought along a felt-tip pen and several lined pages for notes and musings, which she could later place in her binder.

She also liked to loll about on Pleasant Bay. There, Deena read books and magazines and watched for birds. After dinner, she biked to Nantucket Sound and sat by herself, hoping that no one pestered her. She lived for that moment—the precise instant each day when the sun disappeared. She did not need to scan the heavens to look for the moon. She had a sense for the moon's specific location and turned that way every evening. Young Deena was non-scientific. She had read about people's intuition and imagined that hers granted her the talent to instantly search out the moon. This was fun and a gift she decided was exclusively hers.

By the time she was in ninth grade, Deena had achieved her full height. Compact and shapely, she was embarrassed by her curves and chose to hide them by wearing, for the most part, men's oxford long-sleeved shirts, with tails hanging down. In this way, she was able to cover much of her body without revealing the shape of her breasts and hips.

At Lincoln-Sudbury Regional High School, she listened closely to her English teacher. Barbara Falk, in her early twenties, had published poems in two small journals, one based in the Midwest, the other in the South. Originally from North Carolina, she had come to the Northeast to be with her boyfriend. The relationship dissolved when he declared, suddenly, that he wished to be celibate. Barbara and Deena latched onto each other. It was Barbara who said to Deena one day, "You're DT. Deena makes you sound like a housewife. DT has a distinctive ring to it. This is 1962, not 1950 —perhaps a new time," she declared. DT was most pleased. She had never seen herself as a Deena, but it had not occurred to her to modify her given name.

Marsha and Henry were delighted when DT invited Barbara to Thanksgiving dinner, to be held at the Chatham summer home. This was a first. While Chatham did not completely shut down after the leaves fell to the ground, many businesses closed their doors until the following summer. Each of the children was permitted to bring one friend to Thanksgiving dinner. This was a no-brainer for Todd, who asked George. George idolized Todd. Whatever Todd said, George did. Everyone told Todd that he should branch out, but Todd was content, for now, to be George's hero.

Henry drove the Volvo wagon, filled with people (including George, whom they picked up) and food, directly to Chatham that Wednesday. It was a mild, humid, windy night—highly unusual for late November on Cape Cod. A euphoric DT realized she was welcome to comb the shoreline. She knew that Barbara would be a taker and that her mother and father would look kindly upon the venture since Barbara was driving. DT directed her teacher to a beach on Nantucket Sound.

Even as the wind whipped through DT's flowing long hair, the water remained still. Barbara wore a baseball cap embossed with the image of a black Labrador retriever looking out on the world before it. The teacher, long and willowy, and the student, smaller and eager, ran to the water's edge. They approached the passive salt water and stopped. Without a word, they clasped hands and walked together beneath the nearly full moon's radiance and guidance. Soon, they approached a lifeguard's chair.

"This is my one chance," said DT, who scurried up to the guard's seat. Barbara followed, and they squished together. They felt invisible to everyone else, encased within the solid black night.

Barbara began to stretch but then lost her balance and nearly toppled to the sand. As DT caught her, she saw that a book was supporting one leg of the structure. She shimmied out of the chair, Barbara followed carefully, and they lifted the wooden beam to see what kept it in balance.

DT found a Plexiglas box-like container housing a book. She removed a worn, wan paperback volume that read *The Portable Blake*. Beneath the title, a man with frizzy hair, apparently naked, was caught amid flames.

"This is the poet you once mentioned?" asked DT.

"Yes, could I see it?" said Barbara. The English teacher saw that a pink three-by-five card marked a page. She turned to it and presented a circled passage to her favorite student.

DT read: "To see a World in a Grain of Sand / And a Heaven in a Wild Flower / Hold Infinity in the palm of your hand / And Eternity in an hour."

Neither woman spoke. Barbara placed her left hand and DT her right behind the volume, providing a joint backrest for the book. Barbara looked at DT, then the Blake verse, then back at DT. "This is not the name—DT—you should carry with you for the rest of your time," she said.

DT loved to listen as Barbara spoke. She became transfixed with her teacher's use of language, as she sprinkled in, from time to time, words like *métier*, taken from the French. The teenager wondered how Barbara came by her gift. Barbara's timing was always perfect. She seemed to know the precise moment to use an occasional expression from another land.

"You must be a Continental person," DT said softly, not realizing that Barbara could hear the remark.

"My parents were born in France but educated here. I have been abroad only once. Yes, I went to Paris. I feel mostly American but not completely. You're the first to put a finger on it." Barbara paused. "Let's go back up and just sit on the landing."

Silently, the two women, one innocent and the other more experienced, climbed together and sat in stillness upon the white lifeguard chair as the wind whipped about and through them.

Before too long, DT rose from the chair, and, helping Barbara down the steps, led her across the beach and back to the car. DT would have remained forever, but she knew better. She correctly surmised that Henry had begun to fret. Soon, if they did not reappear, he would insist that Marsha and Todd join him for the retrieval ride. Henry was liberal, but his boundaries were clearly marked. He still wanted control over his daughter's life. It was fine if she wished to meander just a bit—but wandering for an extended period was not acceptable.

DT and Barbara pulled into the drive before Henry made his move. The teacher held the Blake collection close to her body with two hands, hoping to avoid scrutiny. Marsha greeted them at the door. "I sliced the batter for chocolate chip cookies the moment you left. They're cooling just now. What perfect timing!"

"Still my favorite," said Barbara. "I just want to thank all of you but especially you two"—she motioned toward Marsha and Henry—"for having me. I so look forward to tomorrow."

Yates family tradition dictated that their arrival in Chatham be marked by a pizza dinner. Marsha had called Red's when they arrived to be certain the order would be filled. She was a bit paranoid about things pertaining to food and restaurants. In this regard, Marsha, otherwise sunny and bright, was dark and pessimistic. She often predicted food shortages. Before she and Henry would leave either of their homes, she would anticipate a lengthy wait at the restaurant. Whenever possible, she made reservations. Hence, the need to contact Red's immediately; she feared that the place would shut down early for the holiday. Privately, Marsha wondered if a pizza shop could run low on pizza.

As DT and Barbara washed their hands, Marsha set the table. Henry, Todd and George watched. Everyone was both hungry and willing to sing. Even the usually reserved Todd joined in as Marsha led them in "I Get By With a Little Help from My Friends." They all drank wine, Marsha and Henry having lifted any prohibitive rule for their children. After the group had dispensed with virtually all of the pizza and many chocolate chip cookies, the parents, asking for pitch-in with clean-up, excused themselves and made for their upstairs bedroom. Todd and George each grabbed a fistful of cookies, went to the recently winterized downstairs porch, turned on a football game, and vanished within the many pillows that were randomly thrown upon the soft sofa.

Barbara and DT filled themselves final glasses of wine and sat at the corners of the kitchen table. DT fiddled with a wooden napkin holder, two white sails gripping the napkins, while Barbara meticulously thumbed through the book. "I cannot believe how well this treasure held together," she said.

The two (whose chairs nearly intertwined) began to read the poems, sometimes aloud, sometimes to themselves. They were thrilled with the stories of boys and girls, the chimney sweep, the nurse, fly, rose, and, of course, tyger. And awed with and by Blake's etchings—the illuminations, as he called them.

DT bent back the corner of the page with "The Little Girl Lost," about a young girl and her vision of the future. She kept turning back to the first two stanzas of the poem. DT said the verse over and over: "In futurity / I prophesy . . . And the desert wild / Become a garden mild."

Finally, she turned to Barbara and said, "I love it, but why am I drawn to this? I feel pulled by an unseen force."

Barbara put her arm around the girl and said, "Because this is you. People find themselves in different ways. The way to your soul is through your name. That passage says it all: Destiny."

She would always recall that particular moment and believed it was pivotal. Destiny began to see the world differently. It suddenly made complete sense that she imagined the specific position of the moon as day evolved into evening. Even so, years would pass before she could fully accept her heightened vision. Her intuitive sense could be difficult. Increased perception jeopardized her sense of the credible, what she thought to be real. This acuity could be off-putting.

Destiny, during those days, had cheerleader good looks. When she looked in the mirror, she was appalled. Her features were fine, her light hair long and lustrous. She yearned, however, to be plain. She knew that boys thought she would be easy, and this dismayed her. Finally, during her thirties, she took on a bit of weight. Her face seemed to round out, matching her figure. Losing her physical allure (at least she thought so), she gained equivalent peace of mind.

At Boston University, she majored in English and learned to write short stories. She loved the genre and contemporary authors like Ray Carver, Ann Beattie, Alice Munro, and John Updike. Destiny tried writing poetry but never felt comfortable reading her own work. She began a novel but felt her best twenty pages were the first twenty.

Unable to configure a potential career after BU, Destiny went to graduate school. After earning a Master's Degree, she worked at a bookstore/café three nights per week and taught a course in "The Blues" at Salem State. Still searching, she enrolled in a psychology class there. She taught one afternoon, studied psychology the next. One of the twelve "Blues" students, eight of whom were women, looked familiar to Destiny. Destiny realized she and the younger woman were both students in the psychology section. Destiny wondered if she had previously met this girl with the long brown French braid. It was Annabelle, who would become Destiny's best friend and protégé.

CHAPTER 5

Annabelle grew up with dogs, cats, chickens, and roosters. It wasn't until a year into their friendship that Destiny and Annie discovered each had attended the same high school, albeit during different eras — ten years or so apart. Annabelle was raised, more or less, in the Massachusetts woods, off Route 2, not all that far from Walden Pond.

Dogs were friends, forever and unconditionally. You didn't sign or form a contract. There weren't any rules, and trust would never become an issue. Annie loved her two dogs. When they died, she would get others. She felt she needed dogs in order to be whole. Dogs and jazz.

Little Annabelle, called Belle only by her parents, placed her fingers on the upright piano in the living room when she was six. Her mother, Lyla, taught her daughter to play but never gave formal lessons. Every so often, Lyla would talk to Belle about playing by ear, searching for black keys, finding different keys for "Oh, Susannah!"

Annabelle found that, aside from running with her dogs up the large hill behind their house, which on a clear day afforded a view of Boston's Prudential Center, she would rather sit on the piano bench and rely on her hands to make music. As she did, the Labs, one black and one chocolate, flopped down behind her and slept.

When she began to master chord progressions before she turned thirteen, Annabelle wrote "Canine Paradise" and dedicated it to her dogs, Cool and Stride. Alone with the dogs, she would call out, "Here, come to Mama, jazz puppies!"

High school allowed Annie the opportunity to work with music teacher Samuel Kent. He was twenty-eight years old but looked years younger when fourteen-year-old Annie met him. Blond-haired and skinny, he constantly pushed his granny glasses up the bridge of his nose. Annie liked Sam from that first day, when he explained that he only played for fun; that when he had fun, he became better; that as he became better, he was more motivated to practice; and that he now practiced for fun.

Annie, when she was working with Sam, enjoyed being the learner. She never felt intimidated. He geared her toward performance, convincing her that if she relaxed herself completely before a recital, she would feel exhilarated rather than anxious. The higher the stakes, the more Sam preached that calm fostered attention—that unless she enjoyed herself, it all wasn't worth, as he said, a fig. She could not help but visualize fig leaves—the kind artists drew to shield Adam's and Eve's genitals. Even as she sat alone in a practice room running scales, Annie thought about this and blushed.

How she loved to watch Sam as he explained, with his arms and pony-tailed hair flying about, how to play the piano. "Releasing muscles," he would say, "means you transfer thought through your body from your mind and eye to your fingers, but always the heart becomes a guiding spirit and presence." The bony fingers of his right hand elevated from the keyboard as if they were gliding in air.

Totally smitten, Annie kept her feelings hidden, never expecting reciprocity.

It was not until the concluding month of the final semester of her senior year of high school that Sam began to admit his feelings.

One of Annie's few friends, Brian Yeager, had invited her to a graduation party. Everyone in Lincoln referred to his house as one of mystery. Never having been there, Annie leapt at the invitation. She did not know Brian well, but during the past half year, Annie had begun to play guitar and piano duets with Alicia, Brian's little sister by hardly more than a year.

Permitted to drive her parents' car to the party, Annie parked and walked around to the backyard. Magical gardens, featuring marigolds, pink rose bushes, and sparkling violet flowers, startled her. A grape arbor surrounded a large in-ground swimming pool on three sides. The black upright piano, placed before the pool, was situated so that anyone who wished to could play.

Samuel Kent sat alone at the keyboard, pushing his eyeglasses toward his wide forehead. Annie approached, and he motioned to her to sit by him on the piano bench. When she did, he waved at the music and smiled at Annie. She began to play. The page read, "Adaptations: William Blake's Songs of Innocence and Experience – By S.A. Kent."

Sight-reading was Annie's forte. That she was asked to play her teacher's composition provided further incentive. "Have fun, relax," she told herself. Before beginning, she swiveled and smiled at Sam to reassure him. No need for him to repeat the mantra.

Every so often, Sam lent harmony to his piece, thereby creating a composition for four hands on the piano. Annie continued to play, to focus, to deflect tension by releasing the back of her neck. She imagined Sam's fingers upon her shoulders. It was not until much later that she acknowledged fully to herself that he had intentionally touched her there.

Annie knew that several girls had become involved with faculty members at the high school. She found this unremarkable: youthful and sometimes soul-searching young men and seventeen- or eighteen-year-old young women— why not? It was the early 1970s. This, to her, was neither love nor exploitation. If it was true that girls were more mature than boys, the chronological age difference was not relevant. If people were drawn to one another, that was more precious than a significant gap in their ages.

She edged closer to Sam near the center of the piano bench. She slid her hip until it brushed up on and then settled against Sam's outer thigh. That accomplished, Annabelle leaned partially but undeniably against her teacher. For a time, she tried to keep playing "Songs of Innocence." Soon enough, however, she stopped and the piece, abruptly, was over.

As Sam nodded and smiled, Annie lifted her lips toward his. He kissed her fully as his glasses fell between them. Laughing, she delicately placed them directly across several of the black keys. She intertwined the fingers of both her hands around Sam's neck, pressed his body to her own, and returned the kiss with all the passion she had silently stored. Annie had assumed, before, that she could control her feelings. She had been practicing for years. Practice, Sam had advised her, should be fun. Keeping the lustful crush secret would be easy. This is what she told herself.

****

Sam Kent had surprised his family, closest friends, and music instructor when he chose to major in English at Assumption College. Having played the piano since the age of seven, in recital several years later, he was on the fast track to musical renown. He felt, however, that reading music meant nothing. Anyone could paint by numbers. Sam longed to explore, not replicate. Unschooled as a writer, he filled a journal with poems. Someday, he would set them to music.

His mentor at Assumption, Rob Schneider, grew up around academic types at Chapel Hill, in North Carolina. Rob's Jewish mother was from Brooklyn, and his atheist father, who taught philosophy, was born in Manhattan but retained childhood memories of Atlanta. Rob had been teaching at Assumption for just two years before meeting

Sam Kent, a student in his "Poets of England: The Romantics" course. Rob wished he had become a jazz musician while Sam imagined himself a beat poet.

Rob was a conscientious objector to the Vietnam War. Sam felt that influence and counseled others to become pacifists.

Rob also passed along his poet of choice, William Blake, to his favorite student, Sam Kent. Sam spent most of his time committing to memory *Songs of Innocence and Experience*. He planned, as a senior project, to write music for the songs. It was quite by accident that he stumbled across Blake's "Auguries of Innocence," written somewhat later.

Living off campus, Sam painted the opening lines on his ceiling, kept a copy in his wallet, and told himself that if ever the opportunity arose, he would encase these in a time capsule.

"To see a World in a Grain of Sand / And a Heaven in a Wild Flower / Hold Infinity in the palm of your hand / And Eternity in an hour."

Sam and Annabelle, as she now wished to be known, were a known couple by the time summer arrived. Before long, she was the superior pianist. Sam had always known Annie was more talented than he was. He would assume the role of creative accessory. He could write verse and lyrics but was less certain of his ability to compose music.

As a musical couple, Sam and Annie prospered. Together, they set poems to music. Sam wrote some and discovered others that he thought would work well in that context. Annie was only too happy to perform. Adored by Sam, she often smiled through a recital. They appeared together at the DeCordova Museum in Lincoln, at a synagogue in Newton, and at a Cambridge chapel.

Accepted at Simmons and Emerson Colleges, Annabelle chose the latter. Sam monitored her course selection. She moved into Sam's Somerville apartment. He commuted to the suburban high school each day, while she went into Boston for classes.

Her problem was a social one. Reclusive as a teenager, Annie wished to maintain that solitude. Sam was enough for her and, in many ways, she was his ideal partner. On weekends, however, Sam wished to meet with friends and colleagues. Annie wanted Sam to herself. They managed well enough that first year. She pushed herself, every third or fourth Saturday, to mingle. He told himself not to rush her—she was young yet. Oftentimes, they stayed home, creating and playing music and drinking red wine until one or both of them leaned, again, toward the other on the piano bench. That became a signal to shut down and move the following chapter to the bedroom.

Emerson, on the other hand, did not fulfill Annie's needs. Sam, for his part, helped but only when she asked. The following fall, Annie selected one course at Harvard extension and another at Boston University and hoped she could someday accumulate a sufficient number of credits to earn her a degree.

Each autumn afternoon, before her "Heroes and Heroines in American Literature" course, Annie sat on concrete steps and listened to three musicians who gathered to sing and play. She imagined joining them but then realized that she couldn't very well carry in a keyboard. The woman with the almost transparent blue eyes became a transfixing guitar-playing presence. A few years later, Annie would discover this was Destiny.

At first, Annie tried to deny that her feelings for Sam were diminishing. Very slowly, she began to acknowledge that she might have mistaken idolatry for love. Yes, Sam was charismatic, smart, and a trusted companion. For a time, she found his protection comforting, if not necessary. As she ventured beyond their apartment, however, she found that she could make decisions, mingle with others, and forge an independent identity.

Grateful as she was to him, Annie could not bear to speak her mind. He, however, must have sensed her pulling away and suggested that a weekend getaway together might, as he phrased it, "provide linkage."

Sam chose a wildlife area in central Massachusetts. He had been there and had a specific reason to return. He had painted for her a picture of a pristine pond with soft baby-blue water that allowed for a clear view of the sandy bottom.

He brought with him a piece of charcoal and a plastic cover. Sam was serene, and Annie, hopeful, took on his mood. It was an easy ride to the rural outpost beyond Worcester.

Annie wondered why Sam took an exit, then doubled beneath the Pike and re-entered heading east. He waved with his right hand as they turned into a small, half-moon-shaped rest area. It wasn't official, and it hadn't any restrooms. A narrow path led into a wooded section behind the cutoff. Sam, taking Annie's hand as she walked directly behind him, led them through a grove of trees. Someone had taken the time to clear branches for others.

The reflection of the sun off the still water stopped Annie, who immediately blocked the glare with both of her hands. She laced her fingers together and peeked out from behind the braiding. Sam, standing behind her, moved Annie gently toward a stone pillar situated across the way. They slowly ambled along the soggy periphery. Annie felt it took forever to reach the pond.

He asked her to join him as he wrote that Blake line that was the basis for one of his compositions directly upon the stone: "To see a World in a Grain of Sand / And a Heaven in a Wild Flower / Hold Infinity in the palm of your hand /

And Eternity in an hour." Sam placed a bold, black WB beneath those words, then drew a heart within which he wrote, on a slant, the initials SAK and AW.

Sam knew the dark chalk would wash away and took care to prevent that from occurring. He produced a see-through cover and strong staples to affix the plastic upon the structure. He carried a small hammer, too, and within minutes the job was completed.

"There, that's good for two or three decades, I would wager," he said.

"A prognostication: Someone, maybe more, will wander out here and find the Blake poem and our initials," said Annie, to herself and to Sam, too. "Should we write the date somewhere or at least leave word from this year, 1972?"

"I had originally hoped to put something like this in a time capsule," said Sam. "That didn't happen, at least not yet. Yes, what is encased, whatever else you add, it all needs notation. Till posterity, Annie."

Sam knelt; Annie jumped aboard his shoulders. He held her knees as she steadied herself and wrote atop the pillar, "Peace and love, 1972 – Sam and Annie."

A few months later, Annie left Sam and the security he represented. She found a room for rent in a Cambridge house. It took her just a week to realize that she greatly missed Sam for his musical encouragement and influence. Yes, she had enjoyed his warmth and humor. He made her feel wanted, and he never forced her in any way. They had made love often and, to her, this was pleasant if not truly exhilarating. As she moved away from Sam, Annie deconstructed and better understood their relationship. She and Sam had been intimate but non-mysterious; romantic but confined and conventional. Annie saw that she needed to find an edge and live closer to it.

CHAPTER 6

Annie stayed in Cambridge for three years before moving to the North Shore. Relocating within an hour of greater Boston with proximity to the beach was ideal: the sea five or ten minutes away and culture whenever she wanted or needed it.

Since the Sam era, she had expanded her musical repertoire, learning folk guitar well enough to play and sing. She bought a battery-powered keyboard that traveled with her wherever she went. It wasn't a piano, but it wasn't a cheap imitation either. She enrolled at Salem State, hoping to carry with her the credits she had earned from Emerson and elsewhere.

Annie changed addresses three times that first year before finally choosing Ipswich, near Crane Beach, as her place. She settled into the second story of a two-family house. The owners, situated below her, had two dogs. It became evident that Annie and the dogs were perfectly matched. Within a few weeks, the Labs were traipsing upstairs to find her and she welcomed the company. Her landlords, busy with their lives, agreed that Annie was well-suited to become honorary owner of the dogs. Except for Sam and a few others, Annie preferred dogs to people.

"I could live on music and dogs alone," she said one day while waiting for her "Psych: Human Development" class to begin. Annie sat on a stone wall and held firm to her guitar case and the instrument within.

"Pancakes, too," said the outgoing woman with golden hair next to her, whom Annie recognized as the teacher of the Blues course she'd taken. "Blueberry pancakes especially. They taste even better when you use a wheat batter. Nobody believes me until they eat the ones I make. I host pancake breakfasts all the time," she continued. "One day, I will open my own place."

"Could I come there sometime? If you say yes, could I bring two special dogs?"

"Goldens, Labs, or Irish Setters and the answer is yes. Small, yappy dogs? I don't want to say no, but, to me, less exciting to have around."

"A yellow and a black Lab," said Annie. "By the way, I loved your Blues course."

"Thank you!" said Destiny. "And now, instead of teaching, I'm a student in psychology—I usually sit behind you, so you wouldn't know. I go with whatever flow," she laughed. "I mean performing and human psychology."

"I will, too, someday," said Annie. "I just need a field."

"I think the dogs need a field more than you do," said Destiny.

Annie opened up with laughter. Had someone else said it, Annabelle could very well have been put off and remained stone silent. But the woman with the bright, circular face instantly put Annie at ease.

That Thursday evening, Annie waited until she saw Destiny before "Human Development." Both women found the course title pretentious. Each felt isolated; both wished for friendship, yet neither felt comfortable pushing for it. They sat in class hoping that the loneliness would ease. The world, during the mid-1970s, was, for each, not all that enchanting. Anyone not comfortable with the so-called Me Generation hoped for more.

After class, Annie turned quickly to catch Destiny's eye, then skipped toward the shorter woman.

"Coffee?" asked Annie. "Iced? Iced tea?"

"Now you have me," said Destiny.

Annie walked along with Destiny.

"It's your real name?"

"Now it is," said Destiny. "It fits me. And yours?"

"Annabelle."

"Sounds Southern."

"I know. Maybe they heard it in California. That's where my parents were born."

"What brought them here?"

"They were living off the land in the Bay Area. They were gardeners, committed and heartfelt. But, they found that they couldn't raise their daughter on the sale of produce. So, they moved East, thinking it would be easier to start a craft shop around here."

"Then what?"

"My mom did open a store: flowers, trinkets, jewelry, greeting cards—a bit upscale. And my father managed to go to law school, then became a poor people's advocate in Cambridge and Somerville. Between them, they were able to raise me and pay for anything I ever needed."

"And?"

"I became involved with my high school mentor. We had an affair, I left, and here I am."

"The simple version, no?"

"But not simplistic. And you?"

"More than a couple of paragraphs, that's for sure."

****

Annie moved a few times, but Cape Ann, rocky and north of Boston, suited her best. Destiny became a close friend and model teacher. Annie enrolled in or sat in on any course Destiny taught. Soon, she played piano as Destiny sang folk songs.

Destiny earned extra money working shifts at the local diner. Annie coordinated a playgroup for working parents. She was underpaid and eventually settled in a mother-in-law apartment attached to one family's home. She brought with her, having more or less adopted them, the precious dogs.

Thrilled to have Annie on the premises, Ben Adamson and Harriette Church charged her next to nothing. Annie became a member of the family, often watching the couple's two young children. When she was not in that house, Annie was at Destiny's home, which was always a work in process. Polly and Jess, naturally, came along.

Destiny acquired a handyman's special, a house with potential, a few blocks from the beach. It was falling apart, and she had not yet learned even basic carpentry. Thus, she apprenticed with a local and eventually became competent enough for her needs. She recruited Annie, who was geometrically savvy and good with angles. The women worked together, at night walked the beach with dogs in and out of tow, and then played music.

The two eventually built an almost symmetrical gazebo-like studio for Annie behind the main house. Annie found herself splitting time between the Adamson/Church house and Destiny's gazebo, where she sometimes slept. The arrangement worked well for a time, but Annie felt pulled toward Destiny. Soon, she and her dogs moved to Destiny's home. When Annie stayed in the gazebo during warm weather days, the dogs wedged in with her, remained outside, or were welcomed inside to play with Destiny.

Annie brought in some money through the playgroup. She accumulated the necessary credits to become certified as a preschool teacher. Taking a job in Salem, her salary rose. On occasion, Destiny was able to step in as a replacement for professors who were on sabbatical; otherwise, she was part time. Between the two of them, the women combined ample funds to easily survive.

Destiny, however, wished to have her own restaurant. Impractical as it seemed, she planned for a day when she could decorate and equip a space, cook for people, and demonstrate, to and for them, what she felt to be a rewarding style of life. She hoped this was a calling.

She improved as a carpenter by partially redoing her house. Her apprentice, Annie, had an eye for design rather than literal construction. The two of them, working by day, drinking wine and listening to or playing music after dark, fully enjoyed each other's company. Destiny saved carefully. When her friend, Gina, sold her fruit and produce shack on the beach, Destiny leapt to buy it outright. By the mid-1990s, with Annie's help, humor, and eye for the possible, Destiny opened her restaurant just steps away from Crane Beach.

CHAPTER 7

It was a full decade after she opened that a couple of old Jewish men showed up at her door. They liked her pancakes, her guitar, and her candles, and the larger of the two talked about her "scene." He had asked for seconds and even thirds. The wiry frowner, on the other hand, picked at his food, eating the blueberries but little else. Now, they were coming back, with their girlfriends and someone else. Destiny wondered what this meant and how these guys could possibly appeal to, well, anyone, let alone women.

Anticipating their arrival, Destiny dusted and cleaned—around the candleholders, all the window shades, the tables and chairs, the low, round coffee table. She even fluffed the pillows. She swept and gathered sand in piles at either door, then scattered spare grains back onto the beach. She cleaned windows and mirrors with a wet rag since she could not tolerate even the faintest scent of Windex. Then, she needed to pick pieces of white lint off the glass surfaces.

The building grew warmer, even more enveloping. Destiny wondered whether it was beginning to sparkle. If so, this could actually become worrisome to Destiny, who thought the appeal of her little place relied heavily on its charm. It was cozy, welcoming. Destiny wanted it to feel lived in, like her home. Yes, it was a place of business but one where everyone should be able to relax and remain in conversation for a while. She had even posted a sign outside that read: "This restaurant remains a haven from society's harried, hurried race. Those who enter will not be asked to leave. Stay. Wait and then stay."

She realized this might puzzle some, but she didn't want to rush her visitors in and out of her restaurant within twenty minutes. Anyone who cared would understand the message.

Music was important to the ambiance, too. Destiny and Annabelle played together each Sunday morning. It was part of the brunch package. Sometimes, they performed an evening or two each week. Destiny asked Annie if she would be willing to improvise "Greensleeves," a tune these old men might recognize. She adored Annie and was concerned that Annie would catch the eye of one of the ancient coots. After all, the younger woman was delectable and Destiny was certain that men were enthralled with her.

****

The nifty new Prius, with Mendel at the wheel, was back on the Pike and would soon approach Worcester and beyond. Mendel seized that moment to pontificate: "Worcester is a first-class dump. Springfield without the Basketball Hall of Fame. Even Holyoke without the Volleyball Hall of Fame."

"As a native of Cleveland, let me add Canton, Ohio, without the Football Hall of Fame," said Morris. "Which leaves Cooperstown, where the best pitcher ever to throw a ball one hundred miles an hour, Rapid Robert Feller, is enshrined. Don't you even try to say something ugly about the Midwest. There, even you could have been a big man."

"You open yourself up for the sucker punch now, Mo. I hear that in Ohio, cows are getting bigger. In your case, that is hard to believe. If only I had been there when you were a little tyke. I can hear, even now, everyone: 'Oy, when will he stop growing?'"

"Zip your lips, Mendel Greenbaum," ordered Gilda. "We can all imagine what you were like seventy years ago, counting pennies and sharing nothing with nobody."

Kiley, preoccupied, said, "This Destiny, she's not Jewish, is she?"

"There he goes again, with Judaism. I got news: she is not Jewish, unless, of course, she converted. This woman looks like she grew up just where and how she lives. She is a calm person," said Mendel. "Some people would say serene. I cannot since I never use that word."

"And maybe with the face of an angel, but don't get me wrong. I mean, she has a sweet look, like maybe she never got mad at anyone. Unlike us. Well, unlike me," said Morris.

"It's just that the way you describe her makes me consider whether she is Jewish. She sounds mystical," said Kiley. "She could be the type of person who thinks maybe something good will happen for us all. Not more bombings, terrorists, wars. Those who believe in Kaballah think a Messiah will actually come—and soon."

"You've never even met the woman," said Morris, "and you got her connecting with some dreamy God in the future."

"Not God but, yes, an expected savior," said Kiley. "The older I get, the more I am praying that, well, after my body is no longer, something else is. So, yes, I hope there is a person. I would welcome that. Maybe this Destiny you keep talking about is special. I, personally, look to religion."

"So we could get him cast in some local production of 'Fiddler,'" said Mendel. "The problem is he looks like a goy but he acts Jewish."

"These days, they got gays playing Tevye, like that Firestone guy," said Morris.

Zena elbowed Gilda, the sisters having been assigned the back seat. "I know, big sis. My man always does this with names. He doesn't even know it's Harry Finestein. And Mendel?"

"No better," said Gilda. "This one cannot remember the name of that president we used to have—called him The Texas Howdy Doody."

"This conversation is getting me tired. You don't mind if I shut my eyes?" asked Zena.

"Every time during this past year when you are bored, you go to sleep," said Gilda, who was soon snoring before anyone else had fallen off.

Eventually, Mendel looked around and saw that Kiley was the only other person who had managed to stay awake. "Looks like it's you and me, Kiley."

"Behind their backs, maybe we can talk about this woman you've found."

"You should see her friend," said Mendel, winking.

"Mendel," said Kiley, "I am beyond such women— which, I might add, was not always the case. In my youth— or, as the kids are saying, back in the day—I had many, many catches."

"Now you will tell me you only wish you had a Jewish girlfriend," said Mendel.

"My first wife was Jewish. In those days, I could not understand. Remember that I was a devout Christian. It ruined the marriage."

"I did not know that you were married even once."

"And you, Mendel?"

"Yes, I was married. The reason I do not talk about it is that the wound is always open. She never should have died before me. Not in our plan," he said.

"Mendel, if you did not cover up all of your sorrow the way you do, you might not be in so much pain," said Kiley.

"I feel fine, Kiley, and it's none of your business."

"It just sounded like you might want to talk."

"About my lovely, I do not. Her skin, almost till the end, was clear and smooth. The woman, for someone her age, had no wrinkles. Look at me! I am making up for it," said Mendel.

"I once thought women were good for holding up men. Now, I realize that as we leap, they tend to look."

"I'm not sure I know what you mean, but let's say I agree with you, Kiley. Maybe it's my memory or whatever but, so help me, I forget. Is everyone else asleep here?"

"That is the truth. They are draped on one another."

"I will tell you this, Kiley. I still look at women. I say this knowing that I truly adore Gilda, but I cannot help myself. When a pretty girl walks down the street, I cannot help but drink her in. You know what I mean? Am I a pervert?"

"This is normal, Mendel. Me, too, despite all my talk of religion. It's true that I am finding out more about myself, but some of it is not so good."

"This Destiny, I tell you, Kiley, she is one of a kind. Salt of the earth is what I think."

"Where did you get that one, Mendel?"

"By mistake one day, I heard it on a public radio broadcast. To you, Kiley, I admit I don't know exactly what it means. Not a word of this from you to Morris or the sisters, please."

"Cross my heart, pray to Yahweh, my lips are zipped tight."

With that, Mendel turned on the radio and drew in 89.7 FM—the Boston public radio affiliate. He listened to the classical selection, quickly whispered toward Kiley, "It's a Beethoven, but I don't know if it's the fourth or seventh."

"Eighth," said Kiley. "Close enough, my friend."

They drove the rest of the way to Ipswich in silence. Beethoven was followed by an interview with Michael Tilson Thomas, now based in San Francisco. Mendel had heard of him, but it was Kiley who explained that the tall, lanky conductor had never become, as prognosticated, Leonard Bernstein's true protégé.

"This Tilson Thomas, he might be Jewish," said Kiley. "Unlike Bernstein, I think. And Bernstein favored Mahler, who actually gave up on Judaism completely. The reverse of me." Mendel did not respond. "I'm sorry, Mendel, but I obsess."

Within moments, Kiley, too, had fallen asleep. Morris, Gilda, and Zena were all dozing. Mendel drove on, visualizing young women while he tried to focus on Destiny's Place.

****

When Mendel turned off the Turnpike to begin wending his way on smaller roads toward Ipswich and the beach, Gilda snapped awake, shook her head, and looked about. "Are they alive, Mendy?"

"You know the answer to your question, Gilda."

"One makes a buzz, the other sniffles. Not so pleasant for the driver."

"Nothing so bad since it takes my mind off the unthinkable," said Mendel. He tried to remember the series of turns they had taken the first time to get to Crane's Beach; failing that, he followed signs. Each time he knifed the car in a new direction, Mendel nodded at Gilda.

"Mendel, you don't have to impress me. I know how important this is to you, this business of driving a car and pretending that God gave you a perfect sense of direction. If this pleases you, fine. You don't have to smirk at me at each corner."

"This is not a smirk. Don't you know the difference between a smirk and a loving glance?" he asked.

"Oh, yes I do. Need I say one additional word?"

Mendel did not answer.

"What a great story for a grandchild: 'Grandpa Mendel and his shiny, new Prius. He used to drive a fancy Mercedes but saw the error of his ways and traded for a healthy and special car.' A little seven-year-old would get some kick out of that!" she said.

Mendel stared straight ahead, but he could not suppress a smile, which emphasized the cracks in his skin but also widened his face, to his benefit.

"Money," said Morris, suddenly awake.

"Come again?" asked Mendel

"Look around you, for God's sake. You got one picture postcard after another. Fields, woods, young girls riding big black horses. You see the ponies, whatever you call them, one minute and the next you lose them. Coming back from somewhere deep in a meadow, here they are. This is like the beginning of a million movies I watched," continued Morris.

"I saw a few stone walls," said Zena. "You going to call them The Ten Commandments or what?"

"Look, this is *goyisha* cash, right here. Another way to put it is old money, going back to the Mayflower even. I don't think you found too many Jews on the Mayflower."

"That I would like to investigate," said Kiley, previously so quiet that his presence was nearly forgotten.

"Listen," said Mendel, "I'm the one who has some serious investments. And, this is what it's all about. You see one home, one estate after another up for sale, that's how people make money. You got enough to buy even middle level, you sell high."

"I was wondering when Alfred Greenberg or Greenspan, whatever his name is, would pipe up," said Gilda.

"Look at that!" shouted Morris. "Myopia Hunt Club — Members Only.' We all know what that means," he said.

"You don't know a thing," said Zena. "You think everyone's out to get you and that it's all about you."

Morris, stung by the comment, had to say something. "We just passed a small liquor store. I think it was called Hartigan's. I say let's go back and buy a bottle of something to bring for Destiny." No one disagreed.

Within ten minutes, they came upon a sign that read:

STEEP GRADE/CASTLE HILL/CRANE BEACH

"Dammit," said Mendel. "I missed it."

"I am going to ignore you, but what is this with Crane Beach? What happened to the 's'?" Morris shook his walrus-like head.

"If you opened your eyes just once when we were here by ourselves, you would have noticed that there isn't any Crane's Beach. Who ever said it belonged to a big white bird anyway?" asked Mendel.

"What's your problem, Men?" asked Gilda.

"I overshot or else I forgot directions, and Morris is so *farhblunget* he can't get anything straight. I thought Destiny's first, followed by the beach. Nu? We're here. Let's explore."

****

Annie hadn't slept with a man in more than six months. She had walked away from the last boyfriend before it got to that. She liked men but, after Sam, Annie chose to keep her distance. Gradually, she had concluded that it would be nice to have someone, and even better if he were a bit older. Sam was chronologically older. But, he was unaware. A devoted musician, he missed out on maturation, perhaps a portion of adolescence.

Annie realized that men's necks still snapped backward when she walked by. This did not disturb her. She was flattered. She continued her daily routine, which included morning runs on the beach, aware that loose clothing piqued the male imagination.

Annie had alerted Destiny, of course, that "the older set of men" and their companions were on their way back to Ipswich. Annie thought they were sweet and non-threatening. The big one seemed to genuinely love the dogs. The wiry crone looked her up and down, but Annie really did not mind. It actually amused her. She foresaw herself lapping up the attention and was more than willing to play along.

She would wear a vintage, almost-see-through peasant blouse that she purchased in the South End. Annie had been saving it for a special occasion. She was fully aware that men edged forward to look not at her fingers but down her shirt when she played the piano. That no longer unsettled her.

She was told, when she reached puberty, to watch their eyes, to relax until their sight lines rested below the curve of her thighs.

Now, though, her legs bowed upon her horse Bonnie, she and her beloved animal moved slowly along the water's edge. She hadn't thought to bring her sunglasses, and the glare off the deep blue-green ocean caused her, from time to time, to look away. Gazing back toward the dunes, she saw something moving and turned the large chestnut toward the entering stairway. Mendel and Morris, spotting her, caught her eye by waving their arms across each other, the windmill gestures never achieving balance. She noticed another man with them.

Annie smiled to herself, realizing that each of these men sought a corner on the charm market, one hoping to outdo the other. As a promise to herself, she pledged not to tire of them. As she came closer, Annie saw that two women completed the party of five.

She wondered what the view of the world was like for the quintet of elderly people who were bearing down upon her. Did they worry about the consequences of, for example, falling over and down? Broken hips, arms, ankles, and wrists at age, what, eighty or so? Was each and every second one of potential high drama?

Did they ever make love? With whom? Did they ever think of finding another partner?

Annie, having loved her gerontology course and subsequent discussions with Destiny, was convinced that many who survived independently beyond the age of eighty believed they were immortal. Their conviction was fierce, and they cared not about mores, societal commentary, and judgment—the rules and evidence. They did what they wanted.

Annie could not imagine any of the three men as passionate, physically functioning sexual beings. Not now. She told herself to banish the topic from further contemplation. That said, the new man's translucent blue eyes enraptured her. He seemed to have an aura about him. Destiny had told Annie to watch for this. Annie wondered how it could be that someone twenty-five or so years older than she could actually bring her to pause even for one moment.

Still, she found herself checking this man out as the group approached. He walked more easily than either Mendel or Morris. Really, she thought, he loped. He hadn't cut his hair and, from the front at least, it seemed full and healthy. He smiled at her, and she realized that she saw something of herself, the WASP part, in him. She was neither heartened nor thrilled but recognized the familiarity of crease lines in his face, his easy gait, the lack of frenzy. How comforting.

She felt herself fiddling with her own hair, wondering if her face was filled with sea salt and when it would wrinkle. Annie, high in the saddle, looking down toward the entourage, rejected a notion to dismount. Instead, she steadied herself and the horse, allowing Kiley, shielding his eyes, to gaze upward at her.

Mendel, unaware that Annie could hear him, yelled toward the sisters, "What did I tell you? Is she not a peach?"

Gilda shot Zena a look, then said, "If you knew one thing about women, it's that you don't talk about another girl's good looks in front of one of us. Where does that get you?"

Morris interjected, "He only meant that Annabelle, on top of her treasured horse, is a picture postcard if ever I saw one."

"You're as bad as your scrawny friend," said Zena.

Annie looked through all of them at the still-silent Kiley. Finally, she said, "I'm so, so happy to see all of you. By previous descriptions, I can figure out just who goes with whom. Except for you," said Annie, nodding toward Kiley.

"I am Everyman, everyone's friend, a sponge, just pleased to be soaking up the scenery, the ocean . . . you."

Annie felt the blood rushing to her face. She studied Kiley's features. His once dark, wavy hair was now streaked with gray, and she imagined hers following suit. His eyes seemed to take on the sea's blue-green hue. It was a combination she loved in herself as well— her rich, thick brown hair as a counterpoint to her eyes. Annie gazed at him perhaps a little too long.

"What, you forgot about us?" bellowed Morris, breaking her trance. "You don't remember the songs you and the Destiny person were singing for us?"

"For once, I side with my fat friend. Annie, this is Kiley. But, we are Mendel and Morris, and we've brought our girlfriends here to meet the two of you. What gives?"

Annie dismounted, slipped the horse's reins over a tall post affixed to a stairway, and, beaming, approached Mendel and Morris.

"I am so, so sorry, my friends. Let's see if I guessed right—who goes with whom?"

"You can probably tell, sweetheart, that Morris and me, we are like peanut butter and jelly," said Zena in an attempt to amuse.

"And the older sister gets the leftovers," said Gilda. "You can't judge the cover of a book," she continued, pointing to Mendel.

"Which leaves me," said Kiley. "Once a goy, now trying to become a Jew. You would never know?"

"I've always been intrigued with Judaism," said Annie. "Kaballah, to be specific. Destiny and I were in a class together. Sometimes I feel like I'm part Jewish."

"I've been thinking of converting," said Kiley.

"Tell me more."

"I could give you impressive reasons such as Torah or certain prayers, but that is not what is in my heart."

"Go on," said Annie.

"Warmth."

"I don't follow you," she said.

"I need to be around people who haven't any ice."

"That's not me," said Mendel. "These days I get chilly just looking at a pond or the ocean — no matter how warm it is outside. I don't have the layers he has," he continued, gesturing toward Morris. "I can easily get in a deep freeze."

"Me, too, since my blood thinned out. For years, I never wore a coat," said Morris. "Now, I got to. Otherwise, I'm frozen when I come in—anytime from Thanksgiving on until April, the earliest. Fat or skinny, it doesn't make a difference."

"That's not it," said Kiley. "Catholics—my family and my friends—tell you how much they love you, but they cannot look at your face, your eyes. Jews? First, I can read how they feel through a scrunch here or there. Second, I can see them—it is actually possible to find them. Do you know what I mean?"

"I do," said Zena. "I hate to say this, but not every Jew, dear Kiley, is such a mensch."

"Some are," said Gilda. "Some were long ago before money got in the way. Once the dollar sign flickers, forget it—Jew, Catholic, Muslim, and anything else you can think of."

"Still, you got a chance with Jews," said Kiley. "I bet this Destiny, if she is anything like what my friends said, is Jewish."

"She's been waiting for all of you," said Annie. "Actually, she began preparing yesterday. Let me take the horse to the stable, trade for my microbus, and we'll be off. I'll lead you."

"No argument here," said Morris as Mendel shrugged.

The women were not quite so certain. "What do we do now?" asked Zena.

Gilda tried to shush her.

"Wait here. Sit in the car. I will return in, maybe, fifteen minutes—no longer," said Annie.

And with that, she turned her horse in an about-face and raced toward the water's edge. She bobbed up and down upon the saddle, and her hair, flowing halfway down her back, followed a beat later.

Kiley, who at first needed to shield his eyes from the sun, was now able to stare fully at horse, rider, and the changeable ocean, which had transformed to turquoise from its earlier deep blue. He watched as Annie sped along the wet sand, turned a corner, and finally disappeared.

"Heavenly," he whispered.

"What did you say, Kiley?" asked Gilda.

"Nothing. The scene—the ocean, sun, and sky—it just about takes my breath away," he said.

"You left out one part," said Morris, raising both eyebrows, but Kiley remained silent.

"Well, I guess we ought to trudge back to that sweet Prius," said Gilda. "And wait so that we can meet her highness."

"You will eat those words," said Mendel.

Destiny dusted with a well-worn broom. She had decorated it with ribbons and turned it into a feathered device designed to reach the ceiling. Barely five feet in height, she needed help when it came to cornering cobwebs. Destiny and ladders did not mix well; she felt better planting her feet on the ground.

She intended to officially close the restaurant to eliminate possible distractions as she played host to the men she and Annabelle lovingly dubbed "the western geezers." Now, she kept the door open but spread glitter all over everything. What began as a toss here and there evolved into high, eclectic art. Everything sparkled.

Destiny cradled her precious Gibson guitar, sat upon her favorite counter stool, and sighed. She played a delicate, inviting melody, then sat in silence. Destiny, during darker days, used music to comfort herself. "We need music. Music is our life," she always said, whether alone or with others present.

"We need music," she began, as the door opened softly. It was Annabelle. She walked quickly to Destiny, embraced her friend, and then looked at the decorations.

"I haven't seen this in . . . well, I haven't seen this," Annie said. "I ran into the entire group on the beach. There's this new man with them, someone called Kiley. He's odd, but his face crinkles while his eyes—they seem almost translucent—widen." She paused. "Here. I brought my recorder." She withdrew from a larger satchel a smaller, soft leather casing. The blond recorder was in three pieces. Annie began to warm up by playing individual notes, extending the tones. She then nodded at Destiny.

Annie sang, "'Tis the gift to be simple, 'tis the gift to be free," as Destiny played chords behind the melody. Then, Annie lifted the recorder and the women played the old song together. Annie excused herself and explained that she would be off to fetch the rest of the contingent.

****

The front door opened slowly. Kiley walked in and everyone else followed. Before introductions could be made, he said, "Annie told us about your song, so please resume." After just a few moments, they began just where they'd left off: "And when we find ourselves in the place just right, 'Twill be in the valley of love and delight." Kiley waved his right hand toward them, then at his chest, and the women knew to pause.

"Meet my friends. Actually, you know the boys. It's the women who are newcomers," he said and waved in the others. "You might call them The Final Four," said Kiley, but only Morris caught the joke.

"This guy is no dummy. He knows basketball. I watch the pros, but each March I begin to get interested in the college kids. The Final Four, you get it?" he asked as he cast his eyes about the restaurant, drinking in its warmth.

"Now, you don't exactly have some big-deal joint here," said Mendel. "But, it's got that little extra, something special in the air, maybe? What? It smells like, what, that Yankee Candle joint we once went to. Remember?"

No one responded.

"Maybe four years ago or something, we went up to see glacial potholes and such," said Morris. "On the way back, we stopped at the candle place for presents. Christian-looking it was, if you know what I mean, but no matter. This is the kind of building I like—it smells good, and it looks good. Tell me, though, does this Yankee have anything to do with the Yankees, Mendel?"

"This is what happens when you grow up in the Midwest. You don't know the difference between a Yankee and the Yankees. My friend Morris, here, is old and has never been the sharpest knife in the drawer. They must spend all their time milking cows in Ohio, no?"

The others watched and listened as the M&M Boys went after each other. Destiny and Annabelle, looked for something, anything, to do. Destiny waved her arms as if to spread good karma about the room. Annie walked briefly into the kitchen and returned with tiny candles. She took them to various tables and lit them before placing them in tiny holders.

"Hey, you buy them wholesale before Chanukah, which is early this year?" asked Mendel.

"We use them all the time here at Destiny's," said Destiny. "For the actual holiday, we light up the place to an extreme, I suppose. Festival of lights, you know."

"See, this is what I like about Judaism," said Kiley. "It is not stuck in place. You have someone here who is really exploring a holiday, presenting it as part of life's fabric instead of extracting. The people I grew up with would be nice to almost anyone on a holiday, even on a Sunday. Then off they go to war, yelling at each other in the parking lot after a Christmas Eve service. Inside, it's lovey-dovey. Outside on the street, it's like being in the trenches."

Destiny picked up her guitar and began to strum chords familiar to everyone in the room. Within seconds, Morris, a baritone, mostly on pitch or just slightly flat, began singing, "Let it be, let it be, let it be, let it be . . ." Everyone joined the chorus the next time around.

The guitarist made eye contact with Annie, who walked quickly to the back room and returned with a medium-sized keyboard. She latched onto the chord progression, holding each note. The sound had a gospel feel with a hint of flair.

"Remarkable," whispered Kiley to no one in particular.

The Springfield quintet and the Ipswich duo came together as seven to sing, drink, and enjoy the evening. Quality was irrelevant. The musical rendering was sweet and pleasing to all of the participants.

After a time, Annie retrieved her recorder and played a simple melody.

At first, Destiny sang it solo: "Children of the future age / Reading this indignant page / Know that in a former time / Love, Sweet Love, was thought a crime."

She urged everybody to sing slowly with her. Several minutes later, with the group halved, the tune was done in rounds. Destiny, lifting her voice to the ceiling, provided further texture.

Annie alternated between recorder and keyboard, singing when she could.

Finally, Destiny drew a circle with her right arm, indicating that all, as they completed the verse, should slowly conclude.

When the song was done, the room grew silent before Destiny exhorted, "Celebrate!"

"Just one thing," said Morris, "before we go on. This sounds like another song, another poem, I found not so long ago."

"Blake," said Destiny.

"The same man," said Morris, simultaneously incredulous and relieved.

"You know him," stated Annie, not entirely surprised.

"I found lines he had written," said Morris. "Something about infinity in the palm of your hand and eternity for an hour. And you?"

"To see a World in a Grain of Sand / And a Heaven in a Wild Flower," she said.

"The same man, the same pen," said Morris.

"The same verse, too," said Destiny.

"The singing we did was wonderful, but I have no idea what you're talking about now," said Zena.

"My little sister speaks for me, too—in this case, I mean," said Gilda.

"These people are talking about William Blake," said Kiley. "A mystic, a man who wanted everyone to be free. No, not everyone, even. The soul and the spirit. To him, confinement meant shackling the mind in chains. He was this intellectual who only wished that we could recapture the innocence of childhood, adding in some sight as we grow older. So that, at our age, including the younger ones, we might, at last, begin to see."

"What if I find, in my eighties, that I was not so good a man as I once thought?" asked Mendel. "What then? Or that my eyesight gets even worse?"

"I don't think Blake saw all as good and evil or white and black," Kiley said. "To him, those opposites are part of one whole."

"So," laughed Morris, "you can be an SOB and get away with it?"

"I cannot answer your every question, my friend," said Kiley. "But, I would assume Blake might comment that those who are mean-spirited only deceive themselves."

"Trust," said Destiny. "Maybe season the soup with belief. If some creative tension results, that is not necessarily a bad thing."

"These days, everyone's a philosopher, nu? Our mother, Sylvie, may she rest in peace, Gilda, she was some thinker. Whenever one of us had a problem, she would stop everything, and I do mean everything, to fix it."

"I don't know, Zena," said Gilda. "Blake, schmake. It seems to me that when you are young, you make mistakes.

And when you get old, like us, you're supposed to make way less. This is genius? It's beyond me."

"That was exactly my thinking until I saw the damned note stuffed behind the Plexiglas off the Mass Pike." With that, Morris launched into a spiel which did not clarify.

"The poet Blake figures in my past. Destiny's, too," said Annie.

"I was never one for poetry," said Mendel.

"Which is surprising, Mendel, since you tend to sit and contemplate. Even during shuffleboard matches, instead of cheering on your teammates, you become very quiet, even pensive on the bench," said Kiley. "And you went off down that hill in the park to ponder, did you not? Morris, here, he's a coach even if he is not so designated. And that's a good thing, too."

"You've been traveling all day. I would imagine everyone could do with some food," said Destiny. "So, let's gather around in the center and we'll put two small tables together."

Before anyone else could react, Annie had the tables positioned. Destiny motioned for each to find a place to sit. She had an eclectic collection of chairs—nothing matched.

"It's like collecting buttons or hair clips, mugs, whatever," she explained about the chairs. "You don't want the pieces to necessarily blend, but you hope everyone can live with clashes—as you do."

"I am tired and I will do as you say," said Morris. Everyone else followed his lead.

Destiny picked up her guitar, began to strum a few chords, and chanted, "Amazing grace! How sweet the sound . . ." Annie was the first to join in: "That saved a wretch like me . . ." Then Kiley: "I once was lost but now am found, 'twas blind but now I see."

The second time around, Morris, with deep volume, raised his voice, followed by Zena and Gilda. Soon, all sang and everyone felt part of the larger unit. Destiny chose not to bother with anything but the chorus, which they sang three times. Kiley's voice was loud, which prompted Annie to raise hers and she did so with precise harmony.

Morris yelped "*L'chayim!*" Gilda and Zena, eying each other while smiling from ear to ear, hoisted their goblets to celebrate the moment.

Mendel, as if lubricating his joints limb by limb as he rose, began to circle the tables. Then, he snapped the thumb and third finger of his right hand together. With his left, he beckoned his friends to join him. Minutes later, all began to weave around the room. Although they were not physically engaged with one another, the seven individuals were rhythmically in synch, asymmetrical, and joyous.

Mendel, the self-appointed leader, began to hum. It was a tune familiar to all, but it wasn't until Morris bellowed, "*Ur'achim, ur'achim, belev sameach,*" that the lyrics to "Hava Nagila" became evident. Annie and Destiny leapt forward, thrusting their arms skyward as if to reach clear through the ten-foot ceiling.

Rejoicing, Kiley shouted, "See, it is a Jewish thing!" and everyone laughed.

CHAPTER 8

Destiny's house was not nearly large enough to accommodate the Springfield bunch overnight. Mendel and Morris had not thought about a place to stay. Carousing and drinking at Destiny's left them without option. It would be neither possible nor advisable to drive back immediately. Besides, they were most conducive to the idea of hanging around with younger women. It was apparent, too, that Kiley was most delighted.

One phone call sufficed. Destiny called the Harbisons, who owned a bed and breakfast near the beach. Annie, a woman of many talents, had done their gardens. They were sweet people whose residence was inland, but they maintained the saltbox house for income. They spent one week in July and another in August in Ipswich. The place was currently unoccupied. With two bedrooms and a pullout sofa, it would provide plenty of space for the travelers.

Mendel pulled into the driveway well past midnight. Rarely were any of them, except Kiley, up at this hour. Always a night person, Kiley often reserved time until two in the morning or later for reading. Eyes wide open, he was eager to investigate as they walked through the front door.

"This is not so bad," said Zena to her sister.

"Simple. Not all that different from what we had in Florida. We never should have moved north," said Gilda. "At our age, no less, we followed the advice of two old goats. And why?"

"There is not an easy answer to such a basic question," said Zena.

The women continued to talk at a rapid clip as if they alone were standing in the small living room of the Harbison cottage. Kiley had already picked up William Faulkner's *As I Lay Dying* and plopped himself in a chair to read.

"Well, Mendel, here we are. Might as well explore the kitchen," said Morris.

With that, the big man lumbered toward the rear of the small home. "Hey," he called, "they got a table here with shells lined up around the rim, I mean the outside. It forms a circle, and some of these shells seem to sparkle. I had heard about this kind of thing, but coming from the Midwest, I don't know a whole lot about life in the ocean. Lemme show you, Mendel. Move your *tuchus* in here."

Mendel, as if on command, followed Morris's voice. Arriving in the kitchen, he said, "I could stand a cracker, maybe, if someone left me one with just a little peanut butter. After that, I better find a bed before I fall on the floor."

The men found only a couple of small packages of oyster crackers, which were surprisingly fresh. They went back to the living room, where they discovered Kiley dozing with the Faulkner leaning upon his chest and chin. The women had disappeared.

"Wake up for five minutes, Kiley," said Morris. "We have to assign some beds and then you can fall asleep for as long as you like."

Zena and Gilda slept side by side on one king-sized bed. Another room held a bunk bed, the type growing boys clamor for and then outgrow.

Kiley said, "I want no part of this. I will sleep on the pullout or that soft chair I slid into before. Good night."

"Morris, let's choose. Loser gets the top berth."

"Choosing is not fair, especially when it is one and done."

"Okay, we will toss out fingers three times," said Mendel.

Mendel won on the third throw, but Morris would not accept the decision.

"I cannot climb up so high. Let's assume I got there. I might fall off or even through. I don't know which is worse."

"Listen, let's do it this way. At this age, both of us will be up at least twice during the night. Why don't we go one after the other? After, we can switch beds. Fair?"

"Maybe it's the salty air, I don't know what. Whatever has got into you has suddenly made you a reasonable human. This is long overdue."

"Maybe next time you will even call me a mensch," said Mendel. "That I would like to see."

"You should live so long," said Morris, mounting the six-foot ladder rung by rung. "I wish I had some practice on a contraption like this one. They didn't have these when I was a boy. It would have scared the living bejesus out of my old man. My mother, she would have pretended it was nothing and then gone off in a corner and prayed."

"Good night, Morris."

"Good night, moon," said Morris. "A kid's book I used to read to my nephew when I got to babysit for him," he explained.

****

Annie let herself in the back door the next morning, having correctly assumed it was left unlocked. The dogs dashed inside and assaulted Kiley, out cold on the sofa, with an array of licks and kisses. Smiling as he fended them off, Kiley spoke to himself. "This is the high life: a couple of grand dogs who just might slurp up anything they can find in your most available crevice—always seeking something rich in salt."

Kiley grappled with the throw, which covered his midsection but not his bare feet. For a moment, he thought about trying to rest further. Then he opened *As I Lay Dying* and pretended to read on for a few minutes before tossing the book into a nearby wicker basket filled with old newspapers and magazines.

Mendel and Morris, hearing the bustle below them, extricated themselves from their beds. Soon enough, the Lewis sisters, freshly showered, dressed, and rejuvenated, emerged.

"Now what?" asked Zena.

"I assume we get something to eat, then drive back," said Morris.

"What's the hurry?" said Mendel, slicking down what hair he had. "Never have we seen much of this part of the state. Let's explore."

"It's a beautiful day for the beach," said Annie. "Follow me. We can get there just as the sun heats up a bit."

"Suits me fine," said Kiley. "I will ride with her," he said, and all eyed him as if he had proposed to the girl. "I just thought it would be balanced. Two in her car, four in yours, Mendel."

"Whatever works," said Gilda with disdain.

The truth was that Kiley wished very much to spend some time with Annabelle. To him, she was totally alluring. He felt touched by the way she cocked her head, moved her neck. Kiley wanted to tell her, but he hadn't any idea of her reaction. She could be offended or put off. He could not decide whether to dive in.

"Just a few words with you, if I may," he said as he slid beside her in her microbus. The dogs were leaning over the seat, hoping to smother him once again.

"Mr. Kiley, the floor is yours," she replied.

"Well, I feel as if I've met you before, but unlike in those short stories and novels I've read where these things actually happen, I am certain this is not the case here."

Annie slowed to allow Mendel, in the Prius, to catch up. At the same time, she loaded a CD. And remained silent.

"Miles Davis," said Kiley. "But, I have no idea when or where. I do know his sound. And that this is not 'Sketches of Spain.'"

"I'm impressed. This is from a live recording," said Annie. "Look over there. It's the Ipswich River. I kayak on it whenever I can, mostly at sunset."

Kiley saw, at low tide, a large stream—to his eye, a purple path meandering between dark yellow stalks, all of which led off into the distance. He assumed that the river at some point fed into the ocean.

"Yes," she said, reading his mind. "These waters join. Sometimes, I just take Jess and Polly"—she waved over her shoulder—"and walk along, looking for blue herons, white egrets, and even a bright-eyed fox."

Mendel just then leaned on his horn, thereby disrupting Kiley's conversation with Annie. Kiley extended his arm out the window and pressed his palm downward, hoping Mendel might understand.

"I'm sorry," said Kiley to Annie. "He's impulsive. He's far more kind than he would ever acknowledge, actually, but impatient. Back to what you were saying."

"Just that more people tend to go to Crane, which I love, too. For reverie, for small, precious treasure, should you ever come back to this part of the world, hike along the bank of the river. But, your shoes, your feet will probably get wet." She paused. "You remind me of my uncle."

"Who would that be?"

"Hiram. People called him H. He was not what you would call a sports guy, at least in the traditional sense. Lousy hand/eye coordination. When he was twelve, a baseball hit him in the nose and bent it slightly. So, with a name like Hiram and a crooked nose, a lot of people thought he was Jewish. Actually, he's a Brahmin."

"My roots are in New England," said Kiley. "I was good at baseball. At least, I could catch one. Not all that much of a hitter, though. They pushed tennis on me. I wish basketball had been popular when I was growing up. Believe it or not, I think Morris excelled at both tennis and basketball. I went from one religion to another for much of my life: Lutheran, Episcopalian, Protestant. Now, Judaism seems, to me, far more tenable."

"I prefer the East. Maybe not a pure Buddhism because that is impossible," said Annie. "But, all of our religions promise solution. I want to allow the current to move me instead of fighting it. You know what I mean?" she asked.

"I only wish I could do so," said Kiley.

Great, soft dunes appeared before them.

"When I was a boy, our parents used to take us to Cape Cod all the time," said Kiley. "Once, I think, we were here but I don't remember it at all. The Cape dunes are darker, coarser. These are almost blond. And, they seem to form a blockade. Is that true or is my imagination speaking? From here, it looks like you have to climb over them to get to the shore."

"Were it not for three sets of stairs, you would be right, Kiley. The stairs and ramps provide access. Years ago, you had to blaze a trail through the sand or follow a partially made path."

"Hey!" yelled Morris from the other car. "Don't let me interrupt, but what exactly are we doing? I thought we would eat breakfast and drive home."

They all piled out of the cars.

"Destiny will have a feast for us after we walk the beach," said Annie. "Remember the time we met here, with the dogs? This is chapter two."

"Not for us, it isn't," said Zena. "I like it, though— reminds me of Florida."

"I don't know it from Cape Ann," said Gilda.

"It's kind of a well-kept secret. Everyone goes to Cape Cod, and plenty of people have discovered the beaches in southern Maine. This is a little harder to find—which is a good thing," Annie added. "It's also a prime spot for teenagers. Actually, couples of any age."

"Va va voom! That is what I like to hear," said Morris, grabbing Zena around the waist and gently pinching her side. She brushed away his hand. "Well, excuse me. I thought this was being affectionate."

"Maybe so," she replied. "Not in public, please."

They walked the beach, the dogs traveling hundreds of extra yards by scampering in circles and loops in pursuit of enticing scents. Annie led her elders in a vain attempt to form a straight line as they skirted the edge of the ocean.

Kiley stepped away from the pack to accompany Annie at the forefront. He watched her as she glanced around every so often to make certain the dogs were reasonably near.

"You love them, I can tell," said Kiley.

"They're my life—Jess, Polly, and, of course, Destiny."

"I would like to hear more," he said.

"Maybe you could spend a day or two out this way. We could talk."

"Or you could drive to Springfield."

"I am afraid I might become the center of attention. Really, though, I would love to visit."

Morris interrupted, "I don't know about the rest of you, but I'm hungry. It's nice here, but French toast or pancakes—whatever she has cooking already—smells better than the salt of this sea."

****

Destiny balanced presentation with preparation. Freeing her imagination allowed her to develop themes for meals. Typically, she awakened no later than six. Anticipating her guests from western Massachusetts, she was up an hour earlier, eager to work and play.

Without advance notice, she would be unable to stage brunch with a fully realized motif. Now, though, she delighted at the opportunity to frolic, to become the foodie of her own dreams.

She dwelled near the ocean by choice. These guests, she decided, were people of the earth, suited to colors of the forest. Destiny, years earlier, had studied abstract painting, and she believed in applying layer upon layer to a canvas until she was reasonably satisfied. Even then, she was forever tempted to resume the work.

Destiny sat to read. She favored Victorian novels, which might have seemed an unlikely match for one who lived so fully in the present moment. George Eliot was Destiny's favorite writer. The woman, Destiny believed, was ahead of her time, liberating female characters and freeing them to experience both carnal and cerebral pleasures. Destiny rarely mentioned to friends that *Middlemarch* was her favorite novel, and it surprised them when she recited specific passages from memory.

Annabelle took note that Destiny was just as intrigued with William Blake's etchings and paintings as with his verse. Destiny bought and framed a number of prints but kept them in her house rather than out for public display at the restaurant.

She had read, with dismay, that a nearly full set of Blake etchings would shortly be auctioned off, each individually, at Sotheby's. Art for dollars? Would no one honor such a combination of passion and dexterity any longer? Would such mercenary greed further mark this era? Destiny asked these questions aloud. They might be rhetorical but, to her, they mattered.

Destiny walked to her back room, raised the screen of her laptop, and penned an email to the *Times*. Never would her words see the light of day, the black and white newsprint. Still, expressing herself was a relief, and Blake would be proud of her protest.

****

The dogs, barking gleefully, announced everyone's arrival. Jess and Polly shrieked with combined joy and alarm, as if a couple of rabbits were dangling in the air before them. Recalling the familiar scents of Destiny's Place, the Labs raised up on hindquarters to celebrate with whoever came to the door.

"Are we here?" questioned Annie.

Destiny was delighted to be summoned. She and Annie had twice spent three weeks, as adults, at an arts/hippie summer camp. There, spirited news announcements for the day were typically delivered with phrasing in reverse. "Here we are" became, in transposition, "are we here?"

No need or reason for response.

Instead, Destiny slid a Beatles CD into a device and it answered with "Here Comes the Sun." Whether night or day, the song was, for these two women, forever appropriate. Beaming, Annabelle led the robust pets and the elderly human five inside.

Mendel and Morris, not to mention their girlfriends, were unsure. Mendel said, "What do we do now?"

Kiley, though, snapped the thumb and third finger on his right hand together and began to gently move to the music from the waist upward. Annie took his hands in hers and led him in a slow-motion version of a jitterbug. The two dogs shook their rear ends, wagged their tails, and attempted to lick faces—all gestures of glee and approval.

Destiny doubled over with laughter. Morris raised both his eyebrows, and Mendel shrugged in either approval or apparent confusion. Soon, Zena and Gilda intertwined fingers and began to hop along to the beat of the music.

"Gimme a slice of salami!" yelped Morris to nobody in particular, even though he realized this request could not possibly be fulfilled.

"We haven't any, but I could get you some hummus and crackers," the hostess replied.

"Of course. What are you waiting for?" he replied, as Destiny, Annabelle, and the dogs retreated to the kitchen.

Kiley danced around once, then ambled over to a chair that he would use as his perch—an observation point. Time, for him, was on hold. He flashed upon the unlikely turns his life had taken to bring him to this point: his Catholic upbringing in Worcester, attendance at Holy Cross, the move to Springfield, and a decision, after a year of teaching, to go into business. He made enough money and left the church. Long past the halfway point in his life, according to his calculation, he came upon Mendel and Morris and all played shuffleboard in Forest Park. Soon, he was a regular at their house for dinner, occasionally spending the night. Then, they left for Florida. There, they had met the sisters. Meanwhile, Kiley had found religion yet again. How could that be—he, a confirmed agnostic, leaning toward and nearly upon another conventional faith?

Finally, the graceful, shining young woman, this Annabelle. He could not help but stare when she was in the room. It was inappropriate and embarrassing, but he could not desist. This Destiny, too, he found transfixing. The two of them.

Kiley sat and pondered, cupping his face within the palms of his hands as he leaned forward. If he wasn't careful, he knew he might just pitch himself onto the floor.

Kiley was certain he had met Annie previously, and she reminded him of his daughter whom he had not seen for months. Susan lived in Burlington, Vermont, a good four-hour drive from home. He usually managed to visit her once a month during bad weather, more often during summer. She was a dancer with a modern company that performed throughout New England at colleges. Susan danced to drums. It was eclectic, never the same. Kiley admired rather than cared for the artistry, but he loved Susan so very much. This Annabelle, though, she was something else.

Kiley often wished to talk about Susan with his friends, Mendel and Morris. He never did, perhaps because he thought it taboo. Morris had a son who lived in the Midwest. Mendel occasionally spoke of his son who lived in Brooklyn; it seemed his daughter had moved far off. If asked, Mendel would speak about them, but he never initiated such a discussion. All three men found it difficult to talk about these baby boom children they had fathered.

Kiley felt the very real presence of these two women with whom he was intrigued. Destiny was the earth mother: comfortable with herself, seemingly aglow with spirit. Annie was an artist and woman of the outdoors. Could she become his muse? Besides, what might this mean? He did not speculate.

He always felt more comfortable speaking with women. Men were, to him, problematic. Even these geezers boasted of scores—notches long, long ago in their belts.

If he and Helen, his wife, had been lucky enough to have another child, she would have looked like Annie. That's what Kiley thought, but how could he and why would he say this to the young woman? Susan, his daughter, would have had a sister. Helen, he knew, would have loved Annie. That was it: Annie resembled Helen—as he met her when they were in their twenties.

Kiley's mind and memory tripped backward by decades. After meeting Helen, after each agreed life without the other was worthless, they had driven, well, where was it: Chatham or Hyannis? The images were alternately blurry then keen, foggy then sharp. He saw the swing set at the motel the morning Susie flew off. He had raced to the spot and caught her just before her head and back would have cracked on the asphalt. Now, he lurched as if revisiting the moment.

He so wished Helen were alive, that she had not died, that they had been correct in the initial diagnosis, that nothing within her would spread, that Susan would soon have a child, that Helen and he might experience many more years together.

Kiley would season his vision with philosophy as he did appearance with reality. He caught himself staring at the open door to the kitchen, anticipating Annabelle and Destiny. His good friends, walking in place, blocked Kiley's view. But, he did not mind. His imagination carried the moment.

Destiny interrupted the reverie. She had changed into an elegant, crème suede outfit. More typical for her were flex-fitting jeans, denim, or flannel shirts in cooler weather and any one of a number of well-worn T-shirts during warm summer days.

Annabelle had not yet returned from the kitchen, but Destiny's appearance stopped all conversation.

"Well," she said, eyeballing each person in the room. "I am a woman. This is a special occasion, a celebration. I picked out something maybe appropriately distinctive?"

Annie walked out wearing what appeared to be a caftan. Kiley realized he hadn't seen such an item in more than thirty years. A becoming, luminous shawl rested upon her shoulders.

On it was a painting of a lanky boy, dressed in pale blue, with a staff in his hand. Behind him stood a flock of lambs. Kiley recognized the picture.

"Blake. It's *The Shepherd*," he said.

"Yes, he—I mean, the writer, the artist, William Blake—has been in my life for a long time."

Morris appeared startled, as he remembered the inscription on the stone he found by the pond near the highway. He looked at Mendel, who shrugged his bony shoulders but otherwise did not react.

Kiley, however, responded. "How sweet is the Shepherd's sweet lot!" he said. "I grew up on William Blake. My parents read *Songs of Innocence* to me. Then, when I was a bit older, *Songs of Experience*. I think they were trying to educate me about sex through Blake. I remember my father emphasizing just how important the body was. This was at a time when certain people would call sex 'the S word.'" He paused. "I know, you're wondering how Catholics and this William Blake came to mix. All I can imagine is that they liked the ritual of the church. They never pushed catechism or communion on me. But, we were told that the sanctuary would provide comfort. I guess, to this day, maybe that's what I miss. Could further explain my interest in becoming a Jew." He paused. "I am thinking the warmth and maybe what I imagine is security."

"This was not what we felt, no way," said Zena.

"They pretended that sex did not exist. We never did learn about babies and pregnancy. Not when I was in that house," added Gilda.

"Us? No. I wish I could say that I made up for it later on, but that's another story."

"I didn't know William Blake from a hole in the wall until Morris came up with this meshugge. Still, who is this Blake? That aside, if this guy was one of the first to say sex is holier than God, I'm with him," said Mendel.

"Well, I'm sure Annabelle did not wear that lovely silk shawl thinking of this," said Destiny. "Blake was a mystic, and tonight's skies will be filled with stars. The moon is close to full, and the air is unseasonably warm."

"Listen, we're tired," said Zena. "I thought we came here to eat."

"Second," said Gilda.

"Surely," replied Destiny. "Annie and I will bring out the meal. Settle wherever you wish."

Annabelle, silent all the while, thought of Sam, their affair, the piano, and of Blake.

****

The lavish buffet spread included cranberry French toast; Belgian waffles; homemade onion rolls; honey wheat bread; various cheeses and crackers; and an abundance of fruit, including melons, pineapple, berries, mangos, grapes, and kiwi. Pitchers of orange, grapefruit, cranberry, and tomato juice lined one table edge.

"Coffee and tea later," said Destiny.

"This friend of yours, Morris, she knows something about catering," said Zena. "She should be in business."

"She is," said Mendel. "This is a restaurant. You haven't got eyes?"

"Shush, Mendel. She was just making a comment, paying a compliment," said Gilda.

"Why don't all three of you keep quiet? It's time to eat, and I don't mind if I start," said Morris.

Destiny and Annie stood behind the rectangular table and paused for a moment. Morris, wasting no time, grabbed a plate, filled it, and retreated to his seat, where he wolfed down a large portion.

The others understood that one of the hosts might wish to speak before the meal began.

Annie raised a goblet and said, "This is to my dearest friend, Destiny, for having created such a loving moment and this plentiful feast for us all."

"And I would like to thank our guests for making the trek to the ocean, for the fine company, and for sharing this precious meal with us." Destiny raised a golden cup and drank from it.

Kiley was surprised and even a bit disappointed that conversation was neither expansive nor revealing during the next hour. He wanted to talk, even explore. He wanted to lead someone somewhere. But, no matter how hard he pushed, he couldn't get anywhere.

He realized that his motive was to get to know Annabelle better, but that would have to wait for another day.

Everyone was at ease and resting comfortably when Morris stood. "Any good shuffleboard courts around this joint?" he asked.

Destiny and Annabelle looked at each other.

"Actually, there's a senior center in Essex. I think they have shuffleboard courts," said Destiny as Annie shrugged.

"Off we go," said Mendel, suddenly jaunty.

"That's the town with the famous clam joint. Mendel and I found it first time through. Even though I am stuffed, maybe in a few hours we could hit Woodcock's." Morris paused when no one responded. "Look, it was just a suggestion."

With that, the boys rose and everyone else followed. Destiny's Place was temporarily vacated.

****

The Essex shuffleboard courts looked abandoned. Broken glass dominated the asphalt, and leaves that had fallen months earlier huddled in the corners of the fenced-in area. There were six courts. Atop one of the posts where a scoreboard once perched, someone had pushed down the head of a child's doll. It smiled wanly as if to remain hopeful even if the odds for survival were terribly long.

Carefully constructed but now splintering wooden frames, upon which scoreboards could be mounted, sat behind zones with numbers 7, 9, and 10. Mendel, in memory, mimed a shot, thrusting his fist skyward as he yelled, "Good 10!"

Every few minutes, someone would stroll or skate or bicycle past the courts. A teenage girl flaunted her good looks. Her boyfriend's shorts hung low, revealing a midsection as taut as an ironing board. Mendel, spying out of the corner of his eye, pretended to be oblivious yet imagined them thrashing about in bed.

Jess and Polly whooped it up, pleased that no other humans entered the shuffleboard area. The dogs figured they might as well claim the spot as their own.

The Lewis sisters wished that they had thought to bring sticks and discs.

Morris, who had been uncharacteristically silent as he moved away from the scene, suddenly shouted, "Girls, Mendel, Kiley! I just found some equipment! In here!"

But, no one knew where he had gone.

It was Kiley who traced Morris's voice up an incline that led to a rectangular brick building. "Not only that," said Morris, "but they got huge bags of popcorn up here, tubs of ketchup, some hot dog rolls. Hurry!" called the big man.

Even during youthful days when Morris played basketball and tennis, he had never been light-footed. Now, he danced by himself within the confines of the seedy brick building. Treating a cue as he would a Lindy partner, Morris spun about, then pushed out as if shooting a disc forward.

Mendel, stumbling through the door, caught sight of his friend in mid-pirouette.

"Now I've seen everything," he said. "Morris Kahn, ballerina. Never could I have anticipated. A regular twinkle toes is this one."

"Well, I found what we're looking for, so why not?"

Kiley, next to appear, began scribbling in the notebook he was carrying.

"What is that, Kiley?" asked Morris.

"I have been sketching: the beach, Destiny's Place, whatever strikes me."

"Since when are you an artist?" asked Mendel.

"I used to draw cartoons when I was growing up in Worcester. Only lately have I thought about it again."

"Well, you got plenty of material right now, with him," said Mendel, gesturing toward Morris.

At that moment, the women, led by Annie and her dogs, joined them.

"Such a couple of days I could not imagine," said Zena. "I mean, Morris described Destiny and she is just that picture. The rest of it, though, I don't know. I just can't tell where I am."

"She gets this way when she's exhausted," explained Gilda to those who were listening. "It's been like this since we were little. If Zena is tired, she will exaggerate, say something she doesn't mean, and often have to apologize the next day. Just give us a few minutes to rest up."

"We came here to play some shuffleboard, so let's play," said Kiley. "How do we make teams?"

"How about the four of us against Kiley, the young girls, and maybe even the dogs?"

"Fair," said Annie, "since my dogs lend spiritual support. You four are the shuffleboard players and we, except for Mr. Kiley, are the pretenders. Sounds like fun."

Annie and Destiny, laughing, agreed to share sticks.

Morris led off. True to form, he overshot the court, his disc rumbling and tumbling onto the sparse grass beyond.

"Bad cue, bad shot," he said.

It was just the start.

Mendel, lurching forward to see if his disc had landed in or at the line on a back right 7, toppled over. He was, however, pleased when Annie, her strong hands beneath his armpits, hoisted him to an upright position. He was unharmed physically, but his cheeks, reddening, revealed more.

The Lewis sisters, attempting to impress, were pitiful.

Only the meticulous Kiley, taking time to line-draw as he awaited his turn, shot with accuracy.

Destiny, pushing off the wrong foot, had fair success, while Annie's primary goal was to ensure that her dogs were happy. She cooed at them, rubbed their bellies, and smoothed their hair with her nails. As a thank you, Annie received drenching dog lickings. Before she picked up a cue to shoot, she would ruffle one of the dogs around the ears and then wipe her fingers on her jeans before finally letting loose with a wayward poke.

Kiley, realizing that his performance was the only hope for victory, attempted to focus on the game rather than his sketch pad. That did not work. Drawing mattered a great deal more to him than did avoiding the 10 Off box.

In fact, he quickly sketched that shape and captioned it, "Recycle Here!" Soon, Kiley excused himself from the game and wandered around a bit before settling beneath a beckoning weeping willow tree at the bottom of the hill.

There, he opened his book, produced a few pencils, and began to draw the tree as it appeared to him from the grass beneath it. He created his own figure as that of an aging man with a shawl—his prayer tallit—draped over his body as he gazed upward. The branches drooped very low, touching the head and face of this immobile figure.

After moving to a new vantage point, Kiley flipped the page and began another drawing. The effect was to create a set of adjacent images of one man and his relationship to the tree. Using a set of markers he stowed in his pocket, Kiley created a soft blue sky, a red-orange setting sun, and a naturally worn wooden trellis upon which vines grew.

He adorned himself with a long silver beard and inscribed the tallit with silver Hebrew lettering. Lost in his project, Kiley was oblivious to time. He continued, between strokes of the pen or pencil, to look upward and saw light green boughs. Would nature protect him?

Destiny was first to leave the shuffleboard area. From a distance, she saw the supine Kiley watching what seemed to be a large cumulus cloud hovering high above him. She walked on her toes as she approached, careful not to disturb him. Destiny perceived a man oblivious to all. She stepped closer to him.

After a while, she could stand it no longer. Bending gently, she whispered, "Blake?"

Kiley raised his head slightly and nodded. "Yes, Blake."

"Why?"

"It's about a journey, is it not, Destiny? Why, other than that, would you be called Destiny? I have re-discovered Blake late in my life—Blake and now Judaism, although I cannot say that the two are related. Within the context of this existence, it makes sense. But, for me to claim that I understand the intricacies of Blake, no."

"My time on this land is at its midpoint, while yours, Kiley, includes a good many more turns," she said, touching his wrist.

"It's just that, as you approach the end of life, you naturally wish for more," said Kiley.

Destiny nodded, "I've been thinking—and sometimes obsessively—about that since I was fifteen and my favorite teacher, Barbara, introduced me to Blake. She had come with us on a family vacation to Chatham during the off-season. We found a book supporting a lifeguard chair and she gave me that *Portable Blake*. I keep it by my bedside always."

"I'm not certain why," said Kiley, "but it seems that for some of us here, however different we are, Blake is a central figure. For me, this is conscious and it's mystical. For Morris, I sense something else. I know, without asking, that he means something special to Annabelle. His art? His revolutionary beliefs? I watched the way she clutched that shawl to her shoulders, neck, and throat. Only Gilda and Zena seem to wish that Blake and maybe you two, as well, would go away."

"How alienating would it be to bring up these thoughts about Blake?" asked Destiny. Out of the corner of her eye, she saw everyone at the top of the hill leave the building and begin the downward trek.

"For now, I suppose we ought to put him aside. Before we leave, and this could be relatively soon, you and I need a few minutes, yes?"

Destiny nodded and smiled. Kiley noticed how her entire face showed delightful dimples when she was pleased. He lifted his lips and opened his eyes widely in response.

The dogs were the first to arrive. They danced around Destiny and were followed by Annie, who loped about gracefully.

Morris was roaring. "If you didn't get stuck in the kitchen for half an hour, we actually might have won," he said, punctuating his points in the air, every so often looking around for Mendel.

"Shuffleboard is not a game of strength," said Mendel. "Just because you are huge what with a football player's neck, that does not mean one iota. You ever heard of the word finesse?"

"I surely have, and you got none of it. Looking like a crow is one thing. This does not permit such fancy finesse you got on your brain."

This talk was oddly musical, familiar, and welcome to Gilda and Zena, both of whom stood to one side. Annabelle and Destiny framed Kiley on the other.

"At least I can understand this," said Gilda.

"Morris is nothing if not a fat fool, but I love him for it," said Zena. "All of the hocus-pocus and Destiny's Place? I don't go for it. If you think I like it, what, are you kidding?"

"I am not a woman whose mind is closed," said Gilda, attempting to be diplomatic. "But did you hear Kiley and Destiny as we were slipping down the slope? You would think this Blake is God or Jesus. This is the new Moses, go know?"

"If you ask me, we should get the boys and drive back to Springfield nice and early," said Zena. "None of us can see six feet ahead in the dark."

"I'm with you, little sis," said Gilda, elbowing the bigger woman in the side.

****

Kiley and Destiny sat on the grass. Annie, sensing that they needed a bit of time, kept the dogs occupied by throwing a Frisbee and letting them chase after it.

Destiny seemed to be tracing a path with her index finger. She would move her hand and Kiley would nod; then the process was repeated. She then watched as Kiley initiated the procedure and mimicked him.

"Muscle memory," said Kiley. "She is an artist. I am a student. She breathes William Blake. My understanding is intellectual. I need more. Perhaps the answer is spiritual. No references to Catholicism or Judaism."

"From what I can tell, nobody around here has much in the way of muscles," said Zena.

"Including you," added Gilda, blowing out her cheeks. "Kiley is talking about something I only heard of when I went back to school. Maybe this is a mix of your mind and your body. Let me think."

"Correct, Gilda," said Kiley. "It is—how to phrase it?—in her fingers. Mine, and I am sad about this, have not yet grown accustomed to drawing Blake. Destiny is able to channel what he understood, in terms of structure."

Annie had been silent while she made sure the exuberant dogs were not jumping up to greet unsuspecting souls in the park. Now, she spoke. "I learned about Blake from Sam, my boyfriend years ago. Well, he was my teacher, my lover, my boyfriend, my best friend. He had this passion for the words of William Blake. Sam was better with composition than playing the actual keyboard, so he wrote the music for some of the poems in the *Songs of Innocence and Experience*. I have to admit that it did not take me that long to become the more proficient pianist. I sat at the piano and sometimes we sang the verses together. Anyway, before we broke up, he put one of Blake's verses in a plastic container and posted it, like a time capsule, off the Pike—near a small pond."

Morris interrupted with a holler. "And I found it! Mendel, schlemiel, this is what I am talking about. This is Blake!"

The sisters glanced at each other while Destiny calmed the dogs, who had been reinvigorated by Morris's outburst.

"For the life of me," said Zena, "I don't have a clue. What is going on? We gotta get home. Without sounding like a know-everything, what I can say is this: Life moves along."

"Blake, Schmake," seconded Gilda. "I never heard of the man. Now, he is right up there with, well, I don't know, Abraham Lincoln?"

"Blake was a revolutionary but expressed it all through one art or another," said Destiny. "Like Annie's friend, Sam, he was musical but such a writer that he set his own words to music just by singing out loud. He really wanted people to blend in with the entire universe. That he was just flesh troubled him. But he could imagine, always, what it was like to be a child, first innocent, then as a person in the world who retained some of the innocence of his youth.

"I was amazed when we had that *Da Vinci Code* controversy," Destiny continued. "Look at Blake's view of Jesus. Blake saw him and painted him as a revolutionary figure. To Blake, Jesus would have been a leader in Paris or Prague in 1968. You know what I mean? Blake's Jesus was a strong, unafraid, and emotional man."

"You know," said Kiley, "maybe all organized religion is doomed. Here I am embracing Judaism, but why? Blake saw good and evil. I am not so certain, and maybe I am reading into this, that the difference was sometimes difficult to discern. That was what he was telling us through poems and etchings. The tension has to be positive—not competitive like a me-against-you. Think about that."

"Could we please just go home?" Zena implored.

"She's right. Enough," bellowed Morris. "My head hurts. I like this Blake as much as the next person. But, for God's sake, I am a simple man."

"If you are so simple, what are you talking wildflowers and sand grains forever, for eternity—all of this?" asked Mendel.

"Look, just because I found the saying doesn't mean I believe in it right away," said Morris. "My mind dawdles. It needs to first consider before drawing a conclusion."

"See this gorilla? He goes back on his word," said Mendel. "It's always been like that with him."

"To me, Blake is music," said Annabelle.

"And to me, destiny—my name," added Destiny. "Eternity is really what we hope for while we live in the here and now. As I experience midpoint and beyond in my life, each instant of time on this earth is even more precious. Music is forever. Allen Ginsberg singing Blake lives on. I know—I have listened. Flesh? Yes, this is finite. Souls, though, do not expire."

"We live on, through generations, as a single person examines a painting, listens to a song, or plays a sonata," said Annie.

"My head also hurts," said Gilda.

"No, it doesn't really," Annie replied. "You and your sister, and Mendel and Morris and Kiley, too—all of us—we are uncertain. We don't know what is ahead. 'What if we have a baby?' my parents must have asked. Do most people examine it all before conceiving?"

"Just a notion at first and sometimes not even that, aside from exceptional souls who might examine consequences," said Kiley. "When I think of the hostility manifesting itself throughout the Eastern world."

Destiny interrupted. "When you are with others, look to your right, then to your left, and I guarantee that you will find someone you wish never to see again—an enemy, a jealous competitor in love or at work. I've learned this and, sadly, Blake would be proud of me. When I was a young woman, I thought in terms of Utopia and ideals. Now, sunrise and a good day—that's enough to make me happy."

Morris fidgeted nervously. "So explain why this Blake is such a big shot. Yes, I was moved, so to speak, when I found the wildflower note. Enough, though. I don't get why this should be so special for someone like me—a Jew who has seen plenty of better days."

"Don't be such a sad sack, Morris. We got plenty to live for," said Zena.

"Just assuming that might be the case, how is this Blake going to help us?" he asked.

"I want my daughter to be able to live to a hundred," said Kiley. "Should she be fortunate enough to have even one child, let that sweet being live into the next century. When we made the turn into this millennium, these notions were not impossibly far-fetched. Now, with the threat of extinction, who knows?"

"I will be extinct if I don't get back home to my bed and get a good night's sleep," said Zena.

Kiley continued as if he had not heard her. "Maybe that is why I turn to Judaism—to make some sense of this world, of those who say they live to die. I do not understand this. Or maybe I just don't want to hear. And Blake was a romantic who valued each moment of life. He wished to celebrate, bring together heaven and hell, and redefine the concept of evil."

"We need to make a decision. Drive back now or spend another night out here with Destiny, Annie, and these lovable dogs," said Mendel.

"Take a vote," said Gilda, the pragmatic mathematician.

"Out of here!" bellowed Morris.

"I second the big man's motion," said Mendel.

The sisters, glancing toward each other, nodded in assent.

Kiley said, "I am not ready to go. Perhaps the women could house me and we will figure out a way for me to rejoin you, my loving, extended family. Soon, I mean."

"We have a couch in the rear room at the restaurant," said Destiny. "You're welcome to stay with us for as long . . ."

". . . as you wish," said Annie, completing the thought.

"Let's go," said Zena. "Not that I haven't enjoyed this: the hospitality, the dogs, the shore, the food."

"And especially Destiny's Place, which I am thinking about even now," said Gilda, surprising herself. "But, it is late."

Within thirty minutes, the original foursome was back on the road, Mendel at the wheel.

Kiley waved as the group departed. He knew for certain that he was in no rush to return to the western part of the state.

CHAPTER 9

The decision, now left to him, was obvious: Kiley dreamt of sleeping at Destiny's that first night. She left the glowing design, including glitter and balloons. He dozed, and his mind wandered as he soaked in the sea's salty and distinctive scent—happy endings.

With a start, Kiley thought of Annabelle. That made him feel inspired and, at once, troubled. His turn of mind could present a problem. Still, he must see her. Perhaps she would come to Destiny's Place. Together, he and Annie would sing "Songs of Innocence." Who knew?

He wished her to be older, even by a decade or so. And then? He caught himself: This reverie was solitary. She responded to him. And so? Was he seventeen years old? This was puppy love?

Maybe she was just as curious.

Annie fought the impulse. Why would she wish to get involved with a much older man?

Or, his years might be helpful. Some wisdom? Since that time, she had had friends her age, male friends her age, and lovers her age, but never a person she could trust. The men she knew were short on listening skills and longer on personal bravado.

She had been observing how Kiley conversed with people. He looked a woman in the eye; his eyes did not lower, surreptitiously or not, to chest level for a quick glance, longer look, or the obvious ogle. Of course, this made her wonder. Then again, he was far past his sexual peak. Annie kept warning herself that this could not be the priority. She desperately needed to be heard. She looked forward to the rendezvous at Destiny's.

When she arrived, Annie found Kiley sitting cross-legged in the middle of the main room. Annie had brought the dogs but left them to their own devices. She always felt better that the dogs had each other. And she had them. A person who too often found herself isolated, Annie more often yearned for company. This, she felt, was not a contradiction.

Kiley appeared to be asleep or meditating. She watched him as, ever so gently, he shifted back and forth, an invisible wave influencing his rhythm. Annie tilted forward on her toes and softly approached.

She held her hand upon his spine and he acknowledged her presence with a nearly imperceptible nod. Slowly, Annie lowered her body until she sat next to Kiley. She began to sway in time with his pace.

Several minutes later, Kiley held steady and Annie followed his lead.

He turned to her, placing his hands upon her shoulders. Leaning forward, she bowed her head and gently smiled.

As they helped each other up, Kiley released a deep sigh. Annie gripped his hand more tightly and led him out the front door of Destiny's Place. She hooked his arm through hers and slowly made her way toward the sand dunes and the sea beyond. She draped her other arm around his waist. She felt soft flesh since he wore a shirt that hid his belt line. Annie grasped the pliable skin and helped keep him upright.

Kiley was quite capable of standing ramrod straight, or at least what he assumed to be vertical. At the same time, he treasured the young woman's assisting touch since he hadn't experienced anything like it in quite some time. He leaned on her, pretending to require the support.

When Annie looked at him, however, she saw that his lips were gently upturned, as if he were striving, ever slightly, to camouflage a smile.

"Go ahead, admit it," she said to him.

"No contest," said Kiley. "You have the gift, the fingers of a sorceress."

"I can't say anyone's given me that title, so I'll take it as a compliment. I never thought of myself as a woman of mystery," she replied.

Before long, they reached a marsh that, Kiley remembered, led across a paved road and then to the beach. To his disappointment, Annie created physical distance between them. They walked rhythmically, but Kiley was certain that Annie wanted space.

It had been a long, long while since Kiley had last engineered a stumble with a woman. He remembered.

Losing his footing as the swamp yielded to the asphalt, he tripped and fell into Annie's midsection, a sweeter place than could be envisioned—pleasantly soothing and inviting.

She drew him to her and hugged him first, then steadied him. Annie was, by far, the stronger of the two.

Several minutes later, Kiley, hesitant to break the silence, said, "Mystery. As you referred to yourself."

"Yes, it is; not me."

"Blake, the swamp, and sand dunes a bit further off."

"Not since my time with Sam has Blake occupied me this way, front and center. Blake in the foremost place of my mind."

"Annie, as I've become older—well, I'm old—I wonder constantly, it seems, about next: next minute, next life, next footstep—eternity. Blake."

"I hear the water's lap beyond the dunes. To me, it is all everlasting. At least, I cannot imagine an ending. Nature is infinite."

"As I grow closer to my time, dear Annie, I hope this doesn't sound like selfish elderly pontificating. While you're probably right about the waves, they are, to me, abstract."

"You speak as an artist, Kiley. Yet, never do you mention your talent, your own piano—music that still lives," she said.

"Nothing, nothing anymore."

"But, you told me . . ." she continued.

"There was a man who wrote music, composed music," said Kiley. "He loved no one in particular, but he improvised. I would not call myself a proficient jazz player but I tried."

"Go ahead, Kiley."

"Well, I thought, at one point, that I would be a musician. I sat in during small-time sessions in Hartford, Springfield, Boston, New York, too. I remember a time when we were outside a college hall, it was in the spring, and we were warming up before a dinner time gig. I remember another instance we were at a Springfield club and—was it Jinxie's?—all of a sudden, this guy appears with his friend. He sat next to me on the piano bench and said, 'You take the top and I'll play the bottom.' Well, I never heard anything like it."

"Why is that, Kiley?"

"It was as if he led with the bass even though I began and was playing treble clef."

"I know that's interesting, in terms of music. But why is it so special?"

"It had more to do with his card. He was one of the few people those days who carried a card."

"What did it say?"

"It said Blake's Blues."

"Meaning?"

"I found out a good while later. It has to do with auras, the blues, Blake's message. No, I mean the flip side of Blake's theme. If we agree that Blake was a positivist, then to play the blues is to contradict."

"Who says Blake is positive?" she asked.

"Marriage of heaven and hell; higher innocence; value of experience if somehow it doesn't become completely corrupted. You know all or some of this, Annie?"

She encircled Kiley's thin wrist with her thumb and third finger and then moved her hand slightly as if to measure his pulse. "You're very much alive," she said.

"That has to be a good thing," said Kiley.

Annie giggled, stopped, took a deep breath, and then laughed hard, so hard she felt her stomach quiver. She rubbed it.

"For me, this is something new," she said to Kiley, holding the tiny fold of flesh between her fingers.

"You're way too thin," said Kiley.

"And one person you are not is my mother," said Annie.

He smiled, realizing that he could not bluff her and that he cared genuinely and deeply about her, probably too deeply.

"I never approached an anorexic state, but I could not tolerate the slightest trace of fat, especially around my middle."

"You're very dear, even now," he said.

They walked along the edge of the marsh as the sea salt began to permeate the air. Annie and Kiley moved together slowly and in rhythm. They had time to consider. Kiley had always thought himself a rationalist. What, then, was he doing with a woman so much younger? Annie was relieved, even optimistic. If she truly believed in each moment, why not savor this one?

She dangled her hand next to his until their fingers interlaced.

The beaming sun matched her mood as she grasped his fingers more tightly. Annabelle realized she was accustomed to the smooth skin of a much younger person. Kiley's fingers were marked—and knobby. She was intrigued and looked down. She saw the blue veins lining the top portion of his hand. Annabelle decided that the complexity was a metaphor for a lifespan long in meaning and intricacy. She would learn about this man.

He was thrilled by her touch. Kiley had forgotten the scent and texture of youth. As he walked along, his mind shifted to Mendel and Morris and their girlfriends; the shuffleboard crew back in Springfield; and his daughter, Susan. No one would believe this, whatever it might be.

Soon enough, they came to the water and Kiley had to shield his blue eyes. The sea before him was strikingly dark and violet, and the contrast with the bright orange sunshine was nearly too much to bear.

He looked sharply downward. "What happened?" Annie asked.

"I felt temporarily blinded. I just couldn't look straight at the water."

"Oh, I remember that moment the first time I was here. Same thing," she said. Then she asked, "What are we doing?"

"Two people walking on a beach. Lovely, sublime day in New England. Who would not wish for that?"

She nodded. "I wish Destiny were here."

But Kiley was gratified to be alone with Annabelle. He was intrigued with Destiny but pleased that she was not with them at that very moment. Destiny's presence was luminous. She filled a room, projected a glow and created a mood.

He said, "Yes, Destiny. It seems, sometimes, that you two complete one composite picture. Perhaps even more."

CHAPTER 10

Destiny loved Annabelle and it pained her to be even the slightest bit jealous, but she could not stop herself. Destiny wished it were she walking to the beach with Kiley. She and Kiley were closer in age. And it had been so long for her. Everyone admired Destiny, found her charismatic, mystical, a source or wellspring. What, however, about her own needs?

Destiny had learned long ago to speak feelings aloud, so she proceeded to do just that, even though she was by herself. She maintained her poise.

"Another day," she said to herself. "Later."

"Destiny, your moment arrives sooner than you might expect," replied her other side.

"I understand that patience is essential. After all, I've been waiting for some time now."

"Dance. Make music. Create and inspire, Destiny. This is you."

"He could not fulfill my dreams. Or maybe he could."

"This moment, Destiny. You understand that and you live that. Indulge yourself but do not speculate. Center yourself, Destiny."

Destiny shook her thick, shoulder-length light hair free of the butterfly clip holding it in place. She leaned forward, rubbed her face until she drew some color—and then smiled broadly. She grabbed her favorite walking stick, which she had decorated with gold, blue, and red stars. Then, shutting the door behind her, she made her way toward the beach. She anticipated the rush of joy she would feel when she found Annabelle and Kiley. Tension no longer coursed through her body. Instead, she felt at ease and non-competitive. Always, Destiny remembered that it would be self-defeating to so intensely compete.

She chose to cut through the reeds. She was hurrying only because she missed her friends. It was a mid-summer sun.

"Savor number nine, ever so sublime," her father used to advise.

He had spent his life treating children and often invented rhymes, jingles, sayings, and even mantras that were specific to each of his patients. Like this one, they were typically imperfect yet endearing. You needed a code or answer key to realize he was speaking of the ninth month.

As she walked, she imagined Kiley and Annabelle as a twosome so that she would not be surprised if she came upon them holding hands. Just then, Destiny saw Annabelle affectionately balancing her forehead upon Kiley's shoulder. They might have been eighteen and thirty.

"Trust them, do not waver," Destiny whispered to herself. She ambled forward, kicking sand, and called out, "The perfect, perfect mid-summer day!"

Jess and Polly approached at full gallop. How did the Labs get out and know to come here?

Annabelle, seeing her friend, sashayed over. "Enjoy this glorious season, dear Des," she called to Destiny, then embraced both animals. She hoped to prod the dogs over to where Destiny and Kiley stood. Annie wanted them all gathered together, within one extended reach.

Instead, it was Destiny (was it not always she? wondered Annie) who raised her arms to beckon the animals. Annabelle said nothing but signaled them all to join hands and slowly surround the befuddled dogs. Polly and Jess jumped about, creating full circles through single leaps, until they realized the adoration was directed at them. Ultimately, they were not to escape. After a few minutes, the Labs sat and, closing their eyes, lopped onto each other as the three humans shared blissful smiles and gentle laughter.

After a moment, Kiley became uncertain of himself, hesitant. Recently, he had grown closer to Mendel and Morris. He wished his old friends were there with him and not across the state. They provided context.

Then he felt suddenly self-indulgent. Who was he to dictate? Mendel and Morris, Gilda and Zena—or was it Mendel and Gilda, Morris and Zena?—were back in Springfield. He could have gone with them.

Now, in Ipswich, he was surrounded by beautiful humans who were new to him and two wholesome dogs. Kiley, a lifetime ago, had drawn cartoons, even developed a flip book that ultimately turned into an animated short film. He featured dogs of all sizes, shapes, personalities, and quirks.

He recalled that version of himself, the youthful visual artist rather than an elderly man who could not stop thinking about a much younger woman. He turned toward Annabelle, whose light blue eyes were staring at his.

"Maybe I should go," said Kiley.

Destiny fastened her grip upon his hand. She led Kiley to the edge of the water.

"It used to be," said Destiny, "that I believed water could cure. However, the passing of each of my parents, despite water therapy—which teaches immersion—and prayer (we tried everything) convinced me otherwise. But I still search for something even more profound. Should I not find it, even I could become somewhat more rational," she said.

Surprised, Kiley straightened. "You don't say. You see, that was one of the many things I did. I wrote and edited copy and even became a fact checker for those writing books about economics. No, I don't look the part now. And, with my newfound affinity for Jewish mysticism, well, nobody would have any clue. Other career stops, too, you know."

"You two are very much alike," said Annie. "It's just that the paths are in reverse."

Kiley smiled at Annabelle. "And you, with your precision but, at the same time, your ability to relax and your spontaneity, thy name is Annabelle."

Annie blushed, cast her eyes downward, and then met his gaze. She did not understand what to make of this man. Typically, she would analyze before proceeding, but it seemed impossible in the moment.

Kiley interrupted her reverie. "Piano training. It's never haphazard. Even those jazz players are constantly at work. What sounds so impulsive is typically practiced into oblivion. It's the ultimate in craft refinement. That was me and, secretly, that *is* me."

"I know that, dear," said Destiny.

Annie was startled to hear Destiny address him with such intimacy.

"He really is a sweet man," she said, sensing Destiny's desperation. Annie needed to be true, to stay close to Destiny.

Kiley extended his arms with the hope of huddling with both women, but the dogs intervened, leaping and licking, carefree and uninhibited. The moment was over. Kiley realized that he must extract himself. Was he too old for such tenderness? Now, he must find his way back to the house in Springfield. He needed to sit by himself, to ponder and consider. Individual reflection and intellectual growth, yes.

But, involvement with this woman, with one of these women? Maybe not.

But maybe.

CHAPTER 11

"I cannot believe that this Kiley, some big shot who pretends he is the living end, who is finding religion, whatever that is, thinks that sweet wisp of a girl will sleep with him," said Zena.

"Listen," said Morris, wolfing down a bagel covered with mounds of cream cheese, "the man is entitled. When was the last time, you think, for him?"

"We are not going to have some discussion of sex after seventy-five. No, you and your AARP Magazine can go sit in a corner. Amuse."

Such a lovely and warm summer day in western Massachusetts teased its inhabitants into believing that this year, as the earth heated, winter would not overtake them. Either that, or they would get a hundred inches of snow. There was no in between.

Mendel and Gilda had gone for a walk to the new petting zoo in the park. It was her idea. Mendel carried his dandy, hand-crafted stick in his left hand. He utilized it only to establish personal space, to be certain that Gilda did not crowd him. Mendel, however much he adored Gilda, found it necessary to keep his "peak options in the flow."

Gilda, understanding that she would never have anyone better than this flawed man, raised nary an eyebrow. She was happy to co-manage Phases, the community center and store, with her sister. She and Zena did better when working together, living beneath the same roof, yet able to spend significant time apart.

She enjoyed the balance as she apportioned work with Zena and evenings with Mendel. She wedged in time to pursue a recently discovered hobby, portrait painting. Surprisingly, her hand had grown steadier with age. Always a person of detail who possessed computational skills, she now had the time to sit, study faces, and paint later on, mostly from memory.

Mendel thought, with envy, about Kiley. How was it that he and Morris had come upon Annabelle and Destiny and yet Kiley might, as they said in the old days, score? Not quite a fair deal, thought Mendel. Then again, he was always skeptical of outcomes—new, fair, real, whatever. Truth be told, he expected the worst. Further, who was he to judge?

He poked his stick through the wire fence at the zoo. A tiny, round bunny pressed itself beneath the wire and ran away into the park. Mendel was certain the intruder would make out with nuts, popcorn, whatever tidbits humans had dropped.

"Gilda, where do you suppose we're going?"

"After this, if I have my way, we'll walk home. No, maybe we'll stop at the courts. We haven't played shuffleboard, you against me, for weeks."

"I mean after we're gone. Where do we go? Where have almost all of our friends gone?"

"Watch the animals, Mendel."

"I don't catch."

"Did you ever see an old dog will himself to die?"

"Actually, yes I did. It was when I lived on the island with my wife. Long Island, I mean. We were by ourselves except for Harry."

"Tell me about Harry."

"He was such a mix you would not believe. We knew of beagle and terrier. But, he had the length of a Dalmatian and he ran like the wind. Like nothing you ever saw in your life. Anyway, I bet Harry was seventeen if he was a day. And, he didn't look that bad. A little like I do now. Bent over, but not totally so. He could straighten if he wanted. He was some *gonif.*"

"A dog is a *gonif*?" asked Gilda.

"He could get what he wanted from us. He had us twisted around that waving tail of his."

"How did he die, Mendel?"

"One day, he stayed outside in the yard until past the dinner hour. We ate at six on the dot each and every day. Harry came in to eat dinner with us. Except not on this day. So, we put out a dish for him."

"And?"

"He was hunched over it and, next thing you know, he disappeared. I mean, he ran off." Mendel shrugged.

"You never found him again."

"Actually, we did. I happen to think Harry was trying to say good-bye, to signal us, that sly thing, that he was ready to move on."

"This is why, dear Mendel, I tell you to look at the animals," Gilda said.

"Now, I catch. They are teaching us what to do, how to cope, everything."

Gilda nodded her head twice.

Mendel continued, "When I was in school, I was always good in math, in statistics and finance, but never in English. Whenever anybody said 'metaphor,' I would signal, like you are now, that I understood. But that word, really, meant nothing to me. Until now. Morris and me, for God knows how long, we've been coming to this park. First, we looked at the animals in the big zoo, what with the polar bear, the elephant, the llamas, even deer. We watched them, and they watched us watching them. Now, we walk to this schleppy little zoo. Still, you can do worse than schmooze with the creatures. They don't answer you back, and they are good listeners. What more could an old man want?

"This old man wants to know that someone will remember him after he's gone."

"Same with Mo, too. Why do you think Kiley has such a thing for visiting this Destiny and even more than simply visiting with that delectable Annabelle? Do you really think he believes that he stands a chance with her? I will answer my own question: yes."

"At least you still got something going on, Mendel," answered Gilda. "The real answer is he wants to live longer and he thinks he can do that with what they call a relationship with this Annie."

Just then a willowy, long-winged bird swooped above them.

Mendel ducked. "What the hell? Is this a sign?"

"This is a heron, a wild blue heron. When Zena and I go off by ourselves, especially very early in the morning, we see that one sitting by itself at the edge of one of the ponds. I will tell you, though, this is an accident. I don't know enough about birds to say if it's lost. But, it doesn't want contact with those animals or with us. Look! It's speeding away."

"I wish I could do that," said Mendel. He flapped his arms.

"Then, you could escape easily. Me, Morris, this life, whatever is pressing down on you," said Gilda.

"You forgot your sister. I don't want her pressing on me no how."

"Very funny, you stinker. Let's get back home."

"Just a minute, Gilda. I got an important topic on my mind."

She sighed. "What is it now? Every time we go for a walk, you come up with something. There's no good Chinese anymore in Springfield. Your arthritis is barking something awful. The neighbors' kids play rock and roll music too loud. Nobody pays any attention to the leash law. What now?"

"Let's get married."

Gilda lost her balance and nearly fell over. Mendel caught her arm, and they were able to steady each other before either tumbled to the ground. She opened her mouth, but her throat stuck. More frightened than astounded, she again opened her mouth and again said nothing. Gilda could not make a sound.

"You look like maybe you are going to part the Red Sea. What's so terrible? If you say no, you're still my girl."

"This is my first proposal, Mendel, and I'm seventy-what?"

"Better late than never, as what's his face said at the end of *Some Like it Hot.*"

"Joe E. Brown."

"Yeah, with the wide lips and smile from coast to coast."

"He had some of the best lines."

"But, he didn't get to cuddle with Marilyn," said Mendel. "What I would have given."

"Mendel, I don't know why we would get married."

"To have a party."

"Stop it, Mendel," said Gilda, watching the heron gracefully flying in the distance.

"We could have a festive time right out here in the park while we still have this weather. Okay?"

She stared hard at him.

"Or, we could plan, instead, for next June or the next summer."

"You're taking some chance that we live that long," said Gilda.

"Don't you realize that you girls got us beat by, what, five years? All of the tables say so. Still, you think that the guy with the pitchfork is at your door."

"You're getting confused, what with American Gothic. But, I know what you mean. It's just genes."

"Oh, so you became an orphan early, Gilda?"

"Well, my parents lived to more than seventy, which wasn't so bad in those days."

"Nu? Tack on twenty years and you still got more than twenty to go."

"Let's say that I agree. Where and when?"

"Central Park in that *farshtunkener* city or Crane's Beach if you want the shore. Whatever."

"This feels like a shotgun. What's the rush?"

"If we're going to do this, let's do it before one of us is gone."

Gilda wanted to jump into Mendel's arms. Instead, she opted to lean softly against his shoulder.

Fortunately, Mendel had backed himself against the reasonably strong wire fence separating eager visitors from disenchanted animals. He wouldn't have had the strength to catch Gilda, but, with the assistance of the barricade, he was able to hold her close.

Gilda reached up and kissed him on the lips.

"What the hell," Mendel said, in awe.

Gilda, the more muscular of the two, straightened them up. Hand in hand, they marched back through the park toward the house, where they agreed to spread the good and, they were certain, surprising word.

They found Morris cutting the grass as Zena supervised from her chair on the front porch.

"I got news, you lug," called Mendel.

"Don't bother me. The wicked witch has me on work detail. If I do it right, maybe I get parole, maybe not."

"Gilda and I, we gotta get a *chuppah*."

"What?"

"I proposed, and she said yes. Well, she really did not say yes, but she did agree. Look at her."

At that moment, Gilda sat in her younger sister's lap to explain how it was that, soon enough, she would be a bride.

Zena looked down, as if disapproving, but Gilda knew she was mostly jealous.

"You do that, you lose something huge on taxes," said Zena.

"Zena, let's walk," said Gilda. The sisters often used "walk" as code for "talk."

They lifted each other up from the sitting position. Gilda took her little sister by the hand and led her off the porch, around the corner of the house, and into the backyard, which included two lots. Mendel was certain that this parcel, within city limits, was the house's prime selling point.

"Why spoil a good thing, Gilda?" asked Zena.

"I wasn't planning on it. I was against it, and I just said yes. This means it's what I want."

"You make no sense when it comes to logic," said Zena. "Take it from me—not smart and who says you're in love?"

"He is there for me. Do I sound like a sixteen-year-old? Well, I never was sweet sixteen. This is the closest I get in this life, and I am not about to let my one chance slide away," said Gilda.

"The least you can do is write up a formal agreement. Don't just go off like fools and have some phony-baloney justice of the peace tie you together till death and beyond."

"Mendel and me, we were just leaning against a fence in the zoo," said Gilda.

"So?"

"You think any of those animals, when they like each other, draw up papers to stay together?"

"Gilda, you're talking about goats and lambs."

"Still, you must see where I'm headed. It's time, for once, that I just do, instead of talking myself out of doing."

"You're the older sister," said Zena.

She continued, however, to push the idea that Mendel and Gilda agree upon terms before they married. Mendel accepted this as formality, while Gilda acquiesced and managed to camouflage her joy.

Morris wanted to involve Kiley and—why not?—Destiny and Annabelle in the process. "That Christian-turned-Jew, he could officiate, or whatever it is they call it. The girls could play music."

"Kiley used to be a guitar player," offered Gilda.

****

A week later, the Destiny, Annie, Annie's dogs, and Kiley arrived in Springfield. Destiny was the first out of the van, followed by Jess and Polly. Annie helped a limping Kiley.

"Jesus, what happened to you?" asked Morris.

"Not entirely appropriate," said Kiley, "given my choice of religion these days."

Before he could continue, Annie explained, "He walked a little too much. It was my fault. From Destiny's to the beach and back twice a day for a total of how many?"

"Look, stiff is one thing, which does not bother me," said Kiley. "If I remember to massage and then to stretch"—he nodded toward Destiny—"maybe this doesn't happen. Then again, with my memory, who knows?"

"Dum dum da dum," sang Destiny to the tune of "Here Comes the Bride."

Gilda reddened as Mendel interceded. "She has not had time to even think about what she might wear," he said. "We still don't know where we will have it."

"You speak as if you two are about to have a baby," said Annie.

Before he could respond, Morris, coughing, sputtering, and stumbling forward, raised his right arm as if to silence a crowd. Mendel rushed to his friend, smacked him on the back a few times too many, and finally said, "Look, this is my idea, so don't go blaming Gilda. She's getting hitched to a person who, with one leg in the coffin, could use a boost. So? So there."

As he spoke, Destiny made her way to the van and returned with a stacked set of attractive, deep red, plastic glasses. She passed them out, poured a bit of Chablis into each, and raised hers high.

"To everlasting peace, love, and happiness. Amen."

Morris opened his eyes wide. The others clapped softly, nodding in assent.

Mendel placed his arm around Gilda's shoulder and hugged her to him. "This might be the best day of my life," he said, then added, "I think."

Morris let loose with a volcanic roar, which he held for a few counts. The noise instantly liberated the dogs, who took off, one after the other, around the house—and on neighboring lawns, too.

"Well, all I can say is *l'chayim!*" said Kiley.

"That is so far from the truth, Kiley," said Annie. "You, since we met, have never summed up anything with a one-word response."

Kiley kissed her full on the lips, a surprise to Annie and a bit startling to the other women. Morris shrugged. Mendel gave Kiley the thumbs up, walked over to Annie, and hugged her to his body.

****

Destiny tried to convince Mendel that a wedding by the waves would ensure his posterity. "Water never stops flowing, Mendel. You will never die. You will constantly refresh."

"When I give out, thanks, I don't especially hope to come back again and again and again," he said. "It's enough to get married when you are a couple of laps over the hill, if you know what I mean. I will say that I would not object to a honeymoon on the water. And, if you think I don't like Ipswich, Woodchuck's, that green sea, you don't know me from a hole in the wall."

"What are you saying, Men? Where do we tie this knot?" asked Gilda.

Kiley interrupted. "Why don't you just go to a temple? You're both Jewish, and Jewish weddings are fun. You got all kinds of senior organizations to help out."

"Some Zen Buddhist you turned out to be!" boomed Morris. "Look at him! He wants to isolate those two. What is it about you deep thinkers?"

"I just thought that we could have a ceremony for you beyond the dunes," said Destiny. "Then, back to my place—no need to invite everyone in the world. It's really not my role to say that. I misspoke. I'm sorry."

"Destiny, we don't use words like misspoke. You are too sweet and too nice for each and every one of us," said Morris. "You and Annie." No one said a word. "And the dogs, Dolly and Jess. Such sweet animals."

Mendel could no longer stifle a reaction. "Not Dolly, you moron. It's Polly."

Laughter filled the air, and Morris coughed until he began to pant.

Only Kiley could wish aloud for decorum. "Wouldn't it make more sense to find a synagogue?" he asked again.

"You goy-turned-Jew, but really just a smart goy, you go to Temple Beth Sholom. The rest of us, we will be on the beach! But, since I can't get there at this very moment, maybe I could use a walk to the little pond. Who will go with me?" asked Morris. He paused, and no one answered. "Well, I will go by myself," he said.

"No, you want company, Mo, and I could use the exercise," said Zena. "Besides, that eliminates two from planning a wedding. I'm too old to discuss marriage."

"Suit yourself," said Mendel, disdainfully.

Morris and Zena quickly slipped on walking shoes and left the house.

They were barely out the door when Morris said, "What does the coot have in mind? He's got money. Why marry your sister?"

"She's a catch," said Zena.

They walked across Sumner Avenue at the traffic light, looking both ways, as if they were schoolchildren who had been scolded, admonished, and instructed to take extra time and care when traversing a major thoroughfare.

"For us, they need a kid to be a crossing guard. For the kids, they need a senior, like us," said Morris.

He steered Zena past the clay tennis courts, along the periphery of the ball field, down a sloping road, and, finally, to the duck pond. Schoolchildren had gathered around the lily-laden pool. A few harried adults attempted to keep some order as the more audacious kids taunted the birds.

Morris was amused. "See that one with the big hair and the shorts falling down his behind? That would be me if I was his age."

"Yes, with the belly hanging over his belt," said Zena.

With that, he touched her somewhat smaller but still pillowy midsection.

She slapped his hand away. "Not with children around, you don't," she said.

"'Opposition is true friendship.' That's what Blake says. That line is somewhere later on in the poem." Morris stopped and then continued. "But, in the *Songs of Experience*, which I have been reading ever since I found that message near the Turnpike, he always comes back to the same thing: the difference between good and bad, black and white, you and me—it isn't such a big deal. I keep thinking about his 'The Garden of Love.' He binds joys and desires with briars."

"I don't understand why you spend so much time with your Blake books. I don't get it," said Zena. "Blake, Schmake."

"Maybe because I am trying to understand, Zena, why I love you so much. And how."

"First Mendel, now you. Next thing you know, you'll ask me to marry you."

"That would make me even happier than having more money than Mendel."

"What, are you serious, Morris? We talked about this before and you said, and I quote, 'Marriage is for the birds—the snowbirds and all the other birds who are coming and going twice a year.' I never knew, even then, what you were talking about. But now? Why would we do such a thing?"

"A much better question is: why not?" he asked. With that, he lowered his lumbering body to the ground, then balanced himself on one knee. "If I could get my weight on my better knee, I would. For now, this has to do. I think if we get married, we will free ourselves. I don't mean that to be so much hokum. I looked up another short Blake poem, 'Eternity,' Zena. 'He who binds to himself a joy / Does the winged life destroy; / But he who kissed the joy as it flies / Lives in eternity's sun rise.'" With that, he hoisted up slowly and kissed her full on the lips. "Well, what do you say, sweet one?"

Zena had been waiting for the day, the month, the year that he would propose. She knew early on that she wanted to marry Morris, but she would never say so. Unlike other Jewish households she knew growing up, she lived in one with parents who were coy. It was impossible to read them, make an educated guess as to their feelings.

"What am I, a young bride? A kind of naive girl or something?" she asked.

"You are not young and you are not a shiksa, but if you're going to live to a hundred, you might as well be with me. You will eat well, that I can promise."

"Some Romeo you are, Morris."

"They missed a letter. Mo, not Ro."

"And neither are you a comedian," she added.

"What do you think, Zena?"

"What I would like is to get married before my big sister. That's if I say yes."

"You mean walk into a lawyer's office and do it right there?"

"Not just any lawyer but a justice of the peace, Morris. Like in the movies."

"Something Henry Fonda would do."

"He would. But, I cannot think of anyone you're less like."

"Should we go back and tell them?"

"Morris, you know what we should do. My question is: Do we let them in on it before or after we get hitched?"

They shrugged, then laughed. Morris kissed her on the lips.

"It seems simple to ask you to marry me. This stumps us? Maybe we should elope, Zena. That would fix that sly fox, Mendel, but good."

"You still need to outdo your best friend? Show him up?"

"He started it," said Morris.

"And you, Mr. I Can Do Anything Better, think that running off and marrying me will actually hurt Mendel?"

"Hurt is not what I am after. He thinks he's so romantic, and I would like him to try and top this."

"I am not yet one hundred percent certain I would do this with you, Morris. I said yes to marrying you, but now I already have second thoughts."

"Zena, you know me."

"I suppose I do," she sang.

"And I suppose I love you, too," Morris returned, with a reasonable rendering of the lyric from "Fiddler on the Roof." Morris and Zena often sang show tunes together.

Now, he grabbed her by the shoulders, clutched her to him with an enveloping hug, and kissed her again directly on the lips.

She resisted at first but then relaxed into his arms, allowing this ancient bear of a man to cover her with his big body.

After a few minutes, her eyes moist, Zena took his hand and pulled him toward the hill just as his cell phone rang. Though Mendel and Morris had each purchased a flip phone, after debating whether to for months, most of the time each would forget its location, even when it was near enough to trip over.

It was Zena who had to grab for the phone through the car keys, pocket comb, and index cards Morris had stashed in his pocket. "Watch what you're doing, Miss. The family prize possessions, you know."

"I hate to say this," she said, "but they're pretty easy to miss, Mo." Into the phone, she said, "Hello?"

"Hello yourself. This is Mendel. What happened to you and the walrus? Destiny wants to know since she intends to go to some farmers' market to fetch supper."

"We just went walking and now we are on our way back. Fifteen minutes at the most," said Zena.

Morris was not in a hurry. He wanted to tell Mendel the news and upstage his friend without seriously insulting him.

Morris needed a few minutes to figure out how to show him who was boss—with humor and just a hint of edge.

"Zena, what do we say?"

"You got the big ideas, you come up with the plan, Mo."

"Seriously, I'm stuck."

"You really are worried. Listen, Morris, these are our best friends, surrounded by these Crane's Beach girls and the dogs, all adorable. What could be sweeter? What you got to worry about?"

CHAPTER 12

Officiating for his friends at the double wedding thrilled Kiley. That it was his inspiration and had been such a popular notion further validated the idea. Morris balked awkwardly when he broke his news to Mendel.

"Men," he announced, out of breath after having hiked home with Zena, "I got something special: Zena and me, we are tying that knot, same as you two, but like tomorrow. How does that sit, my friend?"

Everyone realized that Morris had overstepped. Reading his friends' facial expressions, he tried to backpedal and make his way to the other side of the error. He needed to apologize.

"Well, we just thought the sooner, the better. What are we waiting for? With my heart, who knows how long I will last?"

"Your ticker isn't the problem. It's your stomach, fat boy," said Mendel, obviously perturbed. "You couldn't for once leave it alone, let me enjoy. You always gotta be top banana, Mr. Big."

The sisters remained silent while Destiny and Annie moved to the living room, cajoling and then pulling the dogs with them. Kiley realized he needed to mediate—he saw himself as the only option, the sole choice, and elected to stay with his friends.

"It really does not have to be such a problem. You, my good men, my brothers in this lifetime, have been going at each other forever, or at least since I have known you. Mendel, this is Morris and it is within his character to one-up even those closest to him. He means it until he understands what he has done. By that time, it's too late for him to withdraw, apologize, even retreat."

"Schmuck," said Mendel.

"Wilted weasel," said Morris. "You never could please even one person."

"Look who's talking, limp lily."

"Cease fire," suggested Kiley. "This should be a time of joy. Me, I'm never going to get married again, so I am jealous of you both." He thought of Annie, whom he would never wed. With good fortune, they would remain close friends but Kiley fully understood the implications.

"Kiley, you're a minister and that means that you can perform a wedding ceremony," said Zena.

"Allow me," said Gilda, "as the mathematician of this group. Unless I have lost all my computational skill, what I hear and what I see adds up this way: one wedding plus one wedding makes two weddings."

"A double ceremony!" yelled Zena. "We will all get married together!"

"Oy vey," said Mendel.

"Over my dead body," said Morris.

"The only problem with your dead body, my dear," said Zena, "would be to get over it or around it or whatever."

"His body could sink a ship," said Mendel.

"Well, I suppose it could be worse. He could get married first," said Morris.

"Tie goes to the runner. And, even with my aching bones, I can beat you in any race," said Mendel, extending a fish-like handshake toward Morris.

Morris took it, pretended to squeeze mightily, then toasted and boasted, "To life!" He drew Mendel's hand, clasped in his own, and tried to raise it toward the ceiling.

When Mendel resisted, Morris lifted his friend off the ground as Destiny and Annie, who had returned with the dogs, clapped their hands together and initiated a round of applause.

****

They could have a small ceremony in Forest Park and the leaves would still be resplendent. Or they could celebrate one of these days at Destiny's and then trek to Crane Beach. Or they could wait and invite a small army of remaining friends next spring.

Mendel and Morris, surprising no one, including themselves, disagreed on what to do.

"Get it over with. That is my philosophy," said Mendel. "If I had my way, I would have beaten this galoot and gotten married first. Now, we are in a tug-of-war. If we hold out for a spring blast, and by then one or two of us is dead, what then?"

"Will you stop with this 'I want first' *mishegoss*? You know better. Besides, I am twice your size," replied Morris.

"Your belly does not have a brain," said Mendel. "Why would anyone but a baboon wait it out? All you got, then, is a bunch of time to waste."

"Time heals everything," said Morris. He realized he had botched the saying and, further, it hadn't any relevance. Still, he continued. "With months to plan this, we will toss a celebration all of New England will remember. So?"

"So, consider it a compromise or, if you want to use a word which is nothing Jewish, acquiescence: I will do this, have the wedding over and done with, but only if it is a brunch."

No one said a word.

"*Capisce*? A brunch. Don't just all sit on your fannies. Say something."

"Mendel, are you talking lox and bagels for my one and only wedding?" asked Gilda.

"Belly, nova, some baked salmon, pickled herring, even gefilte fish if you like. Breads, *bopka*—which is your favorite—whatever you want," he replied.

"This is not quite my cup of tea," said Zena.

"I don't like the smell of this whole thing," added Morris.

"Well, those are my terms. Lox and bagels at eleven in the morning. Take it or leave it," said Mendel.

"Thank God you never ran for office, Mendel. With luck, you might have gotten two votes—from yourself and maybe me if I was taking pity on you," said Gilda. "What nerve you got, with your best friends here and these lovely women, even if they are on the strange side. What are you, the king who insists that he gets his way or a two-year-old? I suggest you and your compromise go for a walk while the rest of us discuss the wedding."

Kiley waved his arm as if it were a wand and said, "Should I preside, I have a problem: what to wear. I mean, around my neck. The choices are nothing or a Star of David. Opinions?" No one responded. "A crucifix?"

"If this worm has his way, it don't matter if you wear nothing, Kiley. Who's going to come to a wedding at eleven in the morning?" asked Morris.

"We'd better be going," said Destiny. "Staying here is lovely, but I have to care for my restaurant."

"And the dogs, sweet as they are, have to go home. Me, too," said Annie.

Kiley's shoulders sagged, but he forced himself to stay silent.

"What if we had the wedding in a few weeks — end of summer with warm days and cool nights? It will—well, it will bring tears," said Destiny, her voice beginning to crack.

"Let's go, Des, before we each start to cry," said Annie.

The dogs, understanding the phrase, bumped into each other, flipped their tails, and made for the front door.

Kiley trundled after everyone as half the group made its way aboard the minibus. Destiny collapsed into the driver's seat, and the dogs rumbled in behind. Annie latched her seatbelt. Destiny rubbed her eyes, smoothed back her hair beneath a visor, and sighed deeply.

Kiley arrived at last and knocked, rather rapidly, outside Annie's window. He motioned and said, too loudly, "Roll it down," forgetting that virtually all contemporary vehicles were equipped with power packs.

A smiling Annabelle lowered the window.

She reached out with her arms, pulled his cheek next to hers, and said, "Until we walk on the beach again."

Kiley nodded and smiled with pleasure, but he wasn't quite sure what she meant and whether to assume anything.

As Destiny pulled the van away, he waved good-bye.

The dogs immediately collapsed into themselves: Polly spread across the bench seat, and Jess wedged herself along the floor toward one of the side doors.

"What are you thinking?" asked Destiny.

"That it will be a sweet relief to be home," answered Annie.

"I mean, what are you thinking about this Kiley?"

"Oh, that," she replied. "Well, I'm not certain, but he is smart and sweet, too."

"Annabelle, age means nothing in most cases. But, I cannot think . . ."

"Please, Destiny. It's not that. I like talking with this man."

"He is elderly, dear," said Destiny.

"You just said that age means nothing. My history, Destiny. After Sam, there really isn't much."

"Gregory"

"Greg and I were in need," said Annie. "He was married, and I was without. We fit for a time, but it was all on a physical level. For a time, it was very good for both of us. But it became old and we ran dry on anything more to say or share. We tried. Look at him. He went to law school with the vow that he would become a Charlestown street person's attorney. Instead, he joined a major Boston firm. Is that me?"

They drove on in silence until Destiny said, "That must be the spot. I'm pulling over."

Annabelle recognized the place instantly when she saw the white statue. Morris had mentioned the chip on its base. "Good, we'll get the dogs out and follow the markers. The Blake will probably remain as Morris left it. He said he partially hid the container."

Destiny grasped Annie's hand as they walked from the van through some marsh and grass toward the structure. It had rained for thirty minutes since they left Springfield, but the skies now cleared. It was muggy.

"Just for a minute, Des, I wish I weren't so concerned about the climate. This is delicious. I wish I had shorts and a tank top. It would be perfect. Look at Jess and Polly!"

The dogs had immersed themselves in the nearby pond, splashing and kicking, swimming without purpose.

"Wanna join them?" asked Destiny.

"We could at least wade," said Annie, pushing her jeans upward past her knees.

Destiny did the same. Holding onto each other, the women cautiously slipped into the water.

"Ow, chilly water in this pond," yelled Des.

By now, Annie's pants and her rear end were soaked. Destiny pointed at her and giggled. Annie was looking backward.

"What do you see?" asked Des.

"I was just looking at that angel. Are you sure that's where Morris found a World in a Grain of Sand?"

"He never did say that it was any kind of a religious figurine, I suppose."

"On the other hand," said Annie, "Kiley would be thrilled." She laughed. "Correction: curious."

"You said it, sister, just remember that."

"Kiley is lyrical when he speaks of religion. The decision to fully immerse in Judaism has transformed him." She paused. "He is persuasive when he expounds."

"Since I didn't know him when he was Catholic, I will just have to take your word for it," said Destiny.

"Obviously, I didn't know him either," said Annie, lifting herself out of the water, "but he tells me that he was just about anything other than mystic until fairly recently."

Destiny adjusted herself, pushing water off her lower legs and feet. "Annabelle, he is an older man who is in need, sweetie."

"That part may be true. Me? I am a younger, midlife woman who is also in need."

"As much as I love you, let me tell you: It's not possible to hurry or manufacture love. Friendship? That's very different."

"Des, you aren't my mother. And while I'm still looking at middle age, it's not as if I'm fifteen. I know what to do, and I know what to say for that matter."

Destiny put her arms around Annie and looked up at her. Her friend smiled broadly and hugged back. They began to leave the area when Annie suddenly stopped and turned fully around.

"What if we took the statue?"

"Now I know something's wrong with you. First, how? And second, why?"

"Because we're wacko hippie flower children—whatever name or phrase will stick in a few years."

"I know all of that, dear Annabelle. But, again, why?"

"Kiley would love this, Destiny."

"And am I beginning to see that this man is more than special?"

Annie stopped short, as if she, herself, hadn't admitted it. She took in Destiny's words. She admired Kiley, felt close to him, but was there more than that? It was not in her nature to pursue. Yet, it was possible. She felt a bit short of breath, then panic. She claimed to be an adventurer but, truth be told, that was an exaggeration. Annie was far from a risk-taker. She enjoyed being cared for, coddled. Kiley adored her, but it was WASP to WASP, regardless of his embrace of Judaism. He kept a step away, chose to shake a friend's hand rather than greet even a close someone with a bear hug. He was a cautious, half-snuggling type. When Kiley looked her in the eye, she felt he was glancing ever so slightly beyond her. She really didn't mind. Far from it. He was gentle and personal. That was what she loved and desired. How unlike Blake, she thought. She both appreciated and feared the mystic poet's lineaments of desire, the etchings, the visceral sexuality of it all. Annie thought about it and was stirred. Blake, in his time, must have been wildly passionate. After Sam, she vowed to remain a bit more cautious and, importantly, safe.

She felt Destiny's strong fingers resting upon her shoulders. Des knew Annie well enough not to persist. She would await a response from Annie before proceeding—or not. Annie gently nodded.

Destiny began to hum as she massaged Annabelle's neck from the center and, expanding her fingers, around in a circle, reaching and pressing lightly with a more significant touch. She exerted only enough force to relax Annie, who felt her knees buckle. She sat and swayed. Annie gratefully acknowledged her friend's gift.

****

They never did find the container enclosing Blake's words that Morris often referenced. Riding back to Ipswich, the women discussed this but only briefly.

"Maybe he's delusional," said Destiny. "Not that he meant to make all of it up, but . . ."

". . . just that he did," said Annabelle, concluding the thought.

"They're so different, those two old men," said Destiny. "I mean, Morris is the big, gruff clown. Although he's also really quite sensitive."

"Maybe they're not so dissimilar as you think," said Annie. "Mendel plays the bitter cynic, but that's an act. He's no crone. Look at him when he's with Gilda. Such a sweet companion."

"You're right." Destiny paused. "I only hope the sisters . . ." She didn't finish her thought.

"I've been wondering the same," said Annie.

They drove on in silence until Annie fell asleep. Eventually, the highway lights roused her as the van sped through Worcester.

"I've been dreaming, hoping, that they all live for twenty, thirty, forty more years. It worries me. What if one of those engaging people dies next year?"

"We live in the present," said Destiny, laughing. "Sweet, my dear? Mendel? You must be confused."

"You know what I mean, Des. They are so dear. Not nice — more like precious."

"Now, you sound like me."

"But without the peasant blouses you saved from so many years ago."

"Tack on a couple more decades and you have it," said Destiny.

"Maybe after I get some more sleep, my head will clear," said Annie.

****

At the Forest Park house, the sisters gathered around the dining room table that evening to draw up a preliminary guest list for the party following the wedding. Morris wanted nothing of it and lifted Mendel out of his chair. "This is not for us, little man," he said. "Let's retire to the living room."

"I would rather check out the numbers for Phases," said Mendel. "Figure out why this is such a bomb."

"Bomb, schmomb," said Morris. "You should know it takes more than a few months to get business. Whoever said we were in this to make a fast buck? It might not be until the warm weather comes back around next time that we have any sense of whether this is a financial go or not. If we started this to make money, we are what they now call 'catching fire.' For me, though, it is more than that."

"It takes a little while? You think this is going to take ten years? I got news for you: There is a chance we will all be dead in ten years. I invested my money, and I want to see Phases work. I don't need some glorious profit, but I don't want to go under with a huge loss. Okay?"

Silence.

Kiley spoke—of God, the afterlife, and eternity.

"Save the drama, Kiley," said Zena.

"I don't think he was like this before he discovered Judaism," said Zena. "Now, all of a sudden, he cares, God help us."

"Inside, I always did. It's just that we grew up repressed," said Kiley. "Only now, as an old man, am I learning to speak up. The unspoken rule in my house was never risk, never gamble. Dress in perfectly complementary colors, never clash.

Have your hair cut every two weeks and in the same fashion. Be exceptionally polite and never ever lose your temper. You know what? It left me—it left all of us—filled with rage, internal rage."

"Nu? Now?" asked Zena.

"I never quite say what I wish to, but I am growing ever closer. By the time I'm eighty-five or ninety, who knows? I might even be telling the truth."

"Morris, you want to walk over to Phases with me? It's our business, you know, in case you forgot," said Mendel.

"Yes and right—in that order," said Morris. "But, before I do . . . Kiley, you are my friend. Would you mind if I told you something? Say no if you are not in the mood for advice."

"Go ahead, Mo," said Kiley.

"You will never be a real Jew if you sound just like another goy. With this 'growing closer' crap, it's as if you got a bug or a broom you know where, right up . . ."

Kiley glared at the big man before extending a hand. When Morris grabbed it, Kiley pulled back until the two of them toppled over.

Mendel jumped in and raised both their hands as if declaring a draw.

Morris gathered himself inch by inch, limb by limb, until he finally stood. "Now, let us take a stroll to Phases," he said, walking toward the front door, waving to Kiley and the women with one hand while summoning Mendel with the other.

Kiley called after them, "I know, Morris, where you got that real Jew thing: *Annie Hall* and Diane Keaton. You might be right, but you cannot claim it for your very own."

Morris windmilled both of his arms at Kiley and pushed Mendel in the other direction.

Once the two men were outside, Mendel said, "We are both getting married, Mo. Who would have thought that when we were just two schlemiels waiting to die? Funny what goes on in one short year."

"Look at us now, as some song used to go. We got women." Morris paused. "Well, what else? Happiness, yes. But health? You never know. When my father was dying and he was, what, sixty-two, he said, 'I should have, so help me, Moishkie, I should have enjoyed more fruit.' The next day he was gone, and here I am, a century later it seems like it to me, wondering what he meant."

"Girls; sex," said Mendel as Morris yanked him back to the tree belt before they crossed Sumner Avenue.

"Which makes me think of that Annabelle."

"Let's not beat around any bush. You mean our good man Kiley," said Mendel.

"He's not so lucky as you think, Mendel. Those two are not what the kids call a couple, an item. No. Friends maybe, but that is all."

"Try telling that to Kiley," said Morris. "He is convinced, already, that there will be a wedding for him, too. If he were walking right next to us, he would tell you so himself." He yanked Mendel toward Phases.

"What did you slip me so that I would back this no-good business?" asked Mendel.

"A friendship pill, a small, delicate pill filled with *nakhes*. I know this is a word my own father used when, once in a blue moon, I would do good. I'm telling you, Mendel, that you did this because we got five, ten if we're lucky, years left together. This might be the best thing about you. You got money, and you decided to help out."

Mendel shrugged free of Morris's clasp and shook himself as if he were shedding random dog hair.

"Morris, I put up the money because I thought this Phases would work out and I would lose maybe a nickel but nothing more."

"Come on, Mendel, admit that you did it for me."

"Look at that paint job. It's already peeling," said Mendel, lifting his arm and pointing at the third section of their community center across the street.

Morris dragged his nay-saying friend into Phase III. "You want the Taj Mahal, go there. You want cozy, someone to reminisce with, a game of Parcheesi, come here."

Mendel thought of those few years when he lived in the Bronx. The image of the neighbor's son, Jackie, the boy with the braces from polio, was predominant. Mendel became lost in that memory. More and more, he found himself unwittingly flashing backward in time. He did not wish for such distractions.

"How did your parents produce someone like you who is always on the lookout for the next guy to swindle, as you put it?" asked Morris.

"My father lost his shirt because he trusted one man, just one man. The very next know-it-all might be waiting for me, looking for my hard-earned cash. You never can be too careful. You never know."

"Mendel, Mendel, I am certain that your money is safe. You got plenty and, if I know you, nobody will get his hands on it."

Mendel tried pressing his dry lips together but could not suppress a grin. His head moved up and down, up and down, like a yo-yo.

Just then, his cell phone rang. He bought the device a month before, saying that he wanted to be "with it." But really, Mendel realized the phone could be a lifeline. He was filled with dread that he would die alone because when he did topple over one day, he would not be able to reach anybody.

The phone, if he could hear its music, would save his life. He hardly used it and understood none of its intricacies. Now, he fumbled the thing before it fell out of his hands onto the pavement, where it bounced three times before he could rescue it. Finally, he flipped it open and began yelling, "Hello, god-dammit, hello! Where are you? This is Mendel."

"You were too slow," said Morris.

"What do you know from phones?" said Mendel.

"Looks like you got a message. Press listen."

"There is no such thing as listen. Shush."

Mendel hit a small square in the middle of the phone and was able, after several attempts, to hear the message.

"It was Gilda. She says Kiley got a pain in his stomach. What do you think?"

"I think you switch religions, you get such *tsuris*. Oy, we better go back and check."

Mendel nodded and began to turn. As he did so, Morris spun him around a few times. Mendel, despite himself, began to laugh. "You're a lug, you," he said to his best friend.

"And away we go," said Morris.

****

By the time they returned home, Kiley, claiming indigestion, had recovered and was resting in a recliner. The M&M Boys were not convinced that their friend hadn't suffered a mild heart attack. Never one to shun the spotlight, Morris, with one eye on Kiley, proclaimed, "No double double wedding. One time, for two couples, for four of us, is enough. And nothing in Forest Park in late fall when you can freeze off the tips of your toes and more than that, neither."

"We will marry once," said Mendel, "at Destiny's Prime Time, or whatever she calls it."

"Mendy and me, as usual, we agree," added Morris. "The two of us, we go together like peanut butter and jelly."

"You don't touch that stuff, Morris," said Zena. "Someone just the other day told me it loosens up your teeth."

Morris's face and neck reddened. It was not common knowledge that he stored his teeth in a container each night. Only Zena knew, and he was burning with fury at the implication.

Able to control if not quite quell his angry impulse, Morris continued, "Let's get on task, as they now say. When I was young, it was get to work. Mendel and me and the girls"—he waved his arm in their direction—"it's best for us to make it all official. All good for us in copacetic weather."

Gilda and Zena, exchanging sidelong glances, nodded their heads in rhythmic agreement.

"On the beach at Ipswich it is!" yelled Morris.

Kiley shrugged and then smiled in acquiescence.

"For this, I will drop a few pounds," said Morris.

"I will give you a buck a pound," said Mendel.

"See, Simon Legree is at it again. What you're worth, you could give me a hundred a pound and this wouldn't break even that corkscrew tail of your piggy bank," said Morris.

CHAPTER 13

The day of the wedding, a balmy second summer day in late September, everyone had gathered early at Destiny's to get ready. Even the dogs were going to be dressed up. Annabelle had bought each a new, colorful, hand-woven collar. She remembered how Sam would braid leather belts, collars, headbands, and—his specialty—custom-fitted sandals. She decided to take the dogs out for a run on the public beach. Usually, they would go to the beach near Destiny's and gambol about for as long as they could, journeying far and wide. Annie wanted to explore the other, more utilized section of the shoreline. She didn't know why. She drove slowly up to the ranger station.

"No dogs allowed during the season," said a pimply-faced teenager manning the booth.

"I thought the cutoff was Labor Day," said Annie.

"You thought wrong. It's not till October," he replied.

"Nobody's here, it's early morning, and I thought it would be fun to take the dogs for a quick scoot."

"That would be against the law," the young man insisted. "No dogs."

"You're not going to keep us away so early in the morning, are you?"

"I will report you through my cell phone or walky-talky," he said robotically.

Annabelle backed her bus away, turned around, drove a few hundred yards up the road, and parked. She opened a back door, and the dogs barreled out. Jess caught a scent immediately, and Polly sped alongside.

Typical Lab, any Lab, thought Annie, as Jess sought food. Polly, meanwhile, was still on the move. Ahead, the cattails and high lilting reeds seemed to part. Annie moved close enough to see that water provided separation. Perfect for dogs but not easily traversed by ungainly, inept humans—not to mention ticks. The dogs cut through a short path to Destiny's, traipsing through marsh and grass. Annie trotted to follow.

Suddenly Polly changed course, galloping across meadow and field directly toward the beach. Jess was pleased to run with her soul mate, while Annie hadn't any choice but to follow.

The dogs, unaware that they would be committing a crime by entering the public beach area, sped past the ranger station. The ranger-in-training, complete with safari hat, bolted free of his seat, as if self-releasing from captivity, to hotly pursue the dogs. He seemed unaware that Annabelle, jogging now, trailed him by just a few paces.

The dogs crossed the parking lot and jumped up the wooden staircase that led to Crane. The ranger boy yelled, "Hey, you! You can't go there!" as if the dogs might understand the commandment. Annie laughed loudly at the absurdity.

The few other people on the beach were neither frightened nor bothered. In fact, they couldn't get enough of the scene. The caricature before them, including two lovely retrievers, an adolescent wannabe state trooper, and a former flower child at midpoint of her life, was a hoot and a half.

Annie saw that one of the lifeguard chairs was vacated, although two oblivious people were entwined upon the other guard platform as they grappled and grasped for each other's flesh. Annie, remembering Sam, was envious. Without option, she pushed on.

She thought that Mendel, Morris, the Lewis sisters, and Kiley were still at Destiny's, probably wondering just what had happened to Annie and the dogs. At this moment, she surmised, the M&M Boys were arguing. What Annie did not realize was that the men and women were close by, having followed.

"I say, pop the kid one," said Morris. "Teach him a lesson or two, ordering around a couple of beautiful dogs. I've never seen such beauties. And that Annabelle!"

"Agree with your sentiment," said Mendel, "but this is not a time for walloping some kid. We should get information and turn it over to my lawyer. Sue the pants off some of these good-for-nothing goyisher land barons."

"Look who's talking," replied Morris. "What are you, some philanthropist? Our successor to Brooke Astor or somebody? You watch your money like a hawk, and you won't part with one red cent. You are just an *alter kocker* — crotchety to an extreme."

"Why, for God's sake, must you change the topic, Morris? I just want to milk these stuck-up, nose-in-the-air, high-and-mighty New Englanders for some old money. What is so terrible about that?"

"And then what, Mendel? You are going to give away the reward? No way. You'll keep it for yourself."

"Just what are you talking, Mo?" Mendel turned away from Morris and spat on the ground, then mashed the saliva with his sneaker. "That is what I think of you," he said.

Meanwhile, the young enforcer was making up ground on the dogs, who had charged into the surf and chosen to refresh themselves with a quick swim.

"Hey, you dogs, out of there!" he shouted. A few small kids with buckets froze at the command.

"Just what is your problem?" Annie, closing fast, asked. "My dogs are peaceful, sweet, and more in love with humans than anyone I know."

"They insisted in our training sessions no animals until October. This is too early."

"Use your common sense," said Annie. "Whom do they hurt by jumping into the water on a second summer day?"

"Not the point."

"The point is we are here for a wedding, a double marriage, and nobody is going to ruin our good time." She kicked at some sand in frustration. The spray covered the tips of the ranger's shoes.

"Don't you do that," he said, as if alleging that Annabelle meant to obliterate his footwear.

"If I wanted to mess with you, I would," she said.

The ramshackle group, having paid its entry fee, had arrived on the beach, although straggling, with Mendel and Morris in the lead.

"Look at that," boomed Morris, never all that aware of his vocal power. "Asians."

Even Mendel pressed two fingers to his cracked lips. "Shush, you baboon," he said. "Not right."

"Well, excuse me, but it's not like I called them a name. I was trying to be polite but specific. You want otherwise?"

The approaching Kiley seemed to measure each step he took, as if he might crack an egg if his toes fully struck the pavement.

"Breathe," said Kiley. "Maintain."

"Oy," said Morris.

"Ditto, from the old oy days," added Mendel.

Thus far, Destiny had watched silently from a distance, as the dogs hit the beach with the ranger close behind and as Mendel and Morris, true to form, harmlessly squawked. She wished only to return home, where she could prepare for the wedding, but now approached the group.

"Friends," said Destiny to anyone who might listen, "suggesting that someone breathe is not the worst advice. Remain strong of soul, yet be calm. Tension we try to lessen." She pointed across the high grass and swampland. "Back to my place," she said, without need for further explanation. She had longed to live beside the beach where she could inhale the salty breeze seemingly forever. Her current home, though, sat on a bluff above marshland. She grew to adore the geographic contrast. A marked trail led to Destiny's Place, even if the final walkway was somewhat challenging.

Morris and Mendel exchanged a look, then huddled.

"She's some smart girl," said Mendel.

Morris smacked his friend on the back, sending him close to the earth below. "You are no dummy, but when you say something like this, even a compliment gets lost. Destiny we both like. So?"

"So, she lives in her God's country here, a place where no Jew, no Yahweh believer, could ever get a house. Maybe now it's different, I will give you that. I'm an old enough goat, I don't know."

"This might be the first time you have admitted you don't occupy every inch on the smart corner on everything. I wish I had something to write this down."

"That is not what I meant, Morris," said Mendel. "I got more brains in my pinky than you . . ."

Morris cut him off. "This I have heard a million times. Destiny is the host for our weddings, in case you forgot. So, cut out this crap and keep your mouth shut."

Kiley attempted to interrupt their tirade.

Mendel and Morris, trying not to eye each other, were set off once again. The big man coughed and sputtered, while his rumpled sidekick wiped his brow with a wrinkled, checkered handkerchief.

"If we can possibly move on," Kiley said, "I know that Destiny has outdone herself for the occasion. Her place is, well, it is the picture of comfort, warm and cozy. Annabelle," he called, "please bring the dogs. If they hit the trail, everyone else will follow." Kiley leaned in the direction of the path, hoping someone would catch a hint.

The sisters had caught up with the group at this point. Gilda took Zena by the hand, and the women began, limb by limb, to move.

"Why we could not get married like normal people God only knows," said Zena.

"Maybe because we are not so normal. How many sisters live together for most of their lives?" asked Gilda. "Don't answer because I will tell you: none."

At that moment, Jess and Polly, in full gallop, split the sisters and nosed their way toward Destiny's.

"Follow them," said Destiny. "They know the trail and appreciate my home. Sometimes a place to simply meditate, I've lent maybe the chameleon's touch to it. One day, years ago, I rolled up my jeans and walked all the way through the reeds before the path existed. I was soaked, but I was happy. And I have been ever since, to a great extent."

Nevertheless, the sisters were reluctant. Having lived in Florida, they were used to water and marsh but fearful of anything thriving in a swamp. Explorers they were not. What they did not know they did not trust.

Destiny had begun dreaming of hosting weddings and celebrations decades earlier when she thought of becoming an innkeeper. She envisioned herself growing older among those seeking a weekend in her ramshackle, renovated expanded Victorian. Instead, she found herself a magical place on the hill beyond the beach. This was her castle and a mystery to those who hadn't been there.

Never had anyone been married there—until now. Wedding firsts, she thought.

Destiny's Place awaited all: She had precisely positioned a candle, dried floral arrangements, one glass unicorn, two shining stars (gold and red), a small strobe light close to the floor, and, in a corner, a lovely grid of photographs.

Destiny had also painted intersecting and overlapping rainbows across the ceiling, carefully fading the colors, especially the shade of lavender, so the designs were short-lived panoramic meteors. Life was special, life was fleeting, even if she felt a permanence here on the beach that she hadn't known very often. At this point in her life, Destiny spoke only of positives. She sought the company of people who experienced the present and embraced all the future offered. Destiny adjusted her perspective, finding that it did her no good to endlessly ponder.

The dogs led the way, covering three times as much territory as did the humans. Each clump of marsh or sifting reed required of them specific investigation. Jess and Polly jostled for the door, wagging their tails furiously and waiting for the others to arrive. When Destiny got there, she opened her arms and the dogs leapt, causing her to lurch. She might have fallen hard had Kiley not been there to catch her.

"Would have been worth it to see the look on everyone's face!" she exclaimed. "The dogs, too. I can see their different expressions. Besides, it's not even close to my most embarrassing moment."

"And what would that be?" asked Mendel.

Destiny, though, was thinking rather than talking. She didn't respond. Instead, she carried herself back to an early crush on someone.

She remembered when she was Deena. Her favorite high school teacher had changed it to DT. Neither name seemed to fit when she cast her sights upon Bobby Gold. She remembered thinking of him as Golden, for his hair. She engineered bump-ins with him on the staircase and elsewhere, once skipping an entire class and waiting near the boiler room door so that she might brush chest to stomach with him.

He played saxophone, and when Bill Clinton ran for president for the first time, Deena realized she favored Clinton because he, too, played the sax. Not only that, but Bobby Gold and Bill Clinton had the same hair consistency: wavy, luxuriant, and thick.

When it came to men, Destiny was selective but not absolutely picky. She wanted warmth and humor but nothing flimsy. Stubble was fine with her, as was a hint of belly. The male models with the rippling six-pack abs did nothing for her. Never had, even when she was slender.

She had given up on a wedding of her own. The next best thing was making for others what she might have created for herself. Still, how to plan for everyone? Yes, dream on but for how long? Why not? Those from Eastern cultures—Japan, China, India—knew that each day unto itself was precious. This was how she tried to live: in the moment.

Zena said nothing while Mendel and Gilda allowed the dogs, bumping gleefully into each other, to lead the way into Destiny's Place. Jess, spotting Annabelle, flew at her chest. Not to be outdone, Polly plowed into Destiny, nearly knocking her over again.

First there was music. Destiny had made a mix of show tunes and ballads from the mid-twentieth century: vocals by a young Frank Sinatra, Ella Fitzgerald, and John Raitt; instrumentals by Louis Armstrong, Benny Goodman, and Burt Bacharach. She allowed herself to imagine a skinny young man wearing a porkpie hat sitting at an upright piano in the corner. His forearms were lined with blueish veins. A soft, improvisational background allowed for the legendary singers' voices to carry.

"Where is 'Fiddler'?" bellowed Morris. "Is that or is that not what we agreed on?" he asked.

"If I were a rich man," Morris sang, off-key but with plenty of volume.

"Well, you are not," said Mendel. "Listen to your elders," he advised.

"On this day," said Kiley, struggling to stay calm, "both of you need to tone it down. This is your wedding day, and this will be the last wedding day for each of you. That much I guarantee."

"For the love of Christ, Kiley. Talk about throwing cold water," said Morris.

"Think of the rainbow," said Destiny.

"Gimme the pot of gold. The rest you can have," Morris replied.

"Girls, you're embarrassing me," said Annie to her dogs as if they were her daughters. "Calm." Polly and Jess sat still.

"I will be damned," said Mendel, waving his arthritic thumb and forefinger.

"Mr. M, this is not the place," said Destiny, "on your wedding day."

Morris spun around, nearly losing his balance since he, too, had a quick response to "Mr. M."

"While he would never admit it," said Destiny, "this man is a bundle of raw nerves, a wreck."

"And you couldn't tie your tie, big shot," said Zena.

Determined to defuse the situation, Destiny waved her hand. Annie disappeared for a moment into the back room. When she returned, she was carrying a rustic, yellow-brown harp. Wearing a flowing lime-green dress, she stood by the instrument.

"I never knew. Look at this one," said Mendel.

"Keep it to yourself on your wedding day," said Morris. "But, I know what you mean."

"Actually, this is the second wedding day for the two of us." He paused. "Not that I was planning on saying so." Once again, Mendel took a moment. "Just thinking."

"What's gone is gone," said Morris. "We got no alternative but to look to the future. I admit that someone like Annabelle has a few years on us, more time than us. But, we might surprise people. Imagine, you and me—with sisters no less."

Zena and Gilda wore long skirts that Destiny had designed. She had embroidered Zena's with a glowing, radiant, bright red sun and Gilda's with a soothing, mellow, knowing full moon. Over white silk blouses, each wore a multicolored vest. Annie contributed wreaths of dried flowers she'd been saving.

The air was heavy, indicative of Tropical Storm Harriet, which had smacked Cuba en route to the west coast of Florida. "I once knew someone named Harriet who was all bluster," said Morris. "Same with this one. Not to worry."

The double wedding allowed Destiny to celebrate, through her mind and her mind's eye, this possibility for herself. Yes, she thought, living into and through one's nineties need not be torture. Rather than speculate about the hereafter or lack thereof, Destiny simply sought survival. When others asked her to further articulate, she would smile sweetly and explain that the chapter was a work in progress.

She found herself musing lately about men—specifically, about the place of a man in her life. Not that she had any prospects she found appealing. But, the notion was not nearly as daunting as it had been in the past. She began to wonder who might be interested. Sure, she was not twenty-five or even forty-five but she wasn't bad looking. The real question was, how could she possibly go about finding someone? She never went to a club, generally disavowed organized religion, and pretty much stayed to herself, playing with Annie's dogs, cooking, and making music at her place. It would shock many who knew her, but Destiny was shy. What sort of a dating profile was that?

More important, what or whom did she want?

Destiny relaxed into reverie: A man who understood both machines and people—that was rare enough. Someone who had children so that she, solitary for so long, might reap the benefits of instant family. Yes, it would be complicated but feasible. A person who hadn't a fortune but had a couple dollars more than she possessed.

Younger or older or same age? None of that mattered to her. Nor did height. Back to money. Well, yes. It was important to the extent that she didn't want to have to carry someone else.

CHAPTER 14

"When you get old," Mendel had written in his diary, *"everything shrinks: your bones, your hair, your brain, and the jewels below your belt, too. But, more than that, your world compresses and you are stuck inside. It feels like you're pressing against those cartoon walls, the ones you can push and pull like an elastic. You can breathe, but you never get fresh air. Some people, of course, think this is ideal. After all, you become a recycling maven!*

So it is that when four old goats like us try to plan a wedding list, we make a big fat discovery: We got no one to invite. Some are dead, and others have no energy to get up and do a damned thing. Those that still have some fire probably live in Florida or Arizona or California or even North Carolina for God's sake. What the hell, maybe we shouldn't even let them know.

This Destiny and the sweetie with her dogs, bless them all. I would never say such a thing when anyone is around, but in this book I can say what I want. Nobody will see it until the day I die. First, there's Annie. Like in Annie Oakley or Little Orphan Annie, except you think the first one was sexy and the second one cute. They are nothing compared to this catch. And why is she wandering around this North Shore here with her Labs? Destiny, that is why.

Before I met Gilda, I spent my time thinking about eighty years' worth of history and revising the goddamned thing whenever I didn't like it. This is the price you pay when it's easy to remember fifty years into the past but not fifty minutes ago. Of course, I could live another twenty years, maybe more. Or, they could dig a hole and stick me six feet under tomorrow. If I do get a break, it's also possible no more Gilda. Destiny will live forever, at least compared to me. That's something to consider.

I do expect that I will see ninety-eight or ninety-nine without a problem. I have only one fear, something that keeps me tossing and turning all night: What will it be like to have no one—not one person—left from when I was thirty? This ornery man I pretend to be is nothing but a front. I don't want anyone except Gilda close to me. And she, I feel, most of the time, will outlive even me."

Mendel always carried his most recent journal entry with him. When he was motivated to write more, he wanted it to be in sequence.

He began to adjust his collar but stopped, realizing he didn't see Gilda.

Mendel turned to look for her. But she and her sister were busy fixing each other's hair.

The Lewis sisters had agreed at first to ribbons in their hair; Zena's would be red and Gilda's white. Neither adornment would stay put as imagined. Zena yanked hers off while Gilda, without a mirror, fiddled with hers, hoping to catch the fabric on a few strong locks.

Destiny, standing by, tried to soothe them.

"It just doesn't matter," she said. "Each of you is lovely. We have two perfect brides."

"Not your problem. No need to worry," said Zena. In comparison to her older sister, she remained composed.

"Annie and the dogs disappeared again," said Destiny. "Not much causes me to panic these days. That would, but thank goodness they are back."

"Guess who is not," Mendel declared. "Guess who is missing."

Everyone realized that Morris had not been spotted recently.

How could he have disappeared?

****

"Just keep this thing short and simple," said Morris.

Kiley had pre-recorded music, gathered quotes from poets, and even prepared an ecumenical statement for the ceremony. He also had donned a coat of many colors.

"Nothing fancy schmancy," Morris reiterated.

He and Kiley, lost in conversation, slowly walked the beach. Oblivious to the elements, they talked of life, of possibility, of life again. It was Kiley, lifting his head to make a point, who noticed the darkness. He gestured and looked up.

Morris, following with his eyes, said, "What is this, a whatchamacallit eclipse?"

"Torrential rains are about to douse us, Morris. I will take the blame for getting you to your own wedding late."

"That reminds me: Getting married makes little sense. No, this is all show and foolishness."

"Do you love Zena?"

"What is love? I love her."

"The perfect excuse for a party."

"A party tossed by an earth mother who still believes in hocus-pocus," said Morris.

"Earth mother, Morris, is a good term for her. She is serendipitous but with an otherworldly sense, too. Destiny. A good word I just used, no? Destiny is not at all by chance."

Morris crumbled to the ground. Just as quickly, for a man with such girth, he began to get to his feet.

"What happened?" Kiley asked.

"Sand."

"I know." said Kiley. "Well, I know this is what the future holds for me, too. I mean the present, Morris."

Morris smiled. "Back to Destiny. Maybe that is why I slipped. She is not what she seems. I cannot figure it out, but she is not like the rest of us."

"Ah, my friend, a mystery. Maybe even mystical?" Kiley went on, "Yes, she dances, she spins, she lights candles. So do Jews on Friday nights, for Shabbat."

"You have something there, Kiley. You're the one mixing religions. Next thing I know, you'll be telling me this has something to do with that hero of yours, Williams Blake."

"It is William, Morris."

Clouds opened above them, shards of lightning flashed, but not one drop of rain fell.

The men continued to walk, to talk.

"I am an old man, but the way Destiny and this Annabelle look at each other . . . Kiley, is this her daughter?"

"I am with you, Morris, but I do not know." Kiley put his arm around his friend. "We are talking continuity here, spirituality. Are we all not connected to one another?"

Morris responded, "Now you sound like her—this Destiny, who, by the way, I like. It's just that she's got some strange ideas. Certainly, she is some attractive woman."

"Morris, you are about to get married."

"It's time, yes. What about you, once again?"

"Me? Well, lately, better off single," said Kiley. "If something came along, maybe. It almost did, then it didn't. I have been involved and that is all."

"Aha. Shoot."

"Do you remember when I left Springfield, Morris? Told everyone that I was exploring the coast of Italy?"

"Yes. No. In that order. This was in the distant past."

Kiley took Morris by the arm and edged him to a boardwalk bridge that could serve as a shelter. Claps of thunder continued to prognosticate a threatening storm.

"Well, I knew Destiny when she wasn't known as Destiny, during my Springfield sabbatical—well, when I left for a bit."

"Now you're talking, bubee."

"Morris, just because I studied Talmud and so forth, that doesn't mean I'm Jewish."

"Okay, so you're an honorary member of my tribe. The lovely Destiny?" Morris rolled both eyebrows upward.

"It was a time when she was singing folk songs Monday nights in a small place on the North Shore," said Kiley. "Yes, it wasn't all that far from this spot. I was going through a phase. I lived where and when I could with friends in Cambridge. We wandered up here one evening to walk the beach. Afterward, we went to a café, and that's when it began. Don't worry—it also ended soon enough."

"Suddenly, I remember that I am supposed to get married in, what, twenty minutes or something?" Morris looked around. "You know, there is nothing like water. Freud said it and maybe even your boy, Blake, for God's sake. Run your eyes along the beach and you can imagine this ocean never ends! You get near the end of your life, you get married, but this thing in front of us never stops. Doesn't seem like such a big deal, but it is."

Kiley placed both of his hands around Morris's head. "You are a man of vision, my friend, even when your sight is, as you would say, cockeyed."

They both laughed as a cloud directly above doused them with a quick but strong spray. It seemed to be raining on an angle. Morris, cupping his palms, tried to catch the drops and, in one surprisingly graceful and nimble swoop, sprinkle Kiley. Kiley wanted a photo of the scene. He took out his cell phone and tried taking a series of shots as Morris knelt and tossed phantom droplets back at him.

Chuckling and waterlogged, the pair eventually turned to walk back to Destiny's. Ten minutes later, as they came closer, they heard "The Wedding March" ringing clearly in the air.

"Sounds like a guitar," said Morris. "How could they start without me?"

"Not one guitar, my friend. Something so sweet? It's two, maybe three, players." Kiley placed his arm across Morris's shoulders and let it rest. "There's Mendel. I was beginning to wonder," he said, as if it was Mendel, rather than Morris and Kiley, who had traipsed off.

"When he gets nervous," Morris said of Mendel, "he sometimes retreats, as if he can create a cocoon with a sign outside refusing admission to all others. He's just small enough to sidle, like a snake, and make his way. Not that this ever solves any of the world's problems. Or his!"

CHAPTER 15

While Morris and Mendel proceeded back into the house, Kiley saw Destiny at the bottom of the hill and decided to join her. From Destiny's demeanor, Kiley had surmised that she thought the wedding was hers to facilitate; he, though, hoped to officiate at the ceremony. Kiley stepped forward. He carried with him a small, worn book the size of a notepad. Someone had hand-sketched an angel superimposed upon a stormy sky on the cover. Holding firmly to the thin volume with one hand, he reached the other beneath his garment and into a pocket, pulled out a silver chain with a Star of David and a cross. He slipped the necklace over his head. He had compiled notes and quotes. Now what? Making eye contact with her, he reflexively winked and immediately wished he could take back that awkward moment. Kiley could not recall when he had last winked at anyone. On previous rare occasions, when someone flipped an eye open and blinked at him, he felt embarrassment and was totally unable to respond. How to explain himself out of this one?

Destiny, however, laughed loudly and opened her arms to him.

The two of them hugged. He felt the warmth, first, then the softness of her body.

He whispered, "I got you, babe," and, once again, could not understand how he could possibly have uttered such a phrase. Boorish or boring, what was his problem? After all, it was Annabelle, not Destiny, who currently had his heart.

Destiny, in response, tapped Kiley lightly on the back and gently squeezed his rear.

"No one's winked at me in decades." She hesitated a moment before adding, "babe."

While still in Destiny's embrace, Kiley leaned backward and offered, "We need to have a discussion?" He relinquished at last, but Destiny, having relaxed into him, stumbled forward. Kiley, an aging but surprisingly spry goalie, caught Destiny and steadied her.

"Yes, before this becomes impossibly convoluted, let's talk," she said.

"Where is everybody?" he asked.

"They're in the house and I asked Annie to coordinate. Lots of running about and nervousness. After all, they're . . ."

"Old. At the very least, older" said Kiley, completing her thought as Destiny nodded. He pushed back from her, looked into her deep blue eyes, the hue of which nearly matched his own, and continued, "It is a double wedding."

"Correct," said Destiny, smiling once again.

"Two couples to marry and, come on, complete my thought."

"It takes two officiants, one for each couple."

"Not that each of us needs to name our favorite."

"I didn't mean it that way, Kiley. You know very well."

"Just fooling with you. Let me show you what I have."

"Stop it, Kiley. You're interested in Annie."

"I mean for the service or whatever we call it."

"And I've made plans, too."

Before they could retreat, however, Polly and Jess galloped down the slope and, without pause, into Kiley and Destiny.

"And who sent you?" asked Destiny. "Oh, my delightful Annabelle," she said, answering her own question for the tail-wagging dogs. "I guess this means I ought to escort everyone back down here. Kiley, you stay and be ready. I want to see what they look like and get my recorder."

"What happened to our talk about who says what?" he asked.

"We adapt. Perhaps someday we have that other conversation. Surely, though, the divine plan hasn't made space for us to configure."

****

The dogs, confirming their value as messengers and guides, stayed right with Destiny as she walked. Approaching, she heard "The Wedding March" and realized that it was looping on her computer. As it should be, she thought.

In the house, Mendel, though, could not help himself. "Shut the damned thing down, will you, Morris?"

"This never gets old. It is my wedding, too, and I love the tune. Such a melody!"

As they argued and laughed, Destiny approached. The dogs, newly polite as if they realized a time for decorum, stayed behind her. She smiled as she sized up Mendel and Morris, who were wearing matching gray pin-striped suits. Mendel's flopped at the shoulders, while Morris's jacket barely buttoned across his chest. His stomach would not be denied. Mendel had a light blue handkerchief tucked into his suit coat pocket, while Morris's was lavender. The moment Destiny entered the house, the music ceased. Annie, always beautiful, appeared.

Zena and Gilda, Gilda and Zena. That was it. Neither had previously married. Now together? What were the odds? Through eye contact, they laughed at the situation. It was a joyous, uncertain, and silent exchange. They might as well have been in their early twenties. Jittery and almost but not fully sure of themselves, they listened for and thankfully heard Destiny's voice. Zena and Gilda finally exhaled.

It was time for them to move along. The men remained at Destiny's.

"Annie, can you bring your harp or is that too much?"

"Easily. Here's your recorder, Des."

Annabelle slipped red bandanas over the dogs' heads and onto their necks, and the group, minus Mendel and Morris, made its way to the wedding site.

"Will the grooms know when to come down the hill?" asked Destiny.

"I gave them a little clock, small enough to slip into a pocket but one with large, illuminated hands. It also speaks. I told them to be here by one. They can do that," she said.

"I trust you, the watch, and them," said Destiny.

Destiny and Annie spoke together: "If anything goes wrong, send the dogs!"

Jess and Polly jumped up and around.

"You ready, Kiley?" asked Destiny.

His thumbs tilted toward the sky, and he smiled. Kiley was relieved to see Mendel and Morris about to leave the house.

Destiny, on recorder, and Annabelle, on harp, began to play: "Lean on Me," "You've Got a Friend," "All You Need is Love," "Sunrise, Sunset," and, "Vine and Fig Tree." Before the last tune ended, Zena and Gilda had arrived, hand in hand.

Destiny and Annie put down their instruments and sang in harmony: "And every man 'neath his vine and fig tree shall live in peace and unafraid." That was Kiley's signal to step forward. The women waved to the dogs, who sped up the hill to fetch Mendel and Morris.

The women played the melody of Lennon and McCartney's "In My Life." They then sang the lyrics as the men made their way down the hill.

When all had assembled, the younger women put down their instruments.

Kiley, limber and smiling widely, jumped forward, "Before I say one word, let me pass out these papers so that we can all sing together." He handed each person a pale blue sheet upon which lyrics were printed. And sing they did—in pairs, solo, taking turns, to one another, with the dogs, to the dogs, to Annabelle and Destiny, men to women, women to men, and so on.

Kiley, a deep baritone, led with the first verse of "You make me feel so young."

He waved his hand, stopped, and said, "We cannot sing every word of this even if some of us were around when this song was a big deal. Anyone want to make up some lyrics?"

Zena's hand shot upward. "You make me feel such love, it is as if from God above. Whenever I feel somewhat sad, I just think of you and then it's not so bad. You make me feel such love." Then, she blew a kiss toward Morris, who blushed from the neck up.

It all ended with a rambling embrace that almost caused Mendel to tip over as Morris tried to push his friend forward.

"Oy, hands off me, please," said Mendel. "I have no wind left after my first sing-along in a hundred years or so."

Kiley, grinning from ear to ear, said, "I have something to read, but after that, what is there to say?"

"Suddenly, you're shy?" asked Morris. "Open up your mouth . . ."

". . . and speak," said Mendel, finishing his friend's thought.

"Okay," said Kiley. "From Song of Songs, this line: 'I am my beloved's, and my beloved is mine; that feedeth among the lilies.'"

All remained silent, awaiting something more.

Kiley continued, "Well, Song of Songs or Song of Solomon suggests the union of one man and one woman. This is part of Kabbalah, which, as most everyone here knows by now, interests me. I hope for my best friends, here, only to live in harmony. Destiny and Annie led us here with such music, and may everyone's life here and yours"—he gestured to Mendel and Gilda; Morris and Zena—"on this occasion of marriage, be blessed and peaceful."

"Amen?" questioned Zena.

"Amen," said Gilda.

"It is *amain*," said Morris.

"For once, I agree," added Mendel.

****

Destiny stepped in front of the group and faced everyone.

"I was going to read, but I guess we've shared the words and lyrics of others. I will keep my paper with notes and quotes hidden. There's no need for it, not any longer." She paused and took a few very deep breaths. Mendel tried to catch Morris's eye, but the big man looked directly forward and eluded the smaller man's glance.

"This is about love and growing older, and we are fortunate to traverse life without the fear of loneliness but with the security of, well, camaraderie. Look at us! Look at each of us, in the eye, and watch the dogs, too! Be alone, but when you wish to be, travel along your own path. Cherish one another's presence—which brings me to the wedding couples.

"Mendel and Gilda, Morris and Zena, Mendel and Morris, Gilda and Zena. Really, four couples! Slice and dice and, aside from swapping partners—do not comment, please!—this is what we have. To work with. To love and honor. To cherish. Till death they will never part. Believe it, believe me; these people have one another, and this is not ephemeral but forever."

Morris raised his hand, and Destiny nodded in his direction.

"I have just one question: What about the afterlife?"

Mendel fidgeted. "What about it?"

"Will we stay together?"

"I think I know what ephemeral means, but I'm not sure," said Zena as Gilda shrugged.

"It means, nu, that you stay together and—may I say this?—we stay together," said Kiley. He looked around, "Fear not, I'm not going to read from anything."

Annabelle, making eye contact with Kiley, smiled warmly. "Destiny and I, with the dogs' help"—here, the dogs wagged their tails—"prepared a little something for the celebration back at the house. Before we go, though, I was wondering if the newlyweds were planning honeymoons?"

"Sweetie, this just might be enough," said Mendel.

"Speak for yourself, Mr. Not-So-Big," said Morris. "Zena and I have actually thought about it. And, you will never guess where we are headed."

Silence.

"Okay, I will tell you: Springfield!"

"*Oy! Vey ist mir!* What is wrong with you, you, you good-for-nothing! Why there?" Mendel shook a crooked finger at his friend and continued, "Yes, we have a house there, which we should sell. What else? I will tell you. Cemetery plots. I know I already have one. Yes, do not stop me: Phases, of course. I know. But, this is a city that is kaput. This is where we, all of us, are going on a honeymoon?"

"Yes," said Morris. "Maybe not a honeymoon, but at least a celebration. If you can come up, smarty pants, with a caterer."

Mendel stopped kvetching as if struck. "I got a connection —someone who has an idea about food. Not only that, but travel, too." The image of the much younger woman he had once known, the redheaded Lucy, flashed before his eyes.

Then, without notice, the skies opened up and staccato claps of thunder assaulted the group as buckets of rainwater poured down upon the entire wedding party.

"This is what I get for having no hair, dammit," said Mendel. "A wrinkled scalp and such a drenching you have never seen."

Kiley began walking away, skidding on the sand, squishing his way back up the hill. He turned and motioned for the group to follow, and the dogs immediately raced toward him. Gilda and Zena, holding hands, followed. So did Annabelle and Destiny.

That left Mendel and Morris, who seemed content to stand in the downpour, content to banter and joke while sliding about in the muck like a couple of kids.

"I don't know how I let you talk me into this," said Morris, steadying himself on his friend's bony shoulder.

"You are going down. Don't you remember, responsible one? You put us up to this!" screamed Mendel, trying to catch droplets in his hands in order to toss them in Morris's face.

Kiley doubled back to retrieve the boys, while the women continued up the hill.

"What, really, does it matter who dreamed it up, who told whom? Since I've known you two, you've been at war. Turn around and let's get to someplace dry."

"What happened to him?" asked Morris.

"Where is that man of serenity now?" asked Mendel. "Hey, smooth guy, can't you let two old Jews have their day in the rain?"

Kiley was about to respond when he caught himself, stopped, and stared: His two best friends, watered down to flesh and bone, were actually attempting to snatch falling water in their hands in order to douse each other. And even though they were failing, they were loving it, laughing to the

point of collapse, and, finally, laughing at him. Kiley rolled up
his sleeves and flexed a bicep. Taking a deep breath, he sat
right down in the mud and began to chant. After a few
minutes, a grin spread across his face.

"All right, cough it up, you," said Morris. "What gives?
Just this minute, you look like the cat who ate the canary."

The shower was beginning to stop. Kiley sat there with a
look on his face that indicated he had never been happier.
Finally, he began to rise but, as if skating in butter, could not
quite hoist his body upward.

Mendel and Morris, on either side of him, lifted him until
he was able to steady himself and regain some footing. And
then he slipped, banging into Mendel, which brought them
both down on Morris, who gathered them against him and,
ultimately, bellowed to the heavens.

Destiny, now near the top of the hill, could not decide
whether this was a genial roar or reason for alarm. She turned
and descended, shoes turned sideways, making her way back
down the slope. The dogs immediately leapt in unison,
turning in the air while Annie ambled along behind them.

Zena and Gilda continued toward Destiny's Place.

"Morris must be front and center, whatever they're up
to," said Zena.

"He might be the doer, but I think Mendel's brain is
often behind their shenanigans," said Gilda. "Sometimes, I
think 'What brain?' I mean, that man can be cunning one
minute and a fool to the world the very next."

"You just married him, sister. Me? I got an elephant on
my hands. This one, though, he selectively remembers,
forgets, remembers. If it's about food, his memory is sharp as
a tack. The man knows the first time he ate a lobster. The
problem is that he tells the story again and again and again.
Does repetition equal dementia?"

Gilda laughed. "I think I'm giggling. Imagine someone my age giggling. This is for young girls. As Mama used to say, 'You will never catch a man with a little girl's laugh.' Took me a while, and who caught whom?"

The sisters glanced backward at the still sprawling Mendel and Morris, who held each other as Kiley squished between them, a human sandwich.

"Even ancient boys are still boys," said Zena, turning away from the men down below.

Gilda looked her sister in the eye and signaled with her fingers: one, two, three. In unison, laughing, they said, "Boys!"

Destiny, first, then Annie and her dogs, slid to a stop and came upon the newly upright and somewhat steadied duo of Mendel and Morris. Kiley, too, was on his feet. The M&M Boys burst out laughing.

Destiny breathed deeply, hoping that she could calm them. Only Annie responded. Polly and Jess, reacting to Mendel and Morris, bounded forward and succeeded in tripping Kiley, who slipped and fell into Morris, who in turn tripped and took down Mendel with the rest of them. The dogs took the opportunity to lick any face they could find.

Annie whistled sweetly, which is what she learned to do while playing piano as a teenager. Sam had asked her to whistle a melody while she played a bass line. Now, she produced, without thinking, "Ode to Joy" from Beethoven's Ninth Symphony. Morris, the music lover, remembered seeing Leonard Bernstein conducting the piece. He loved it then and was thrilled to hear it now, as the sun broke through the clouds. Mendel, too, stopped. All looked upward, where, instead of a luminous rainbow, the sun glittered.

"Let's go home," said Kiley.

"Could we come with you?" Annie was asking on behalf of herself, Destiny, and the dogs.

Mendel shrugged.

Morris said, "Speaking for us and our brides, back to Springfield!"

CHAPTER 16

Lucy, having previously worked at hotels, health clubs, and with the elderly, was certain she had finally found her true calling as an event planner. Just on the other side of forty, she convinced herself she looked younger: Every man told her so. You wouldn't notice the crow's feet etching her eyes unless you were close enough so that it didn't matter.

Mendel had called her yesterday from the beach.

She learned he was newly married and so was his friend with the big gut. Truth be told, she never did mind a few extra pounds—on someone else. She was primed to create an unforgettable reception for these guys and, she admitted, might as well since those deeds were done. After all, she could not realistically have imagined a life as Mendel's bride. She was drawn to him, yes. And there would have been perks, no question. Now, though, it would be convoluted. Why those haggard sisters? she wondered.

Not that what she thought mattered. She resisted the temptation to fixate on that scrawny Mendel and his potential. Stooping that low was too much. She would maintain the friendship. Show him, really wow them, with a wedding shindig they wouldn't soon forget.

She drove to Forest Park and around to the Longmeadow side, where she hoped to gain free entry. As she did, Lucy pulled down her top, sucked in her stomach, and tried to sweet-talk the middle-aged guy at the entry booth.

"Barney Estate," said Lucy.

"Three dollars, please," he replied.

"Look, I just need to go in and talk to the dude who runs the estate, since I'm in charge of a celebration for some newlyweds. You know, work a deal."

"You can walk in for free or pay me three," he said.

She knew he was proud of the ditty and figured she could cajole him.

"I will only be there five minutes. I understand what you're saying, but come on, help me out."

"Three bucks is gonna break you?"

Lucy bent over as if she had dropped something on the car floor, unbuttoned the top of her blouse, and leaned deeply out the window.

"Give a girl a break?"

"Another button gets you in for a dollar."

Lucy yanked her shirt out from her jeans, pulled it wide, and opened the driver side door fully, which allowed the attendant to drink in the scene.

"Have a sweet day," she chortled, recalling the accent of her native city, Tidewater, Virginia, and drove right through without even checking her rearview mirror.

I should have walked, she thought to herself. Not to save the money but to get some exercise. I could split these jeans right on the spot. Next time, buy relaxed and forget the skinny till I drop at least five pounds. Look at that guy. Whatever the asking price is for a small party, I'll get it down easy.

She approached the carriage house and a man sitting on a rocking chair on the front veranda. He looked her age, but she was sure he was younger. Anyone trying to be forty-five should be able to grow out a scruffy beard. This one had the disposition of a job seeker rather than a park ranger.

"How can I help you?" he asked.

"Well, at least you're more of a gentleman than the money-grubber at the gate," said Lucy.

"He's not the sweetest cup of cocoa. I'm Bill. And you?"

"Lucy. I am arranging a party for two, well, really four—of my friends who just had their wedding ceremony across the state. They want to celebrate in Forest Park, where they live. Why not here, don't you think?"

"The place has charm and history," Bill replied.

"So do they. The youngest of the men might be seventy-nine or so," said Lucy.

"Everybody's welcome."

"What are your prices?" she asked.

"The season is still alive. We are at a minimum of three thousand for rental. The rest is you—I mean, your party."

"No discount for seniors, huh?"

Bill shook his head from side to side.

"They won't live all that long, hon, please."

"Illness?" asked Bill.

"One of the men and one of the women," said Lucy. "Luckily, not a couple. But that means each of them is down one, if you know what I mean, before too long. Not saying that any one of them is sick. More like a hip here, a knee there. Chipping away. So, I just want to make them happy. Know what I mean?"

As she fibbed, Lucy realized this was now a habit. Mendel, when he called, had mentioned nothing about cost. Besides, she was aware that the coot had loot. But, it was fun to flirt with this guy who thought himself pretty special.

As they talked, Bill motioned her into the building and Lucy's eyes opened wide. He began to tell her of the estate's history, Mr. Barney's legacy as "the man who put America on skates," and the eventual restoration of this, the only building still standing.

On this weekday, when nothing was scheduled, Lucy allowed herself to envision her own wedding: She saw a slim young woman strolling outside onto the veranda on the arm of a dark-haired, dapper man who might be a financial advisor. Yes, that would be good, she thought.

They would have imported vines and foliage to approximate the late nineteenth and early twentieth century when this estate must have flourished. Before she could dream about her own wedding, Bill interrupted by asking, "Second floor? You want to go upstairs?"

"Sure, sugar, whatever you say."

They went up the staircase, and Lucy imagined servants walking with trays to individually serve family members who wanted breakfast in bed. "This was probably a bedroom a long time ago, right?" Lucy asked about a meeting room.

"That I could not say," Bill replied. "Maybe."

"I bet you could see the river, in the old days, from way up here. Wake up with a sweetie beside you and glance out the window. See blue water as you were opening up your eyes," she said dreamily.

Bill snapped his fingers. "We book steadily during the season. What were you interested in?"

Lucy remembered Mendel being vague.

"Soon. The sooner, the better," she answered. "This isn't the actual wedding." She knew she had him. The questions were: How far should she push this guy, Bill? Moreover, why? Mendel and his friend certainly had plenty of cash. Still, she could not resist and stepped to his side.

****

It was now the day after the sweet wedding, and the soft beige sand at Crane Beach was nearly dry. The wedding attendees were assembling, preparing to caravan across the state. Mendel promised "a party to end all parties." No one believed him, least of all Morris.

"Mendel is tight. Sometimes it's a good thing. But, for a party after a wedding, as that Irishman who played tennis said, 'You cannot be serious!'" He reddened and punched the air.

"This is different, Moishkie," Mendel said. "My last wedding is going to be my best."

"You act as if you had six or eight."

"Two is plenty."

They ignored the women, who stood nearby, until Destiny said, "Relax and pay attention, as my college theater instructor used to implore. Annie and I want to frolic and not fight. Yes, Mendel and Morris? What about you, Kiley? Which car?"

Kiley motioned toward the van and said simply, "More room."

Not especially accustomed to receiving advice from a woman, Morris nevertheless found himself replying, "Yes, of course."

Mendel twitched his head up and down.

"Well, I'm glad we all agree. Annie, Kiley, and I will take Jess and Polly in the van, and we will follow right on your tail, boys. Newlyweds into Mendel's Prius, yes?"

Zena and Gilda were elated—on their way to explore their future as wives for the first time.

"But first," said Gilda, "let us all say *l'chayim*. If it were not for such beautiful younger women, these men of ours would still be squishing around in the muck!"

"That's my big sister," added Zena. "Well said. Now, let the two of us stretch our legs before we get in the car."

Mendel, while awaiting the women, plucked his flip phone from the case attached to his belt. Pushing his eyeglasses upward, he pressed "Contacts" and then found himself sneezing and needing to grab his handkerchief. He pushed the phone toward Morris.

"Find Lucy and get her on the phone," he said.

"This is not the same Lucy with the hips, is it?"

"Just hit her name on the list, would you please? Hips and lips."

Morris began to laugh. "Just why? We got hitched not all that long ago—in case you got short-term memory loss."

"Shut up, Morris. It's about the reception."

"Even better, you want her at the party?"

"She's organizing it."

"What?"

"I knew she was in the area, close enough, and no one is a better event planner."

"She certainly planned a nice event for you. I thought you were going to have a heart attack the minute I saw you leave her room in the motel way back when."

"Look Morris, I want this to be a day to remember—for all of us. She knows the business. Don't cause an uproar, just call her please."

Lucy, taking a break from dealings with Bill, was walking around the carriage house when her cell rang. She had entered his name in capital letters: MENDY.

"Sweetie pie," she answered.

To which Morris replied, "Morris calling for Mendel."

"Oh," she chortled, "the best and big friend!"

Morris handed the phone to Mendel.

"Sugar," said Mendel.

Morris, in the background, couldn't help himself: "Lump or grains?"

Mendel shushed him.

"Sugar, how's it going with the party?"

"We were just wrapping up," she lied as Bill raised his eyebrows.

"Good, because price is not an object," said Mendel. "Not in this case."

Lucy held her hand over the phone as if Bill might be eavesdropping on the conversation.

"Shoot for the moon," said Mendel.

Morris grabbed for the phone and shouted, "The sun and the stars while you're at it!"

Lucy loved this estate. It was easy for her to imagine, a century ago and more, people staying overnight. She wondered where the bedrooms might have been; there were no longer any. She thought about guests walking, skates tossed over their shoulders, to one of the ponds, lacing up, and then gliding smoothly beneath a full, apricot-colored moon.

Bill's voice brought her back to the present. "I can maybe come down a few hundred as a, as a personal favor to you."

"What is my part?" she asked.

"Stay here."

"But for how long and do what?" she whispered under her breath.

"This is a lonely job. Gives me time, but it makes me deliriously bored. Humor me. Anything more I take as bonus," he replied.

Lucy recreated her youthful, Southern dialect, which she called upon infrequently. This was fun, and it was just beginning.

"Dear, I've been there, done that, and more than once. Just not what stirs my mixed drink these days, if you know what I'm saying."

"I do," said Bill. "Even an innocent massage would work."

"Clothes on?" she asked.

"Absolutely." With that, Bill led Lucy up a winding staircase.

Lucy pulled at her shirt, which had been but was no longer tucked in. As they entered an innocent enough room, which included a love seat and oak desk, she wondered why she hadn't made up an excuse. When he sat on the couch and motioned for her to sit beside him, she quickly obliged. Staring at her from the opposite wall was a photograph. Lucy imagined it was Barney himself. He seemed to be smiling at Lucy.

She often wished she were of another time but the same place as her birth: Virginia or further South during the early rather than later part of the twentieth century. She would be better off with high-collared blouses rather than Ralph Lauren shirts that tempted her to flit about with all the buttons undone.

"Okay, Billy, what now?"

"Just a short back rub?"

"Then we talk about a deal?"

"It's my job," he said.

Lucy had trained to become a physical therapist but left the program early. She was not shy and admitted to enjoying the process. Knead somebody's back and shoulders? A piece of cake. This guy, Bill? Not so bad. He could use significant toning, but maybe a five or even six on a scale of one to ten.

"That's all I have," she said, giving his shoulders a drumroll.

"Made my day, Lucy," he replied and extended his hand to shake hers.

She took his hand within hers, a gesture of warmth she learned from her late father. "Show a man you care," he had advised her.

Now, however, Lucy knew she could use a walk—by herself.

She wondered about Mendel and why the old dude would, from time to time, call her. Sure, she was affectionate toward him that day, more than a while ago, in the motel. He had money, he was funny, and he certainly liked her. She hated gold diggers, though, and wasn't about to become one. Was her extension of friendship dishonest? No way she could hang on an eighty-year-old.

She swerved to elude a family of geese.

"Get out, honkers!" she sang.

Lucy needed to discuss details with Mendel. She didn't even know how many were coming to this affair—ten or twenty? Why such a swanky place, with a big-time price tag? What if one of the geezers died right there on the spot? She would probably have to call the ambulance. After all, this Bill guy wasn't the brightest bulb.

She sauntered along and found herself surrounded by a number of butterflies. Why, growing up in the South, had she never paid one iota of attention when her Mom tried to educate her about flowers, birds, even insects? She wished she could identify these incredible winged creatures; they were black and orange with white dots on the very edges. And this overgrown bush with a million white petals? What was that? Geez, what an ignorant human I am, she thought. Well, at least she was getting some exercise. She hadn't especially relished moving up to size 8, and now she could barely fit into that.

Lucy strode across a red wooden bridge that crossed a lively stream. Suddenly, two dogs, one a chocolate Lab and the other a comical mutt, splashed into the stream. Before she could escape, the dogs shook themselves dry, depositing a mixture of water and sand on her. So, she walked back up the hill toward the estate and sat down on a wrought iron bench to dry. She carefully pressed the soft fold of flesh above her waist so she could pretend her stomach was flat. The advantage of being with older guys, not to mention an ancient bird like Mendel, was that they really didn't care. In fact, her experience was that they kinda liked playing with the excess. Anyone thirty-five or younger talked abs, which, in her case, had vanished. Good thing her chest remained alluring.

Soon, she began to doze. When she awoke, she hadn't any idea how long she had been out. A parade of geese made its way into and then through a pond filled with lily pads.

****

Across the state, members of the wedding contingent, bogged down in traffic on the Turnpike, took turns complaining. About one another. The boys and their brides were obviously nervous. About life as newlyweds?

Annie, Destiny, and Kiley were satisfied with their scene.

"Better having the dogs, I think," said Destiny.

The women had coaxed Kiley into driving since they wished to get some time together.

"What about either of you two?" asked Destiny. "No plans to take vows?"

Annie glanced at Kiley, who was looking back at them through the rearview mirror.

"I would not mind marrying," said Kiley. "Not so lonely," he added.

A man who often kept to himself, who found Judaism an intellectual religion with a cultural warmth and spirituality that attracted him, Kiley felt safe as a scholar studying Torah. But he remained uncertain of his place in the world. Would or could he allow for an intimate relationship with another human? He wished to consider.

Kiley added, "When I counsel, I always advise others to find someone—not embarrassing for me to say so."

Annie figured she might as well speak. After all, Destiny, her dearest friend, would surely support.

"I, well, two is just a better number—many more possibilities. Not as shut down or closed off as I currently am. I mean, I don't want to be this way forever. How do you date when you're not eighteen or twenty?" she asked, not anticipating a response. "I was practically a teenager the last time I had a serious boyfriend," she added.

"I've been just plain serious much of the time," said Kiley, clenching the steering wheel. Annie and Destiny noticed, but neither let on—so Kiley, humming, drove on. He felt he might have overstepped and, rather than spin around to see Annie's reaction, Kiley reached backward whereupon one of the dogs drenched his hand with saliva.

"Unconditional love," said Kiley.

"Is Mendel in love with this Lucy?" asked Destiny.

"No, not love," said Kiley. "Would he accept a massage from a woman much younger? I believe so."

"This is the woman arranging the party?" asked Annie.

Meanwhile, in the other car, Gilda asked Mendel, "Just how many people are coming to this big bash you are staging?"

He liked driving his new Prius and loved to brag about it. He also kind of missed his weary Mercedes. Mendel was aware that, soon enough, the little pond with that William Blake poetry Morris was so obsessed with would come into view. Mendel briefly contemplated crossing the Pike to revisit that scene, show the women around, and recapture a precious moment, but at first he did not—because he could not easily turn about. Mendel tried, unsuccessfully, to ban Lucy from his mind. He was looking forward to seeing her and persuaded himself that she not-so-secretly anticipated his arrival. What was he thinking? He was newly married.

"I have seen this look of a bandit a million times on that crinkled face of yours, and it means something is up and nothing good about it," announced Morris. "Out with it."

"Let's go find the Blake," said Mendel. We will take the next exit and make our way. "

"For once you got brains. Since the girls are suddenly dozing in the backseat, let's go dig up that thing I left there." Morris bounced a bit in his seat.

"According to you, this eternity saying, this ditty, means good luck, Morris."

"Now, you are talking sense!" Morris boomed for all to hear. He, however, could not recall just what had become of that short verse. Did he bury it or did he take it with him? If the latter, he would not know where to look. And, if the former, exactly the same: Where was it? He hadn't a clue.

"Mendel, I cannot for the life me, dementia schementia, remember what I did with that damned piece of paper. The Blake, I know only that it is there. But where?"

Starting back in the opposite direction on the Mass Pike, Mendel found the spot where they had pulled off the highway early in the summer. Together, he and Morris got out of the car and headed toward the woods to begin the search for the elusive Blake. After struggling through the brush and coming up empty-handed, they were about to give up and start back to the car.

Morris turned too quickly toward Mendel, caught his foot, stumbled and tumbled directly into his friend. Both went down, but neither was badly hurt. Lifting himself, Morris grabbed onto a hollowed out branch and felt something wedged inside. He pulled and, to his utter amazement, found that the precious Blake verse, yellowed yet still encased, had survived. He waved it at Mendel and shouted, "Someone or something is looking out for me! Hooray!"

****

Meanwhile, Kiley, maneuvering the microbus to keep on Mendel's tail, experienced a midday reverie: What if the forthcoming celebration included him? Why not Kiley and Annie? It had a ring to it, yes? Well, to answer his own question: First off, they were not married. This could be achieved by a JP, of course, but how and where would he ask her? Yes, he was so much older but he was certain that she cared for him. That was different than getting married, though. What was he thinking? On the other hand, he might have many good years ahead. A child? Was he out of his mind? Finally, was he taken with her or her image or, more accurately, what she represented? Youth and longevity. He thought of her smooth hands and fingers, pretty and delicate. His own were wrinkled and crumpled; this he despised. If only she would hold his hand . . .

CHAPTER 17

Mendel, thrilled that he managed to help Morris snag the Blake, and still leading the caravan, chose to go directly to the Barney Estate rather than the house or Phases. He figured he might as well introduce Lucy to the group. Well, Morris would know who she was if the galoot hadn't lost every one of his marbles. They would all understand: He had a younger friend who was an accomplished event planner. Why not? What, though, if Gilda sniffed this out and got suspicious? She had one smart schnoz and it worked for her like a sensor. Even so, this could not possibly derail the marriage, he convinced himself. On to it: presenting Lucy to his friends and to his wife.

****

He found her rocking back and forth on the porch swing and humming, as if she were in her youth. Mendel looked at her and it struck him that Lucy was on the cusp of middle-age; no longer an ingénue.

Creaking as he extricated himself from the Prius, Mendel called to her before anyone else opened their doors. "Lucy, sweet, guess who?"

"Men, baby, you didn't even call. What are you folks doin' here on such the early side?"

"You get used to early bird, dear. This is what we do," he joked as she nodded.

"So, nu? How you doing?" he asked as the others gathered. Before she could answer, Mendel began introductions—he cared about looks except, perhaps, when it came to himself.

"I met this guy named Bill, sugar. I mean, you and Bill are both sugar-sweet. Anyway, he is just a dream and he's the one who schedules weddings here. So, I mean we are able to get this little party together through him and fairly soon," she said and then paused. A sweet party is what you're after?"

"A shindig is more like it," said Morris, attempting to bow but tripping and falling forward for his effort. "Not for all hours, but something so we can celebrate. What say, Mendel?"

Mendel agreed. "That is exactly what we could use, Miss Lucy."

Morris raised his fist, but Mendel stood unknowingly. Morris picked up his friend's hand and said, "Make a fist." Mendel obliged, and Morris gently touched his fist to Mendel's. "Fist bump is what the kids call it," said Morris.

Mendel shrugged and then grinned. "You know, Jewish holidays are always a consideration in the fall."

"Like I'm not aware. First, we are happy and then we are sad. I never understand the backwards timing, even to this day," said Morris.

Kiley walked in and overheard the conversation.

"It makes sense," he said. "The good and then the sorrowful."

"Tell us," said Mendel.

"I will say this is parallel to Blake. The opposites. Or, as R.D. Laing used to tell us, the line between sanity and insanity is nearly invisible. Well, I'm paraphrasing," said Kiley. "Maybe that is more what I think."

"What I know is that I don't care about taxes anymore," said Morris. "Nothing doing."

"Which means sex is on your mind all of the time, you son of a?" asked Mendel.

Lucy, previously perplexed, quickly came to life. "Well, boys, now we're talking."

Kiley, appearing to be fully immersed in his thoughts, said, "On the one hand, Morris, you and Mendel are on very different poles—surface complements. The sisters, though different, are far from studies in contrast. One of you is with Zena, the other with Gilda. Why?" he asked, not looking for a response.

"Morris is maybe what I sometimes think of myself," said Mendel. "Big, loud, and ready to bring down the house. Meanwhile, I'm always thinking the worst— like that particular house will fall on my head," he continued.

"And I'm wishing, sometimes, that I would shut up," said Morris. "No can do? I fear this is true. Silence is, to me, worse than death." He paused. "Dead."

"The equalizer," Kiley said, summing up.

Mendel pointed at Morris and said, "You do not know whether shush is better than nothing. After all, you're not gone yet. Why don't we take a nice long walk?"

"While we can," said Zena, giving the sisters a voice.

"Yes, you boys have never shown us one end of your beloved park. Always, it's about the ancient white polar bear with the single eye or the elephant they shipped off to Los Angeles. I never really knew about the mansion."

Mendel eyeballed Morris, who slowly nodded his head up and down as if he were an aging lion too fatigued to roar. Mendel had once mused about those animals' lives while he wandered the park. They all had fewer choices to make: where to find food and where to take shelter. Within the confines of the park, they were coddled, more or less.

Now, however, it was time to explore. Off they went, but not briskly. Zena complained about her knee, and Gilda, trying to assist, strained her back. Morris, sensing that all was not well, signaled Mendel to hasten his pace. Lucy, just behind Kiley, concerned herself with her waistband and the encroaching flesh threatening its flexibility. She pressed inward only to watch a protrusion.

They had barely wandered a third of the way down the sloping hill before coming to a halt.

"Listen," said Mendel.

"As if you got great hearing? You cannot even hear when someone takes a shower," said Morris.

In the distance, someone sang, "Keep on the sunny side, always on the sunny side, keep on the sunny side of life. It will help us every day, it will brighten all the way, if we keep on the sunny side of life."

"Is that you, Kiley?" asked Lucy, finally allowing herself to breathe.

"Keep on the sunny side," was the response, followed by a whistle of the tune.

Morris, hoping that collective limbs were intact, beckoned the group forward. "This is the wannabe Jewish minstrel," he announced. "Whoever knew he had such pipes? A reformed cantor?"

"Just what we need: a cantor who just maybe is becoming a Jew," said Mendel.

"I've been singing forever, but not in public," said Kiley. "Part of the altar boy tradition, too. This tune works for all faiths." He began again.

"So, share. Teach us," said Gilda.

Kiley took a deep breath and turned to everyone behind him. "Repeat after me: Oh, you can't get to heaven," he said slowly.

"I know this game!" shouted Morris. "Oh, you can't get to heaven! Get it? We all join in." He motioned to his friends, encouraging them to participate.

Gilda and Zena joined hands, as if they were teenagers. "Oh, you can't get to heaven," they said.

Kiley sang the next line: "On Morris's belly."

"On Morris's belly," boomed Morris and then the others.

Kiley: "Because Morris's belly."

Group: "Because Morris's belly."

"I know this because I'm getting one—look!" said Lucy, finally releasing her tummy and watching it jiggle. "It shakes like jelly!"

All: "It shakes like jelly."

Kiley said, "With some harmony," and everyone followed suit: "Oh, you can't get to heaven on Morris's belly because Morris's belly shakes like jelly."

Kiley went solo: "I ain't gonna grieve, my Lord, no more."

The response: "I ain't gonna grieve, my Lord, no more."

"That's some Yiddish folk song?" asked Mendel.

"I tried to find out," said Kiley. "Either it's from the Bible or handed down from generations in this country."

"Not helpful," said Mendel.

"So, who cares?" Morris asked. "What's the difference—Jewish, Christian, American? "This is perfect," said Morris.

The group strolled along, singing, joking, and making up verses. Given their speed, they failed to cover much territory. Lucy, aware that she was easily the youngest member of this contingent, eventually succeeded in leading them back toward the carriage house.

Huffing herself, she pushed the front door open and led them into the parlor room, where Bill sat, puffing on an unlit pipe. "Hello," he said. "I don't smoke, but I do miss it," he explained.

"I am Mendel. This is Morris and our brides. Kiley, our leader, wants to be Jewish," he added. "We are all here to celebrate—prepare to celebrate."

"Luckily, I can oblige," said Bill. "I am a minister. By the way, Mr. Kiley, I could hear you leading them with that tune from up here. Where did you learn it?"

"From my children," said Kiley.

"Go know. You got children?" asked Morris.

"We all have children," said Mendel, slowly looking around. "I mean, the boys do: Morris, Kiley, me." He paused. "The girls know."

"I cannot say he hasn't mentioned it," said Gilda, glancing at Mendel. "But, I have never yet seen one of them in person."

"Me neither. I would like to meet his son," said Zena as she pointed to Morris.

"Maybe these are just stories for another day, sweethearts," said Lucy. "Me? No kids. Although with this, I feel like maybe I could have one," she said, patting her stomach.

Bill looked at her and said, "The present, the future: Don't look back, someone might be gaining on you or something like that."

"This is a saying my father, if he could speak English, would have loved," Morris said and then shrugged. "Mendel, Mr. Big, let me tell you something: Sex is not such a bad thing. In fact, I agree, but I remember that day and he never finished the sentence. He started to sneeze, of all things. What was he going to say?"

"You just be quiet about your father, Morris," said Zena. "Let the memory sit. Gilda and me, when we moved to Florida, we were much younger—in our fifties. A couple almost old enough to be our parents, I am guessing, gave us a room in their house. We met them—where else?—on the shuffleboard court. Even then, underage, we were playing tournaments and all. Anyway, we knew them as Nan and Paulie since that's what she called him. Our guardian angels, if Jewish people can have them. I don't know."

"Let me pick up here, Zena," said Gilda. "So, we were each working and a year later we had enough money to move out. We landed at the place where we were living when you two boys found us. Nan and Paulie had us to dinner, and we had them over, usually, to watch our TV since we had a better one. In the end, it was Paulie who went first—not by cancer or his heart. A stroke was the reason. He didn't die, but he wouldn't live. I am sure you know what I mean."

"We went to the funeral, of course," said Zena. "It was there we found out that they were Jewish but not interested in religion. That would have been enough. But, this was the real shocker: They weren't even married. How could that be?"

"My dear Mendel and my dear brother-in-law, Morris, maybe we should have kept it the way it was," said Gilda. "We girls were lucky enough, so why push our luck?"

"Not get married and live in sin forever?" Morris looked upward as if he wondered whether God would or would not approve.

"He's never serious," said Mendel before beginning to sing. "Love and marriage, love and marriage . . ."

". . . Go together like a horse and carriage," the girls chimed in.

"Yeah, but what about the party and Bill and planning?" asked Lucy.

"In the end, this is in the beginning, sweet one," said Mendel. "And listen, Gilda, you are truly my sweetheart. So, I talk this way to a younger woman? So what? Anyway, maybe someday we can celebrate her wedding, all of us. For me, there is you, Gilda. And for Morris . . ."

"I will always have my Zena. Just to prove it, I will go buy you a ring, which I did not have a little while ago. Any kind, any color," added Morris.

"Any price, any stone?" asked Mendel. He looked around. "As they say today, some rock. Ruby, for sure. Push him and you get diamonds." He shrugged and glanced at Morris. "Okay, one diamond."

"So, the party is off?" asked Bill.

"Not so fast, junior," said Gilda.

Zena jumped in. "What we are saying is that there might not have been a reason to marry. A party, though, that is another story. Why not?"

"Here, here," said Kiley. "This is about lasting—surviving—and why not forever?"

"Ding dong, ring me, the event planner," said Lucy. "Everyone back to the carriage house for drinks and we will see if we can throw together something quick, something impromptu. What say you, Bill, honey?"

He slowly nodded and gave Lucy the thumbs up. She took Bill's hand, and they led the group back toward Barney's. Soon enough, Bill fingered the soft tube around Lucy's waist, grasping the flesh between his thumb and forefinger.

Zena noticed. "Don't worry, sweetheart. On you, it looks good. He loves it."

Lucy winced, then shrugged as if adding the pounds was inevitable.

By the time they reached the estate house, everyone, except possibly Kiley and Bill, was exhausted.

"Enough for me," said Morris, plopping himself into an easy chair.

"Maybe it's Bill and me who ought to get married," said Lucy, lapsing into twang.

"At least you two might live a while. Not like us geezers. No more hikes for me," said Morris. "The only place I will walk is from the bedroom to the kitchen to the living room and back to the kitchen."

"That's not the only place," said Mendel. "Zena knows which room I'm talking."

"Shush, you," said Morris, making a playful fist and shaking it at Mendel.

"Copacetic is what I say," said Kiley. "As long as these two are at war, the rest of us live in peace. *Amain* and not amen," he added.

"Such a Jew you never saw," said Mendel.

"Honey, talk to me about your religion," Lucy said to Mendel. "You told me you would way back when."

"A story she wants?" asked Mendel. "Well, how about the time two old couples were all set to get married, then were considering it a bad idea to fiddle around with a good thing. The argument must have been that you do better at the bank when you are single," he said. "I have news: no matter, as marrieds, we will do fine."

"Bill, do you think you might like me enough to get married?" asked Lucy.

"You look good, sweetheart," he said. "But, I don't know if hitching myself even to a sweetie like you is the best move. For sure, I will need to get to know you better."

A flock of geese flew by and then suddenly turned around and headed south.

"What do those honkers know that we do not?" asked Morris.

"I don't know about that, but what I feel is this: It is a good thing for Jews and people like me, who are not born Jews, to be together." Kiley looked around and continued. "The worst thing is wandering alone. We are together. The old people, us, and the not-so-ancient—like sweet Lucy and this man."

"Billy boy," said Lucy. She noticed when she spoke that the corners of Bill's lips moved upward and he nearly smiled.

"These two might as well get married twice, at least if he wants it, since she, as certain as the sun is shining, does. For the senior citizens here, as we are called, it doesn't matter so much. These sisters are better than what my two shuffleboard-playing hombres deserve. Boys, take them before they leave!" Kiley lifted his arms as he spoke.

And with that, Morris placed an arm around Zena's shoulders and eyeballed Mendel, who took Gilda's hands.

"May the spirit in me, now and forever, bless you," said Kiley. "The Lord should shelter you forever and, with a pinch of good fortune, this second childhood will carry you into another lifetime." Kiley looked back at the hill in time to see Destiny and Annie, who had hopped in and out of the car, now opened doors so the dogs could freely tumble out. Kiley turned toward them and winked, first with one eye and then the other, and finally smiled wide. "Thank you for that opportunity. I wanted to say this the first time!"

He snapped his fingers, and the dogs galloped at him. He might as well have tossed them slabs of raw meat.

Kiley bowed at the waist and said, "Raise these glasses Lucy gave us. To the lineaments of desire!"

Morris, lifting a thumb upward, laughed with great force, then said, "I know that guy's words. He wrote that poem about the sand and all. Remember, Mendel?"

Mendel winked back at him, looked upward, and said, "Please help us, God."

EPILOGUE

Later, however, Mendel, seeking solitude, made an excuse: "All of this carrying on is just too much for me. Let me go for a walk." So, he did, making his way to the park and that ravine he felt he had discovered. Skidding to a halt on the sandy edge of a smallish pond, he was glad to get a foothold. "Now, how long ago was it when I was here?

"Crap. That is all over the place here. That is what I think about when I am not with Gilda, not with Morris, not even with that Kiley. My God, that man cannot decide: first a Christian, now a Jew. What next? I will tell you what. A surprising run of life is my prediction. You think, up there, that I will have a password for the pearly gates? I got news for you. Hold the phone, since I'm planning on hanging around here. Finally, I have someone to stand by me, as that song goes. Always Morris and now Gilda, too."

He picked up a stone and tossed it into the water. Stooping and then sitting, Mendel began to untie his spiffy sneakers. He carefully took off his socks and placed one inside each shoe. Then he tiptoed cautiously into the water, shuddering just a bit. "Cold? No. Like everything else, you get used to it. Now that I have us talking about what might or might not be and God has blessed the four of us, late in life, is it so out of tune to ask what happens next?"

Aware that he would not get a response, Mendel slowly walked several yards until he was standing in the middle of the pond. He scooped some water in his hands, raised his arms, and allowed drops to fall through his fingers onto his bare head. "Never any chance that I would be baptized. This is the closest I get. I would like to say grace since I have never lived in a household where this was done. Except for this: I cannot say grace without thinking of that girl with the flawless, pale skin, Grace Kelly, who became ungodly rich when she was a princess. Like a fairy tale."

And so Mendel Greenbaum, barefoot, stood as tall as he could in the middle of a brownish pond deep within Forest Park, Springfield. He gazed toward the sky, spread his arms as if they were wings attached to the oldest bird in the world, cleared his voice, threw some water above him, and sang, "Every time it rains, it rains, pennies from heaven."

"That is all I will want when I get there," he said. "A few shining, newly minted pennies!"

ACKNOWLEDGMENTS

For her love and for consistently standing behind or ahead of or beside this author/her husband: Betsy Pirtle Sokol, the best ever life partner.

For support and love: Jason Sokol, Scott Sokol, Nina Morrison and Ashley Sobel.

For her belief in this book, its author and for her mentoring: Linda Cardillo.

For editing the manuscript: Erin Binney.

For recognizing this author's promise as a writer: Tom Ford and Caroline Shrodes.

ABOUT THE AUTHOR

Fred Sokol, in semi-retirement, writes novels and plays. Hence, the previously published *Mendel and Morris* and the current book. His scripted work includes *The Forever Boys* and *The Lewis Sisters*. His next work of fiction, *Summer of '65* focuses upon four months in the life and times of a young woman, then eighteen, in 1965. Fred also continues to review professional theater in Connecticut and the Berkshires for talkinbroadway.com. He co-authored *Muses in Arcadia: Cultural Life in the Berkshires*. Fred enjoyed four decades as a community college and college professor—and directed 45 theater productions. He now teaches a small, lovely acting class through his local library. Fred and his wife, Betsy, live in Longmeadow, Massachusetts.